SHOOTING STARS OVER THE HIGHLANDS

LISA HOBMAN

Boldwood

First published in Great Britain in 2025 by Boldwood Books Ltd.

Copyright © Lisa Hobman, 2025

Cover Design by Alexandra Allden

Cover Images: Shutterstock

The moral right of Lisa Hobman to be identified as the author of this work has been asserted in accordance with the Copyright, Designs and Patents Act 1988.

All rights reserved. No part of this book may be reproduced in any form or by any electronic or mechanical means, including information storage and retrieval systems, without written permission from the author, except for the use of brief quotations in a book review. This book is a work of fiction and, except in the case of historical fact, any resemblance to actual persons, living or dead, is purely coincidental.

Every effort has been made to obtain the necessary permissions with reference to copyright material, both illustrative and quoted. We apologise for any omissions in this respect and will be pleased to make the appropriate acknowledgements in any future edition.

A CIP catalogue record for this book is available from the British Library.

Paperback ISBN 978-1-80483-690-3

Large Print ISBN 978-1-80483-691-0

Hardback ISBN 978-1-80483-692-7

Ebook ISBN 978-1-80483-688-0

Kindle ISBN 978-1-80483-689-7

Audio CD ISBN 978-1-80483-697-2

MP3 CD ISBN 978-1-80483-696-5

Digital audio download ISBN 978-1-80483-693-4

This book is printed on certified sustainable paper. Boldwood Books is dedicated to putting sustainability at the heart of our business. For more information please visit https://www.boldwoodbooks.com/about-us/sustainability/

Boldwood Books Ltd, 23 Bowerdean Street, London, SW6 3TN

www.boldwoodbooks.com

For Gee, my very own shooting star.

PROLOGUE
APRIL 2023

'I got the job!' Esme Cassidy said to her mum as she ended the call with Lady Olivia MacBain of Drumblair Castle. A little rumble of excitement made her stomach flutter. She had loved the castle, which sat on the picturesque shores of Loch Ness on the outskirts of Inverness, since her childhood when she saw the Laird and his elegant Lady interviewed on Highlands TV. They had given a tour of their home with its many rooms, lofty ceilings and ancestral portraits and at the tender age of ten Esme had dreamed that one day she would be a famous actress and would buy the castle with her millions earned from blockbuster movies. She could see herself floating down the sweeping staircase in a ballgown on her way to an awards ceremony that would, of course, be held in her honour. It was a dream that had stuck with her right up until her late teens but that she now knew had been crazy, since her parents had convinced her acting was 'a nice wee hobby to do at weekends, amateur dramatics or panto and such,' and that 'hardly anyone really makes it, you know. For all the Kate Winslets in the world there are thousands of Dolly Daydreams that fall by the wayside.'

Now, even as a twenty-three-year-old adult, she was still sad that she had turned down her chance to attend the Conservatoire in Glasgow to study acting and stagecraft in favour of pursuing 'a proper career in something like travel and tourism'. Deep down she knew her parents were right about choosing such a *shoot-for-the-stars* career, but someone had to make it. Why couldn't it have been her? She had watched her talented friends from drama club head off to pursue their dreams and she had been the dutiful daughter; taking a course she knew she could ace, but that would give her no goosebumps or auditions. And certainly, no chance of starring opposite her teen heartthrob Zachary Marchand.

'That's great news, love,' her mum, Sally, said with a warm smile, dragging her from her reverie. Esme had inherited her mum's long dark wavy hair and green eyes as well as her love of music and film. Looking at her mum was like looking at a future version of herself. 'I knew you'd get it though,' Sally continued. 'She'd be mad not to employ you with your qualifications. You're overqualified to be a PA, if you ask me. But if it's what you want to do…' She gave one of those sympathetic tilts of the head as she placed a mug of coffee in front of Esme on the kitchen table. 'It's good to know you're taking steps to get on with your life. And now maybe you can make that fresh start you've been hoping for since you got back from Australia in February, it's been so hard to see you moping around for the last couple of months.'

Esme tried to ignore the twinge of pain that shot through her chest and instead focused on the trail of steam swirling up into the air and disappearing. 'It's much more than just a PA job, though, Mum. There's a lot more to it,' she replied, feeling a little defensive. After graduating with a first-class degree in travel and tourism, she had taken a year out to travel – much to the panic of her doting parents – and had returned broken hearted from a trip around Thailand, Australia and New Zealand, thanks to a man called Rhys who was thirteen years her senior.

Her mum pulled out the chair opposite her and sat. 'I know you're still missing Rhys, love, but it's all going to work out for the best. You'll see. He just wasn't *the one*. And the age gap…'

Esme jerked up her head and said through gritted teeth, 'Can we, for once, *not* talk about Rhys, please?' She was aware she had snapped and immediately felt guilty.

Her mum smiled and nodded but there was a clear crumple of hurt to her brow. 'Of course, love. Sorry.'

Esme closed her eyes briefly. 'No, Mum, I'm sorry. I know it's stupid to miss him after what he did but…'

Her mum reached out and took her hand. 'I do understand, you know. He seemed so genuine. And at first he seemed to care for you. When we flew out to visit, Dad and I were both impressed by how he treated you. Although I must admit the age gap worried me, but if he had carried on treating you properly it wouldn't have been insurmountable.'

Esme smiled and squeezed her mum's hand. 'I know. And like you say, this is an opportunity to start over. Make new friends, use my degree. It's good. It's definitely good.'

Why did she sound like she was trying to convince herself?

'Has he been in touch at all?' her mum asked, her efforts to sound nonchalant failing miserably as her voice was strained and a little too high pitched.

Esme shook her head. 'Nope.'

'Good… good.' Esme didn't miss the silent sigh of relief that her mum expelled. 'So, when do you start the new job?'

A knot of anxiety took hold of Esme's insides, and she gasped. 'Monday. Oh, my word, Mum... I'm not sure I'm ready.' She felt the colour drain from her face.

'Of course you are. You'll smash it, love. It's the perfect job for you, working for Lady Olivia.' Pride was evident in her eyes. 'I remember when you were wee.' She giggled. 'You were obsessed with Drumblair Castle. Whenever we drove past the big iron gates you'd tell us how you'd live there someday. You were so determined and wouldn't hear of it when we told you it would never be up for sale.' She laughed lightly.

Esme could picture such occasions as she sat in the back of her dad's truck, gazing longingly out of the window. 'I did love the place.'

'And like you said to Lady Olivia, now you get to work there. It may not be the same as living there but it's the next best thing.'

The front door opened and closed again. 'Hey, honeys, I'm home!' a sing-song male voice bellowed in an Irish accent as Colm Cassidy made his way along the hallway of the semi-detached house.

'Hey, Colm! Your daughter has news,' her mum replied, not even attempting to hide her excitement.

'Oh, aye? So do I!' the tall, dark-haired man said as he entered the kitchen, a wriggling bundle of smooth beige fur tucked under his arm. 'And, erm... I think I might have to go first.' He placed his lunch bag and flask on the table with his free hand, and handed the snuffling bundle to Esme with the other.

She gasped and her eyes welled. 'Who's this?' Immediately the little chunky pug began licking her face to catch the escaped salt water while yipping excitedly. Esme laughed through her tears and peered up at her dad, a tad confused, but oh so happy about the occurrence. 'But Dad, I don't—?'

Colm scratched the back of his neck and cringed. 'I just know how sad you've been since you got back home, and I thought you might like a wee friend. She's only two years old, bless her. A guy at work was getting rid of the wee thing for his son who's moved away for work, so I thought…'

'She's so gorgeous. I can't believe she's mine!' Esme said as she cuddled the pudgy animal, and her broken heart warmed a little.

Sally stared open mouthed for a few moments until she finally found her words again. 'Hang on a second, Colm, we didn't want a dog. Why can't the guy at work keep her?'

Colm's brow furrowed. 'He's allergic. Been in a terrible state while he's had her but wanted her to go to a good home.'

Sally shook her head. 'But this has never been mentioned, Colm, Esme hasn't even asked for a dog, so I don't…?'

'To be fair, Mum, I may not have mentioned it recently but I was always asking for one when I was little, and you always said we couldn't take care of one properly due to work or whatever,' Esme said as she gazed into the sad dark eyes of the animal. 'And she's just perfect.'

'That's not a word I would've used,' Sally mumbled with a curled-up lip.

Ignoring his wife's derogatory comment, Colm's eyes lit up. 'So, you'll keep her then?'

'Absolutely!' Esme said without hesitation, nuzzling the dog's warm fur. 'What's her name?'

Colm chuckled and shook his head. 'That's the only unfortunate thing. The former owner named her Betty.'

Esme cuddled the dog to her chest. 'That's not unfortunate, Dad. It's like the Taylor Swift song that I absolutely love!'

Sally scoffed. 'It's hardly a dog's name, is it? We have a neighbour called Betty, for goodness' sake. How will we explain that?'

Esme continued to nuzzle the dog's fur. 'It's a lovely name. *You're* lovely, aren't you, Betty?' she said in a soft voice that the dog seemed to like, and it licked her chin again as if agreeing. A smile had planted itself on Esme's face and she couldn't take her eyes off her new little friend. It was safe to say it was love at first sight.

'Anyway, pet, you've got news?' Colm asked as he reached out to scratch the dog behind her ears.

In all the excitement Esme had almost forgotten about the recent phone call. 'Oh, yes! I got the job at Drumblair Castle. I'll be PA to Lady Olivia MacBain... or whatever her name will be after her wedding this weekend. MacLeod, I think.'

'Grand! That's grand. I'm so proud of you, darlin'. After all those years of dreaming about living there too, eh?'

'I just said the same.' Esme's mum beamed.

'And now you'll be able to put that arse of a man behind you and move on with your life.'

'Colm, love,' her mum said, shaking her head, her eyes wide.

Colm scrunched his brow. 'She knows I'm right about him, Sal.'

Sally nodded her head sideways at Esme. 'Just leave it, eh, love?'

Esme remained silent. She knew her parents detested Rhys for what he had done to her. And she knew she shouldn't still love him. And she didn't... not completely as she had once done. But she had been deeply in love, and you couldn't just switch that off, unfortunately.

Colm huffed. 'Aye, well, I'm off to get a shower. I need to get the reek of malt off my skin.' Colm worked at the whisky distillery on the outskirts of Inverness and, more often than not, his clothes too were a dead giveaway for his employ as the pungent, earthy aromas clung to the fibres. He tramped up the stairs, heavy footed with apparent exhaustion, leaving Esme, her mother and Betty, the newest member of the Cassidy family, in the kitchen.

'We'll have to go out to the pub to celebrate your new job. Maybe the Drumblair Arms. Anyway, I'd better go and finish this edit that I'm working on. The publisher needs it by the end of tomorrow.' Sally kissed the top of Esme's head. 'And stop worrying. You'll be fine, you'll see. I hope you're house trained,' she added with a pat to the dog's head. Esme knew she'd warm to Betty soon enough.

Sally Cassidy was a born worrier but always tried to put on the appearance of optimism. She had worked as a freelance editor for a large publishing company since Esme had been a toddler, meaning she had always been around to look after her daughter. This had created a strong bond between them, but it was sometimes stifling these days as Esme tried more and more to step out on her own. The year away travelling hadn't been a popular suggestion with her parents once she had finished university, but they had relented when she had agreed to check in with them regularly. Now that she was home, she missed the freedoms she had once experienced. Of course, she knew how fortunate she was to have such loving and devoted parents but being an only child had meant their focus had been entirely on her and her alone since she was born. She was beginning to think her independence would be a good thing for them too. Once she had settled into her new role she intended to find her own place.

In the silence of the empty kitchen, she thought back to the moment she first laid eyes on Rhys Carlson...

'Let go! Please let go!' Esme screamed in a combination of anger and distress at the opportunist thief who gripped tight to the handles of her shoulder bag as he tugged and yanked, trying to free it from her grip. His masked face left only glaring brown eyes that appeared almost black in the Thai sunshine. She had just stepped off the plane at Suvarnabhumi airport to begin her solo travelling adventure and this was not the best start.

A tall, blond-haired man who Esme guessed to be in his early thirties came charging over and punched the assailant square in the face, knocking him and his getaway bicycle over.

'You heard the lady! Now bugger off and get a bloody job, you arsehole!' The cyclist let go of the handbag, picked up his bike and pedalled away at speed, chuntering words that Esme couldn't understand.

Initially Esme was relieved but then annoyed. She tugged the straps back into position on her body and huffed. 'I was fine, you know.'

The handsome Australian smiled and his blue eyes glinted. 'Yeah? You looked pretty terrified to me.'

Raising her chin, she yelled, 'I'm a strong, independent woman who doesn't need a man to protect her!' The scripted words were delivered with the utmost conviction.

The man feigned seriousness and held up his hands. 'Well, in that case I apologise and promise not to intervene next time you're being mugged.' The humour in the crinkle of his eyes wasn't lost on her. 'Seriously, though, are you okay? Can I take you for a brandy or something?'

Knowing she should probably be grateful to the stranger, she softened a little. 'I'm fine... really. Thanks, though.'

He shoved his hands into the pockets of his shorts. 'Look, there's a bar over the road and I've never tackled a mugger before.' His eyes widened. 'Shit, he could've been armed.' He shivered as the reality of the situation apparently dawned on him. 'Bleurgh! I think a stiff drink is definitely called for, don't you?'

Against her better judgement and with her parents' voices screaming in her head – 'Don't accept drinks from strangers! Don't talk to men you don't know! Don't go anywhere with anyone you have just met!' – she smiled. 'Okay, just one drink and I'm buying my own.'

He shrugged. 'Fair enough. You could buy mine as a thank you.' She rolled her eyes as he beamed a hundred-kilowatt smile at her.

The place was busy but not oppressively so. They took two stools at the bar and Esme ordered their drinks.

'I should introduce myself seeing as I just saved your life,' the man teased. 'I'm Rhys, I'm thirty-five, divorced, from Sydney in Aus, and to put your mind at ease I'm not a creep, I'm here taking a sabbatical from my job as a sound technician on movies. You?'

Oh yeah, I'm Esme, I'm twenty-two and a supermodel on a break from my job as the muse for Giorgio Armani, she scoffed inwardly. 'I'm Esme, from Inverness,' she stated bluntly.

Rhys smirked and nodded. 'Okay, I suppose what I just said *did* sound a little farfetched,' he said as if reading her mind. 'But it's all true, I can assure you. I can even prove it and tell you some of the features I've worked on.'

'I didn't say a word,' she replied.

He gave her a knowing glance. 'You didn't have to. The disbelief is written all over your beautiful face.' She had never been called beautiful before. Well, not by someone who wasn't her dad, anyway. Apparently accepting he was going to get no further personal details from her, he asked, 'So, what brings you to Thailand? You can share that at least, eh?'

Choosing her words carefully, she paused. 'I'm... taking a gap year. Just finished uni.'

His eyebrows shot up. 'Oh, wow. You really are a youngster.'

She scrunched her face. 'A *youngster*?'

'Yeah. I mean, you do look young, but I was kind of hoping you were one of those lucky people who doesn't age like the rest of us.'

She tilted her head, thinking how presumptuous he was. 'And why is that?'

He gave a shy smile that didn't really correlate with his hitherto seen personality. 'Because I was going to ask you if you fancied getting dinner with me while you're here. But you're probably not interested in an old bloke like me.'

She couldn't help the laugh that escaped her. 'You're thirty-five, not sixty-five.'

His eyes lit up. 'So, you'd consider it then?'

She cringed, realising she had dropped herself slap bang in the middle of an offer she would struggle to refuse. She felt heat rising in her cheeks as her parents' voices sprang up once again. 'Oh... I don't know... I've only just arrived and...'

He nodded and held up his hand. 'Say no more. I understand.'

She fell silent, strangely a little disappointed that he hadn't pushed the issue. He was rather gorgeous. And his accent was quite sexy. But he was a complete stranger, albeit one who had rescued her from a mugger. But no, she was here to experience Thailand and then would move on to Australia and New Zealand. It was a trip paid for with inheritance from her beloved grandma and she didn't come here to find love;

certainly not with a thirty-five-year-old divorcee from the other side of the world.

They parted ways after their drink and didn't exchange any information. Esme located her hotel, checked in and sent a message to her parents to let them know she had arrived; of course, leaving out the startling details of the events since her arrival on foreign soil. Nothing would've have brought her dad out to Thailand faster than hearing the words, 'I was almost mugged and have been for a drink with a man thirteen years my senior who wanted to take me for dinner.'

The following morning, Esme stood in the hotel lobby, waiting for her taxi that would take her to her first lodging house, when someone tapped her on the shoulder.

'Well, well. If it isn't Esme from Inverness.'

Esme turned and looked up into the crystal-clear blue eyes and chiselled face of Rhys and smiled.

And the rest... as they say... is history.

1

FEBRUARY 2024

Even now, after eleven months of working as PA to Lady Olivia MacLeod, née MacBain, the heiress and owner of Drumblair Castle, Esme still buzzed with excitement as she walked away from the castle down the long tree-lined driveway after work. The job had turned out to be so much more than a typical PA role and her level of responsibility was increasing month on month, just like her job satisfaction. Okay, it wasn't her original dream of becoming an award-winning actor, but it still meant something and she was well respected in the Drumblair household. Lady Olivia made it known often that Esme was an important cog in the machine that was the stunning castle.

Lady Olivia had inherited Drumblair instead of her older brother Kerr MacBain and had set out to open the ancient building to the public to pay for its upkeep. The castle was now a massively successful business which was expanding each month thanks to Olivia's unique ideas; the latest of which had been the barn conversion that had been opened as creative spaces for artists to come and work and hold exhibitions. Olivia had her own studio on the upper floor of the barn and had, just prior to her daughter Freya's birth in December 2023, made a return to the fashion design career she had so passionately loved before her surprise inheritance.

Esme discovered – from other staff members – that Kerr had disappeared a short while after the will had been read after causing trouble relating to the inheritance. He had felt, quite strongly by all accounts, that the castle was rightfully his, but his mother had evidently thought otherwise and, therefore, a deep rift had formed between the siblings.

Kerr was now back in the family fold, however, and seemed to be making amends. He had found a passion for arboriculture and had retrained and was now in charge of the plant nursery that had been a part of the castle's estate for many years. He was making a huge success out of it too.

Esme had heard – although she wasn't one to gossip, unlike some of the staff – that she had been employed to replace the woman who'd previously been Olivia's PA. The reason being, said woman had broken Kerr's heart and announced that she was, in fact, the mother of a child he didn't even know he had fathered around fourteen years before. *Honestly, you couldn't write this stuff*, Esme had thought on hearing the gory details of the MacBain family drama. Olivia was such a compassionate and caring person and had taken the decision to let her PA go in favour of her brother's wellbeing; an admirable thing to do, Esme thought, especially after the *other* rumours she had heard about his many attempts to sabotage her plans for the castle.

Along with the art barn, house tours and nursery was another upcoming venture. Both Olivia's husband Brodie and her Uncle Innes were knee deep in preparations to open Drumblair Castle distillery in another of the larger, newly converted outbuildings. After he and Olivia had got together, Brodie had taken on the role of site manager for the castle, ensuring repairs were carried out, but more recently the distillery had become his pet project and when he wasn't looking after his daughter or spending time with his wife, he could often be seen with his nose in a book about whisky. He oozed enthusiasm when he talked about the distillery and he and Innes were a little like kids about to be let loose in a candy store. Drumblair's own whisky was a long way off, however, as single malt had to undergo a maturation of a minimum three years – something Esme already knew thanks to her dad's job – so Drumblair Gin was to be launched first, followed by a whisky blend. In the meantime, the next, even more exciting event was due to begin.

During the previous year, the castle had been scouted as a filming location for a Georgian-era movie called *An Unlikely Inheritance* which was about a woman whose story bore a striking resemblance to that of Lady Olivia. The original start date for filming had been delayed out of respect when Olivia had gone into labour a little earlier than expected and baby Freya June MacLeod – named after both Olivia's and Brodie's mothers – had been born just before Christmas and two weeks before she was due. But things were now on track and the crew were set to arrive imminently.

Through conversations, Esme could tell Olivia was both worried and excited about the shoot in equal measure. She knew that the sizeable sum the castle was set to receive, and the publicity, would be wonderful for business but she had also mentioned concern about her ancestral home feeling like it no longer belonged to her during filming. It would be more intrusive than the house tours which had limited access to the more private areas.

She was also worried about the safety of the valuable furniture pieces and artwork that could easily be damaged by ill-placed equipment. And then of course the other matter was 'movie tourists' when the film was released. Esme had tried her best to ease Olivia's mind, assuring her that locations were always treated with the utmost respect from what she had read.

All of the stable apartments had been booked out for the duration of the three-month shoot, and the café would be doing much of the catering, so it had been an opportunity too good to pass up. There was also a buzz around the village about the film with many residents hoping to spot, and even fraternise with, the stars, and local businesses hoping they too would see a return on the emotional investment Olivia was making.

For Esme, however, it was going to be bittersweet. On one hand she would witness, first hand, what a real working movie set would be like, but on the other she would witness, first hand, the career she had dreamed about since childhood, and missed out on.

* * *

Every day at Drumblair was different for Esme. One day she would be taking bookings for the art space and dealing with enquiries, another she would be in contact with the production team of the film, and another she would be carrying out interviews for staff in Olivia's stead. The variety made it exciting and never did she feel like *just an assistant*.

In addition to the immense job satisfaction she had discovered while working for Lady Olivia, Esme had made a whole new friendship group, something she had missed since everyone from high school had moved away to start new lives and careers, and they had all lost touch. These days she looked forward to lunch breaks with her closest friend, Parker Duff, the marketing assistant who had started his role at Drumblair on the same day she had, and they had become fast friends. All she needed now was enough money to buy a car, so she didn't have to rely on her parents or public transport, but after her travels her savings had been completely wiped out and she'd had to start from scratch. A car was a little way off yet and she was saving every penny she could, much to Parker's dismay. He was continually trying to cajole her into attending the work nights out, but she rarely made it.

Behind her now, the castle was illuminated by the amber glow of spotlights as the sun was on its descent, taking with it any semblance of warmth. She pulled her jacket higher up around her neck and continued to make her way to the bus stop as her breath clouded before her in the crisp early-evening February air.

'Esme! Wait up! I'll walk with you!' a male voice called from behind her. She turned to see Parker jogging towards her.

'No car today?' she asked.

'Nah. Dad had to borrow mine as his is in for repairs and he was going to see my granny,' he replied, a little out of breath when he arrived beside her. 'How has today been for you?'

'Full on! Baby Freya has been a bit feverish, and Olivia ended up taking her to the doctor, she was sure she was just suffering "new mum syndrome" but said she wouldn't rest until the baby was checked out, so I was holding the fort for a while.'

Parker's face crumpled with concern. 'Oh, no, poor wee Freya. I've never known such a quiet and happy baby so it must have been worrying if she's been off it. I think I'd be at the GP's office every time my baby so much as sneezed if I had one.'

Esme giggled. 'Me too. I'm not sure how new parents cope. Thankfully they were sent home again as it was nothing serious, but Olivia was exhausted from worry and a sleepless night, so Brodie ordered her to rest. Can't say I blame him; she needs her strength.' As they walked towards the bus stop at the end of the lane, Esme inhaled the bracing air, filling her lungs and smiling to herself at the lack of fumes she'd no doubt be inhaling in most other places. 'The phones have been manic today. So many artists asking questions about the barn spaces but they're all fully booked into the late spring and we're having to limit changeovers with the filming taking place, so I've had to disappoint a fair few people. Anyway, how's your day been?'

'Oh, great. Really, *really* great. I was dealing with some well-known social media influencers today about the promotions we're commissioning for the new season, although it's probably not necessary thanks to the film but I'm not admitting that to Lady Olivia.' He chuckled and then sighed. 'It's a bit of a dream come true, working here, isn't it?'

Esme smiled as she glanced over her shoulder at the vast stone structure slowly receding into the distance, its frost-covered exterior glistening in the light of the setting sun. 'It is. I used to dream of living here when I was little.'

Parker shrugged. 'Well, I suppose working here is the next best thing!' Her mum's exact words rang from his mouth. 'Are you looking forward to the am dram auditions next week?' Esme had joined the Inverness Amateur Dramatics Society soon after meeting Parker, and even though it wasn't quite the movie career she had envisaged for herself she was excited to be acting again. Parker had insisted he came along for moral support, and they had both had minor parts in the previous Christmas production which had been such fun. Esme had played a fairy and Parker an elf in a production written by their director.

'You really need to show them what you're made of, you know. You're far better than all of them put together and I think you'd make such a good Juliet. Although I fear your Romeo might be limited to Bryce Roberts and he has slightly fewer teeth than I imagine Romeo would have. He's no Leo DiCaprio, that's for sure.' He chuckled. 'And I'm not sure a gay Romeo would work so I'm out of the equation. I think I'll audition for Mercutio so I can play it like Harrold Perrineau did in the original movie.'

Esme giggled. 'You do know the Leonardo DiCaprio version isn't the *original*, don't you? I mean, you do know Shakespeare wrote the play in the 1500s, don't you? Before film was invented.'

Parker rolled his eyes and nudged her with his shoulder. 'Well, obvs. But it's the best version in my opinion, that's what I meant. Anyway, enough ribbing me, Miss Oscar-Winner-to-be. A few of the café staff and tour guides are going for drinks at the Drumblair Arms on Friday. Paisley is going too. Are you in?'

Christmas wasn't yet a distant enough memory and she had spent rather too much on gifts for her parents and Betty, so cash was a little tight. 'Erm... Oh, I don't know... I mean, I'm a bit skint.'

'Oh, come on, Esme! We all need to let our hair down sometimes. You hardly ever come out with us, so you miss out on all the good gossip.' As if noticing the disapproval in her expression, he added, 'Not that *I'm* condoning the gossip, of course. What I mean is simply that you'd learn so much more about the place from those on the frontline so to speak. And even though we're work besties, I feel like there's so much I don't know about you, even after all this time,' he said, linking arms with her. 'I've already info dumped on you about Benoit, but I've barely heard anything saucy about your love life, so you need to come out and drink enough so you'll loosen up and tell me your secrets.' He gave a theatrical wink.

'The reason being it's non-existent,' she replied.

In spite of the fact Parker was indeed a gossip of the highest order, she had immediately liked him when they had been introduced on their first morning and the feeling had been mutual, much to her relief. They shared a love of all things Taylor Swift which had bonded them immediately, along with their mutual adoration of their dogs and their love for amateur dramatics. Parker was slightly younger than her, having finished his degree more recently. He was tall, extremely well dressed and very smiley. His strawberry-blond hair was neatly cropped, and his green eyes sparkled with humour and mischief.

The info dump he had mentioned had occurred one lunchtime during their first week when Esme had discovered Parker was back living with his parents too after returning from uni. Like her he too had a dog; a chihuahua called Gladys that he had acquired surreptitiously under the radar of his former landlord at the flat he was living in during his degree. Gladys had been a rescue whose former owner had surrendered due to her 'being far too dramatic and needy'. Parker too had a tendency for theatrics, so their personalities were well matched in her opinion. Although Esme adored Betty, she wasn't planning on dressing her up in silly little outfits, however, unlike Parker did with Gladys.

'Please come. Benoit was supposed to be visiting this weekend, but his flatmate had the flu and has kindly passed it on, so he feels like death on a stick, bless his heart.' He rolled his eyes and curled his lips downwards, clearly disgruntled with the state of things. Parker was in a long-term, long-distance relationship with a man called Benoit Barbier whom he had met during his first year at university. Benoit had returned home to Normandy after graduation but visited as often as his work would allow. When Esme didn't reply, he nudged her. 'You wouldn't abandon your work bestie on *another* staff night out, would you?' He stuck out his bottom lip and fluttered his eyelashes. 'You can come and stay at mine after, my folks are going away to visit my aunty in Yorkshire. And Gladys would love to see you. She adores you, you know.'

Esme rolled her eyes at the attempted guilt trip. 'Oh, good grief, I'll come.' She laughed.

Parker clapped his hands. 'Yay!'

* * *

When Esme arrived home to her parents' house in Dores, Betty greeted with her usual excited yips and her curly tail wagging frantically. She lifted the little dog into her arms, and Betty licked her chin before she nuzzled the dog's soft fur.

Her mum and dad were both waiting at the kitchen table for her. 'Had a good day, pet?' her dad asked in a hopeful tone.

She beamed. 'Yeah, really good. Great, in fact. I was sort of in charge today as Lady O had to take baby Freya to the doctor.'

Sally gasped. 'Oh, no, is everything okay with the bairn?'

Esme nodded. 'All good. Just a temperature. She's home again now.'

Sally smiled. 'That's a relief.'

Esme placed Betty on the floor and grabbed a biscuit from the plate on the kitchen table. As she munched on it, she broke off a little piece and offered it to Betty who took it greedily. 'I still can't believe I get to see all the bits of the castle the public don't get to see. It's quite surreal but amazing,' she announced with a wistful sigh.

'Grand... grand,' her dad said before her parents exchanged furtive glances.

Sensing something was amiss, Esme swallowed the crumbled baked oats that suddenly rasped like sandpaper in her throat, and glanced between them. 'What's up? You're both looking shifty. What's happened?'

Her mum pushed up from the table and walked over to the worktop to pick up an envelope. 'There's... erm... there's been a letter for you.'

Esme chuckled. 'Oh? Why do you look so worried? Is it from the tax office?'

Sally sighed. 'Your dad didn't think we should give it to you what with everything going so well for you at the castle now, but I think you have a right to see it.'

Esme scoffed. 'Of course I've a right to see it if it's addressed to me. I presume it *is* addressed to me?'

Colm rubbed his hands over his face. 'Aye, it's addressed to you, pet. I just didn't think you'd want to be dragged down by the likes of that rat when you're doing so well with your fresh start.'

Esme felt the colour drain from her face as her heart fought to pump blood back into it. 'It's... it's from Rhys?' The man she had given her young heart to hadn't been in touch since the previous February when he had unceremoniously dumped her at the airport, in the most heartless and callous way. And now, in a rather strange turn of events, he had chosen to write via 'snail mail' rather than the obvious email that would have arrived sooner. He had often talked about how letter writing was a dying art so she shouldn't have been surprised really. He felt that a handwritten letter meant more, and was far more personal. This only added to the dread she felt about reading it.

Sally nodded and held out the envelope.

Esme snatched it and, with a pounding heart, pushed past her mum to go up to her bedroom as Betty followed on hurriedly, her little nails tap tapping on the hard wood flooring of the hallway. There was no way she was reading a letter from her ex in front of her parents. All that would do would be to fuel the fire already burning in her dad's gut about how the older man had treated her and how he wanted to 'punch his lights out'.

Once in her room and the door closed firmly behind her, she dropped her bag onto cream carpet and walked over to her dressing table. The familiar green eyes peering back at her in the ornate cream-framed mirror were circled with shadows; a feature she had acquired since her break-up that had only begun to fade recently. She still clutched the envelope, the crumpled paper spiking into the palm of her hand to match the pain that had appeared in her chest. She slumped onto her bed beside Betty, who had lain down in her usual spot, and glanced at the offending article which did, indeed, display Rhys's handwriting, and the postmark was, of course, Sydney.

After staring blankly at the scrawled script for a few moments, she tentatively tore open the flap at the back as if it might contain one of those snakes that jumps from the cans you buy at joke shops. She opened up the sheet of paper and began to read:

Dear Sweet Esme

I know things ended abruptly between us last year and for that I'm sorry. And I'm also sorry that this letter has been such a long time coming. But I had to let you readjust to your old life until such time as I knew this letter wouldn't make you miss me all over again as I've missed you. I also felt it was time I explained my actions. I chose to write it down on paper as, well, first of all you know my thoughts on the impersonality of emails, and by its very nature this is incredibly personal. And second, more selfishly I suppose, the process is quite cathartic for me.

I know back at the start, when we first met, I said I wasn't ready to have children and be a husband again just yet, and that there was no pressure on you, but the thing is, I realised I am ready to settle down and be a father after all. You're still young, and from our conversations I knew that being tied to dirty nappies and sleepless nights wasn't something you'd be looking for at this point in your life, or at least it shouldn't be. So, it was better to end things before we fell too deeply. This way we can both look for someone who will give us what we each need. I want you to be happy, even if it's not with me, and I'd hate to think I'd put you off love forever or something crazy like that.

If you'd been older or I'd been younger things would have been so different. But I did care deeply for you, Esme. I hope you know that. I can't get the look on your face at the airport out of my head even now. And I hated that I'd put it there. But I did it all for the best reasons, please know that. I know I seemed cruel. But it felt like the right way to deal with the situation. If you hated me it would be easier to say goodbye. I do regret the way I handled things, though. And I hope someday you can forgive me.

I'm sure your folks hate my guts, and I can't say I blame them. They seemed like such great people when they flew out to visit. I reckon me and your dad could've been good mates. But that's maybe the issue. I'm closer to his age than to yours. The age difference was never an issue until I realised I wanted a family of my own and I couldn't imagine you wanting the same thing. I didn't address the matter with you because I didn't want to risk you agreeing to settle down with me when you had such a bright future ahead of you. You may have ended up regretting that and resenting me and I didn't want to put either of us in that position. You have a long life ahead of you before you should think about kids and marriage, and I couldn't ask you to forgo what's left of your youth. So, admittedly it was cowardly, but easier for me not to discuss it.

The age gap became this big deal. It took on a life of its own and I couldn't get past it. Every minute we spent together then just highlighted our differences. I tried to ignore it, hoping my feelings would change but I'm not getting any younger and I realised I don't want to wait ten years and be a new dad in my late forties. I think part of the wakeup call came after I had been offered the job. You see, I found out through a mutual friend in the industry that my ex-wife is married and had just found out she was pregnant. The news tugged at me in a way I didn't expect. I didn't mention that at the time as, again, I didn't want you to feel pressured and agree you'd have my baby for the wrong reasons. My heart and my head were all over the place, still are really. I'm just sorry I dragged you down with me.

I know this is probably of no help at all but I needed to give you a proper explanation now I have had plenty of time to reflect on my awful actions. I really do hope you find someone your own age who makes you happy and who loves you as much as you deserve to be loved.

Take care

Rhys

Esme stared at the words on the page through blurry eyes as tears cascaded down her cheeks. Betty, sensitive soul that she was, nuzzled her arm and Esme immediately scooped her up and nuzzled her fur as anger and sadness knotted her stomach. How dare he waste a year of her life? How dare he say one thing and then change his mind when she had already fallen for him? And how dare he wait over a year to write to her and apologise

– if that's what you could call it. It sounded more like a raft of excuses to her. Excuses not to be with her.

The thing that pained her more than anything was that she would've been happy to have his child in a few years. Surely he could have waited. If he had proposed, she would have said yes without hesitation. But he hadn't even given her the opportunity. He made the decision for her. For both of them. Treating her like the child he almost accused her of being. The fact turned her stomach and made more tears fall.

There was a gentle knock at the door, and it opened before she could ask for privacy.

'Hey, love, are you okay?'

Do I bloody look okay? Guilt tugged at her heart even though she hadn't said a word. She nodded. 'I'm fine... well, maybe not exactly fine but I will be.'

'What has he said? He hasn't asked you to go back to him, has he?'

'No, Mum, quite the opposite. He's doubled down on his decision to end things between us.' She stared at the pink furry slippers by her dressing table. They reminded her of something a five-year-old would wear and anger bubbled up again. 'While you're up here, I need to say something.'

Her mum reached for her hand and took it. 'What can I do for you, sweetheart? Anything to make the pain go away. It's so hard seeing my baby girl like this.'

Esme snatched her hand away. 'That's just it, Mum. I'm not a baby. I'm an adult. I can't carry on behaving like the little girl everyone perceives me to be.'

'No, love, I didn't mean—'

'Dad was going to hide my mail from me. Do you know how ridiculous that sounds? My bedroom still looks almost the same as it did when I was at school, right down to the posters. It's like some kind of shrine to my childhood and I've been too lazy to do anything about it but now is the time, Mum. You chose my degree course for me when I wanted to do something completely different with my life.'

'You can decorate if you want to, it's just never come up before.' A wide-eyed, panicked expression took over her mum's features. 'And we only wanted what was best for your future, Esme.'

'But that's it. It's *my* future, Mum. I've just turned twenty-four years old. I should be out there making my own life. Not letting you cook and clean for me and have Dad give me lifts to meet my friends. You know, Rhys mentioned our age gap so many times in that letter that it makes me sick to my stomach. I need to stand on my own two feet.'

'But you travelled Asia and Australia, love, you are standing on your own two feet. And you don't need to prove anything to that... to that...'

Esme shook her head and swiped the moisture from her face. 'No. I travelled with Rhys. A man who wanted to look after me because that's the vibe I must be giving off to the world. But I don't need to be looked after. And he's made it quite clear that he thinks I'm too immature to be married and have kids so I may as well get out there and bloody live a little.'

'Wait, at the start he told you he didn't want kids. That's why me and your dad—' She clamped her mouth shut.

Esme glared at her. 'That's why you and Dad what?'

Sally smoothed down the fabric of her black linen trousers and sighed deeply. 'That's why me and your dad relaxed over the age gap thing. We were so worried he'd trap you if he was the settling down type. That he'd pressure you and you'd end up tied down to a baby and a house on the other side of the world. We wanted different things for you. Dad and I were so young when we had you that we wanted you to have a life before you had all this,' she gestured around the room, 'to contend with. But when he said he didn't want kids we were... well, relieved, I suppose. We actually thought you'd be the one to get tired of him and end things between you.'

Esme stood and turned to face her mother where she sat on the pale pink floral bedspread. 'You're as bad as Rhys. You all keep making decisions for me, and the stupid thing is I keep allowing you to. But these are my mistakes to make, not yours. Well, no more. I'm looking for my own place. I need my independence, Mum.'

Her mum's chin trembled. 'We only ever wanted what was best for you, love.'

There was that guilt again, drip, drip, dripping into her mind. She sat beside her mum again and put her arm around her. 'I know you do. And I'm grateful. I really am. I know I'm very lucky to have such caring parents. But if this thing with Rhys has taught me anything it's that I need to grow up. I can't hide behind you and Dad forever.'

2

By Friday, Esme found herself in somewhat of a catch-22 situation; she definitely needed a night out but wasn't sure she had the energy to go. With Olivia being instructed to rest by her doting husband, Brodie, Esme had been left holding the reins which had meant she was rushed off her feet. Uncle Innes, as everyone affectionately knew Olivia's relative, and Brodie were meeting with the Food Standards Agency to dot the final I's and cross the last remaining T's for the distillery so, unlike normal days, neither were available to help. To add to the workload, one of the gift shop staff had called in sick on Thursday and Paisley, the gift shop manager, had been unavailable, so Esme had even spent a couple of hours covering in there.

Even though the castle itself was closed over the winter and wouldn't normally be due to open until Easter, the café and gift shop were still thriving. Things were about to change dramatically, however. With the film crew set to arrive after the weekend, castle tours were going to be drastically reduced for the first part of the 2024 season due to restrictions being implemented by the production company so as not to impinge on the working set. With this in mind, Esme had been in charge of implementing a new booking system with limited availability in advance of the new season. The stable block apartments had been fully booked out for film crew and actors and certain areas had been designated as no-go zones, which would reduce the footfall of general public into the grounds. Things were about to get busier in whole new way, although it would be quieter on the visitor front which would be strange for Esme. It was all very exciting and overwhelming simultaneously, like stepping into the unknown.

At three o'clock, Esme knocked on the door of the drawing room where Olivia was holed up with her baby girl.

'Come on in! Please! I'm starved of adult company!' Olivia called from inside.

Esme pushed open the door and found her boss on one of the squashy old sofas, Freya fast asleep in the crook of one arm, and a book in her free hand. There was a roaring fire in the grate and a wall of heat hit her, which was welcome as the castle boiler was under repair for what felt like the hundredth time that year, and it was only 1 March. 'Is there anything I can get you, Lady Olivia?' Wilf and Marley, the two pale golden dogs, lay protectively at her feet and wagged their tails in greeting.

'A new back to replace this one that aches non-stop these days?' Olivia giggled. 'And for the love of all that is fluffy and has paws, please, *please* just call me Liv, or at least Olivia. You've worked here ages now and I'd like to think we're friends as well as colleagues.'

Esme felt her face warming and she cringed. 'Sorry, force of habit. How are you feeling?'

'Bloody tired out. But at least this wee one is on the mend now,' she said, smiling lovingly down at the sleeping bundle in her arms. 'Anyway, how are you?'

Esme nodded and plastered on a smile, even though she too was exhausted. 'Good, good. The enquiries about the art space are off the charts and Eilidh from the film company has been in touch again. I said everything was on track for Monday as you'd instructed, and explained about Freya being poorly. She said not to bother you further and that she'd see you on Monday.'

Olivia rolled her eyes. 'Oh, heck, thanks. I really should've called her back. She'll think I'm avoiding her. It's awful, really, I should be grateful that they chose Drumblair as their location because the boost to our finances has already been immense. I just feel quite daunted at the prospect of loads of camera equipment and cables being scattered all over the place. Not to mention the crew and actors.'

'I'm sure it'll be great fun when we're in the swing of things and once we know how things are being run. It's just the fear of the unknown at the moment.'

Olivia sighed. 'Yes, I'm sure you're right. I just seem to have acquired the ability to worry about every little thing since Freya was born. Anyway, enough about me. I'm aware this week has been a nightmare, how are you doing? And how's that cute little pug of yours?'

Esme nodded. 'Oh, Betty's lovely. I'm not sure what I would do without her. We're both doing well, thank you.' She thought back to sobbing into Betty's fur after reading *the letter*.

Olivia tilted her head and narrowed her eyes. 'What's wrong, Esme? You're not your usual self. You seem a little out of sorts. Is everything okay? This place isn't getting you down, is it?'

Esme was shocked at how perceptive Olivia was and her chin began to tremble, she chewed the inside of her cheek and tried her best not to cry in front of her boss. 'No, no, absolutely not. Please don't worry, I'm fine, honestly.' She shrugged, knowing deep down that both her actions and her words were unconvincing.

Olivia patted the couch next to her. 'Come on, I think I've grown to know you quite well and I can tell when something's off with you. What is it?'

Esme sighed in what felt like relief that someone cared enough to enquire and she walked over and sat beside Olivia. Wilf, the golden retriever, stood and rested his head on her lap as if he too knew something was wrong. She stroked the soft pale fur of his head and took a deep breath. 'I received a letter from my ex this week. And my parents are being far too overprotective of me, so I'm feeling a little stifled as well as heartbroken.' Tears spilled over onto her cheeks.

Olivia placed her book on the coffee table and reached out to take her hand. 'Oh, Esme, I'm so sorry to hear that. I didn't realise you'd had your heart broken. You've hidden that so well, even from me and I'm like a detective.' She smiled and nudged Esme's shoulder. 'Is he trying to get you back? Your ex? Is that why he wrote to you?'

Esme scoffed. 'Nope. He sort of apologised for how he had treated me but doubled down on his reasons for doing so, so it was like being dumped at the airport all over again.'

Olivia gasped. 'Hang on, he dumped you at the airport? This wasn't when you were on your way back home after your travels, was it?'

Esme nodded. 'It sure was. I was so angry and confused. He'd told me how much he loved me only hours earlier. It was a total bolt from the blue.'

Olivia squeezed her hand. 'Look, I know I'm not your mum but... if you wanted to talk about it, I'd be happy to listen.'

Esme shook her head and waved a dismissive hand. 'Oh, I don't want to waste your time with my problems. You've got more important things to think about.' She reached out and gently stroked the fine auburn hair on the baby's scalp.

Olivia gave a sincere smile. 'Freya's sound asleep so I'm not going anywhere for a while. And if I can help at all I'd like to. You know what they say about a problem shared.'

Esme took another deep, calming breath and began the harrowing story of how her life came crashing down around her at Sydney's Kingsford Smith Airport...

* * *

After that fateful meeting the morning after the attempted mugging, Esme and Rhys had spent almost a year travelling Thailand, Australia – Rhys's homeland – and New Zealand and had quickly fallen in love with each other as Rhys acted as tour guide, taking her to all his favourite locations. He expressed his feelings for her very quickly and even though she was rather shocked at his admission, she couldn't deny her own feelings. On the nights when they couldn't be bothered going out, Rhys played movies on his laptop, and they watched them, wrapped naked in each other's arms in bed together. Sure enough, his story about being a movie sound technician was true and he delighted in pointing out his name in the credits of each film he had worked on.

Esme couldn't quite believe how lucky she'd been in meeting him when she wasn't even looking for love. But wasn't that always the way? Rhys was taller than her by four inches, which was quite nice seeing as, at five feet nine, she had always been tall and had towered over many of the boys her age at school. His light brown hair was sun kissed blond at the ends and his tanned skin made his eyes appear surreally blue, as if he wore contacts. He was the image of perfection to her, and she adored him, but he made her laugh too, a more important trait in her humble opinion.

The age gap of thirteen years didn't even register in Esme's mind and the more time they spent together the deeper she fell. He wasn't interested in rushing into having a family and had made this clear from the start; she wasn't sure if this was a warning or a reassurance. Although, as time went on, she discovered that his now ex-wife had had an affair while they were married but then divorced him because of his lack of desire to start a family.

The truth was Esme's feelings ran so deep she would have done anything for Rhys. And that included having his baby, or even passing up the chance to be a mother – whichever was relevant. Although she didn't voice this at the time.

Something was off, however, on the day of her planned return home – a date she had been dreading but couldn't afford to rearrange – and she couldn't quite eradicate the unsettled feeling in her stomach that caused a non-stop churning. Rhys had come into the airport with her as far as he was allowed but he proceeded to fidget with his necklace. He persistently chewed his nails and kept glancing at the departure board. Esme put it down to the upset he must be feeling about her leaving, she felt it too. In fact, she realised, that's probably what the churning in her stomach was all about. *Of course!*

They grabbed a coffee at one of the concessions and found a table in a quiet corner. People around them chatted animatedly, no doubt excited for whatever adventures they were about to embark upon, but their *own* conversation was decidedly lacking.

Eventually Rhys spoke. 'Look, Esme, I know I said I'd come over to Scotland soon but...' He sighed and was evidently struggling to make eye contact. 'We should be realistic about things.

It's over 10,000 miles away from here to where you'll be, more like ten and a half... and as much as I care about you...' He lifted his gaze and fixed it on her with clear determination. 'And I *do* care about you... I just don't think long distance will really work.'

Care about me? Ouch. She shook her head and forced a smile, not really appreciating his timing, nor his sense of humour. 'Ha ha, very funny, Rhys.'

His brow crumpled and he shook his head. 'I mean it, Esme.' His voice was filled with a sad resolve. 'I'm being serious. I... I think it's time to let go.' His chin trembled and he cleared his throat. 'I'm sorry,' he whispered.

His words were like a sucker punch, pulling the air from her lungs so that she was unable to speak for a few seconds. Her eyes stung as she fought back tears. She searched his gaze, hoping for him to burst into laughter and tell her he'd *got her good* like the prankster he was; plastic spiders on her pillow, jumping out from behind doors, and so on. But alas, that didn't happen and the weight of the realisation that he *wasn't* joking pushed her down until she felt sure she would disappear into the tiled floor beneath them. Her heart squeezed uncomfortably in her chest and her mind raced, fighting for the right words whilst trying, desperately, to make sense of *his*.

This can't be happening. Not now.

She swallowed hard, her throat dry and restricted by a hard ball of emotion. 'But... I-I don't understand. Only last night you said you were sure we could do this. You said you loved me enough to make it work. In fact, it felt as though you were trying to convince *me*, as if *I* was the one on the verge of backing out. And now you only *care* about me? You have to be joking. You can't be serious, Rhys. Please don't do this now.' She tried hard not to sound like she was begging but she could hear the desperation in her own voice.

She couldn't bear it. Her heart was shattering into a million pieces, and she was about to get on a flight that would take her to the other side of the world. Over 10,000 miles away, as he'd just pointed out. She was acutely aware that the chance of sorting this madness out once she had left Sydney would be virtually non-existent and the thought that she might never see him again took her breath away once more. Her heart pounded at her ribs now until it was almost painful, and she placed her hand over her chest. She saw stars dancing before her eyes and a ringing sound reverberated in her ears, almost drowning out the whooshing sound of her blood pumping way too fast, but not completely. The voices of the other travellers receded until they became echoes at the end of a long tunnel.

Oh, God, please don't let me pass out.

He reached out and patted her arm in a rather poor and patronising attempt at comfort. Then, as if realising his actions were useless under the circumstances, he withdrew his again rapidly and ran his fingers back through his thick, floppy hair and cleared his throat again. 'I know. I know I said that,' his voice wavered, 'but I've been thinking about it all night. I've hardly slept because I just don't see how we can do that. The time... and the expense...' He shook his head and sighed.

Esme took slow, quiet, deep breaths, willing herself to calm down. 'You said you had enough money to fund a few trips, and I said I'd do the same once I get a job. You even talked about looking for work in the UK. You said the film industry in the UK is buzzing right now and you'd love to be a part of it,' she said, as if jogging his memory with his own words would miraculously change his mind. 'So... *again*, I don't understand.' Tears escaped and slipped silently down her cheeks, but she swiped them away as quickly as they fell.

He lowered his gaze and fiddled with the paper coffee cup on the table before him, this was clearly difficult for him too so why the hell was he doing it? 'The thing is, Esme, I was offered a job. A production company here in Sydney. It's a huge deal and an offer I simply can't pass up. It's with Gadigal Films.' He lifted his chin and pleaded at her with his eyes as if she should completely understand the weight of this news. 'They're massive, Esme. This is a fantastic career move for me and I'm ready to get back to it. I wasn't expecting to be offered anything so good after taking a year off after the divorce, so you've got to understand how big a deal this is for me.'

She clenched her jaw hard until it ached. 'But you'll get vacation time, surely?' *Stop it now, Esme, you sound pathetic*, she warned herself inwardly. 'I've already applied for my return visa; with your encouragement, I might add.'

He leaned towards her and locked his determined gaze on hers once more. 'Can we just...' He shook his head and opened and closed his mouth a few times as if trying to find the right words, his nostrils flared and he swallowed. 'Let's just part on good terms, eh? Remember the fun we've had and move on with our lives.'

Her stomach roiled and she placed a hand over it. 'The *fun* we've had? It was a little more than that, don't you think? You told me you were in love with me after a week of us meeting. A *week*. I thought you were crazy, but you've told me repeatedly how much you love me since then. And I've done the same, because I meant it. Doesn't that count for anything?'

He reached across to take her hand, but she swiftly snatched it away and a look of hurt flashed across his features. 'Of course it does. We've spent some magical, special times together. I care deeply for you, Esme, and I'll always remember what we've shared. I'll look back on it all with such fondness and it'll be...' He shook his head and closed his eyes briefly.

She felt her lip curl. 'Something to keep you warm on long winter nights?' she sneered as the sickly words fell from her lips.

He sighed heavily. 'That's not what I was going to say. I was going to say—'

'Answer me one thing. Why have you chosen *now* to tell me? A couple of hours before I leave. How is that fair, Rhys?'

He scratched his stubbled chin. 'I know the timing isn't great, but... It would've been so much harder to tell you before now. It would've been awful for us both living together with that hanging over us for a whole month.'

Her stomach plummeted earthwards once more. 'A *month*? You've known about this job for a month, and you said nothing?' She realised her voice was a little too loud now but frankly she didn't care. 'You've let me believe that everything is great between us when all that time you've been working out how to end things with me and all over a damn job?'

His cheeks coloured red, and he glanced around uncomfortably. 'It's not just the job... it's... There are other factors.'

'Other factors like what? Come on! Tell me the truth. You owe me that much! What is it? And why the hell couldn't you tell me before?'

'Never mind, Esme. It won't help matters because my mind's made up.' He sighed deeply and his shoulders slumped. 'And like I said, I didn't want your last month to be awful.'

She stared incredulously at this man she thought she knew so well. 'Oh, well, that was so kind of you.' Sarcasm dripped like putrid syrup from her mouth. 'So all that crap you spouted last night about us spending our lives together, about us eventually getting married on a beach in Byron Bay, then relocating to the Highlands someday to bring up our kids, and how you were sure we'd make this work, it was all blatant lies? Because you painted a pretty bloody vivid picture for it to be a counterfeit.'

He spoke through gritted teeth. 'No... no, it wasn't like that... not exactly. I was still weighing things up. Trying to figure out what I wanted most of all.'

She scoffed and shook her head. 'What *you* wanted *most of all*?' She was aware she was repeating him in the manner of a sarcastic and bitter parrot but really didn't give a shit at this point. 'Well, lucky you to have decided so conveniently for both of us just as I'm about to go back to Scotland.' She thought back to the morning they had shared in bed and her skin began to crawl. She rubbed the goosebumps on her arms, leaned forward and hissed, 'We had sex this morning, Rhys. We've had sex countless times in the last month since your deception began; if you hadn't been stringing me along from the start, that is. How could you be so damned cruel? Why would you do that if you were going to dump me? Have I just been some casual fling to you? Telling me what you think I want to hear to get me in your bed?'

He glanced around again. 'The sex has always been great between us, you can't deny that you've enjoyed that too, Esme,' he almost whispered.

A pain shot through her chest, and she gasped. 'I enjoyed it because it *meant* something to me. I thought we had a future. You *said* we had a bloody future.'

He clenched his jaw, his cheeks colouring a deep pink. 'Please lower your voice, Esme. People are looking.'

Had he expected her to be completely fine with being lied to and dumped like that? And in such a public place? If that was the case, he was sadly mistaken. She wasn't prepared to let him off easily after how he had treated her. She stood rapidly from her seat; the force pushed the chair back until it landed with a loud clatter on the tiled floor. 'Let's give them something to look at then, eh?' She picked up her cold coffee and threw the remainder at his face, causing him to gasp. She glanced around and, sure enough, all conversations had ceased, and every eye was on them. Thankfully, however, there were no phones pointed in their direction. The last thing she wanted, or needed, was to be internet famous as a jilted psycho.

She puffed out her chest and straightened her spine. 'Don't worry, Rhys, message received loud and clear. You've lied to me by omission for a month and even with that knowledge you've continued to use me for your own gratification, which says a whole lot about you as a person. Thanks for nothing. I'd say it's been nice knowing you, but I don't think I actually ever did. Goodbye, Rhys.' She grabbed her suitcase and her backpack and stormed away in the direction of the departure gates.

* * *

Olivia hissed in air through clenched teeth before huffing it out again, her eyes wide and eyebrows raised. 'Wow. What a total shit. You deserved so much better than that, Esme. He's an absolute rat for treating you that way. I can't believe he did that to you at all, never mind that he did it at the bloody airport. What a coward! And what did his letter say?'

'That at the time he dumped me he had just discovered his cheating ex-wife was pregnant with the man she'd had the affair with, and it made him realise that he wants kids sooner rather than later. He also said that he thinks I'm too young to want that so breaking up was the best thing to do.'

'Oh, God, it sounds like you had a lucky escape. He clearly

has issues he needs to work through. Am I right in thinking your mum and dad are worried about how this will all affect you?'

Esme nodded. 'They're wrapping me in cotton wool and it's driving me mad. I really think it's time to find my own place and move out as soon as possible. I found out my dad wasn't even going to give me the letter when he realised who it was from. It's like they think I'll fall apart at the mere mention of Rhys but I'm tougher than they realise. I can't continue being treated like a child and I fear that as long as I live there that's exactly what will happen.'

'Have you started looking for somewhere?' Olivia asked, her brow etched with genuine concern.

Esme sighed. 'I have but there's a serious lack of property for rent just now, especially ones that are dog friendly. And the ones that are for rent are either tiny, huge or I wouldn't let a pig live in them.'

Olivia fell silent for a few seconds, a pensive crease between her brows. 'I may have an idea. Leave it with me. And in the meantime, I hear the staff are having a night out. You should definitely go. I think you need to remember what fun is and get that man out of your system.'

3

That evening, Esme sat at her dressing table, putting the final touches to her makeup. She had packed an overnight bag with her essentials and had chosen jeans and a long-sleeved t-shirt in a deep plum colour that made her green eyes even more vivid. She dragged her fingers through her long dark brown waves and then applied her favourite burgundy lip gloss.

Her canine companion sat on her bed, her head tilting as she watched Esme's every move with intrigue.

She swivelled on her chair to face the little dog. 'Well, Betty, I'm ready. Although I think I'd rather stay home and snuggle up to you and watch movies or something.' As if agreeing, the pug gave a single bark. 'Don't worry, I'll spend the day with you tomorrow. I'm going to stay at Parker's tonight though, with Gladys.' This time the dog whined and lowered her head onto her paws. Esme walked over and crouched down before the dog. 'I still love you the most though.' There was a knock at her door.

'Come in.'

Her dad appeared in the doorway. 'You look lovely, pet. I'm

glad you're going out; you should be enjoying yourself. Anyway, I'm ready to go when you are.'

Esme scratched Betty behind her ears and stood. 'I'm sure I could've got a taxi, Dad. I feel bad for taking you out when you've been working all day,' she said, guilt niggling at her for accepting his offer of a lift when her usual taxi company was fully booked. *Ugh, after everything I said to Mum about wanting my independence.*

'Don't be daft. You know I don't mind. I'll see you downstairs.' He turned around to walk away.

'Dad.' He stopped in his tracks and glanced over his shoulder at her. 'I do love you, you know.'

His eyes became a little glassy and he cleared his throat. 'Aye, and I love you, pet. Now come on, we don't want your friends to be left waiting.'

* * *

Esme stood at the doors of the Drumblair Arms in the chilly evening air waving as her dad drove away. Once he was out of sight, she inhaled a deep breath in a bid to calm her racing heart. She felt like the new kid at school all over again, which was silly considering she had known these people for months now. She pushed through the doors into a welcome blast of heat from the roaring log fire over by the bar. The place was busy with people enjoying the end of their working week and the atmosphere was buzzing with lively chatter. She spotted the group of her castle colleagues standing by the bar as Ed Sheeran was playing on hidden speakers. Parker spotted her and made a beeline in her direction.

'Esme!' He hugged her. 'You came!'

Esme hugged him back. 'I said I would, didn't I? And I wouldn't want to let my work bestie down.'

He fluttered his eyelashes. 'N'awww. I've told Gladys that you're coming to stay over, and she can't wait to see you! I just hope Betty isn't jealous when you get home and you smell of a different pooch!' He twirled her around and sang along with Mr Sheeran about Bad Habits. 'I love a bit of Ed almost as much as I do our Queen Taylor,' he informed her, as if they were friends or relatives of his. He suddenly stopped and gripped her by the arms and his eyes widened. 'Speaking of Taylor Alison Swift, you've remembered what's happening next month, haven't you?'

Esme giggled and shook her head. 'Well, durr. She releases *The Tortured Poets Department*. As if I'd forget that.'

He linked his arm through hers and led her to where the others had gathered. 'Oh my God, I can't flipping wait. We're having a listening party on release day. It's only a month away so we'd better start planning.'

Esme grinned. 'Sounds good to me.'

As they reached their group, Judd Cowan, one of the nursery staff, smiled widely but didn't make eye contact for very long. 'Hey, Esme. It's good to see you. To what do we owe the honour? You don't usually come out on work get-togethers.' As well as working for Kerr MacBain, Judd had also begun working with the grounds team at the castle and, following the retirement and relocation of another gardener, had moved into one of the cottages in the castle grounds next door to Dougie, the head groundskeeper, and his wife Mirren.

Esme hadn't spoken to Judd much as he always seemed quite shy and often had AirPods in when he worked. He was a tall man in his late twenties with light brown hair and kind chocolate-brown eyes. His skin had an earthy, tanned tone to it, possibly due to the years of working outside at the nursery since he had been employed there when it was run by his uncle, long before Kerr MacBain took over. She was used to seeing him with smudges of dirt on his face and lots more on his clothes, and his hair was often slicked back with sweat, though tonight he was clean shaven, smelled fresh and woodsy and there wasn't a speck of dirt on his designer polo shirt or his jeans. He was quite handsome, something she hadn't really noticed before.

He reached out and surprised her with a hug, the shock of which almost toppled her over. He grabbed for her. 'Whoa there. And that's before you've had anything to drink.' He chuckled. 'So, what brings you out tonight?'

'I dragged her kicking and screaming, didn't I, Esme?' Parker said with a nudge to her shoulder and a wink.

She laughed. 'Ignore him. I was neither kicking nor screaming. I'm just... I don't know.' She shrugged, unsure how to finish her explanation without sounding silly.

'We don't bite, you know,' Judd replied with a wide smile. Then he leaned closer and in a theatrical whisper said, 'Well, some of the others might but I can assure you I'm not a vampire. Although I know some women find the whole blood-sucking thing quite sexy, don't they? I mean look at *Twilight* and *Vampire Diaries*. Although they're all too good-looking to be real vampires in my opinion.' He shrugged and then his cheeks flushed bright red as if embarrassed by what he'd said. 'Not that I think vampires are real or anything like that. I'm not into that stuff. I've just heard... things...' He cleared his throat. 'Anyway, what are you drinking? I'll get us a round in.'

Parker interjected, 'I'll have a G and T, darling, what else?' he stated as if it was the most obvious thing in the world.

'Make that two... please,' Esme replied as she tucked her hair behind her ear. Judd gave a swift nod and walked the few steps to the bar. As he walked away, Esme heard Judd whispering to himself about being an arse and why couldn't he at least try to be normal in front of other people. She smiled and shook her head.

'He fancies you,' Parker said in a low voice.

'He does not, you just like to match make,' Esme said as she felt her own face heating up. Parker had been nicknamed *Granny Isla* by the gift shop staff, apparently after the grandmother of a former employee of the castle who was well known for her attempts to marry people off.

'I'm being serious! Did you see the way he looked at you when he saw you walking over and then couldn't make eye contact, and how he blushed just now?'

'That was because he was embarrassed that he'd mentioned blood sucking and good-looking vampires, you wee dafty,' Esme replied, rolling her eyes.

Ignoring her reply, Parker continued, 'He is rather yummy though, don't you think? In that rugged and unwashed kind of way.' Before Esme could reply that he wasn't 'unwashed' tonight, he grabbed her by the arms again. 'Ooh, ooh, speaking of yummy, have you heard who's coming to the start of filming?'

Esme had been heavily involved in the organisation of the film crew's imminent visit and had seen the cast list. In fact, it may as well have been tattooed on her brain seeing as she seemed to be running through the cast lists, dietary requirements, flat allocations and whatever else in her sleep. She wasn't particularly excited about any one individual person, except perhaps the lead, Ruby Locke, who was pretty much living Esme's dream. She was the typical 'girl next door' who had shot to stardom following her role in *The Girl and the Rose*.

Esme shrugged. 'I know everyone who's coming, why, who has you all in a tizzy?'

Parker scowled incredulously as if she was insane. 'Zachary Marchand, who else?'

Esme crumpled her forehead and shook her head. Her heart skipped a beat, and she stuttered, 'He-he isn't even in the film.'

She'd had a massive crush on the actor since he was in her favourite teen romance movie set in the heart of London. She had watched it probably a hundred times and had been smitten. Utterly head over heels in love. In fact, his poster was still on her wall in her unchanged bedroom – another reason she clearly needed to move out. Back then when she had been a starry-eyed sixteen-year-old wannabe actress, Zachary Marchand had been around nineteen and had been ridiculously handsome with thick, wavy dark brown hair and deep brown eyes that she would happily have got lost in. He was very well spoken with a Home Counties accent that somehow made him even more dreamy. He was muscular without being an over-the-top body builder type and, of course, his clean-shaven face had been sculpted and smooth as if carved out by hand by a total perfectionist.

These days he had aged like a fine wine. Not that he was old in any way but he was now manly in the best possible way, rather than the fresh-faced teen she had always adored. The last film she had seen him in had been a thriller and he was most definitely all grown up. Stubble had graced his angular jawline, and his hair had been shorter but still thick enough to run your fingers through and grip in the heat of passion. She had watched the movie at the cinema with her mum and had been rather embarrassed at the unexpected love scenes where he had been completely naked, although tastefully covered where it was necessary. But he was still the most gorgeous celebrity she knew of by far. And now, Parker was telling her she was going to be in the same location as him.

'Earth to Esme!' Parker said, clicking his fingers to snap her out of her rather steamy daydream. 'You drifted off for a minute there.'

With firm resolve, Esme stuck to her guns. She knew the cast list like the back of her hand. She had dealt with every aspect of each of their wants and needs for the upcoming shoot and he definitely wasn't involved. 'No. I think you're wrong. He wasn't mentioned anywhere in the paperwork.'

Parker scoffed. 'Uh, no, I'm 150 per cent right. He was cast as the younger brother of the leading man.'

Esme again shook her head. 'No, no, that's Dean Winterburn. The guy from that really good cop show on TV. I remember because I was quite surprised he had transitioned into movies so easily. Although I suppose they do look similar so I can see why you'd make that mistake.'

Parker's eyes widened. 'Don't tell me you didn't know? Dean Winterburn was fired for... well, no one really knows or cares why he was fired, he's a two-bit celebrity, but Zachary was hired in his stead! It was all over TikTok. Don't tell me you didn't see it?'

Esme wasn't as big a consumer of social media as Parker was, after all, it was his job, but she was sure she would have known about something this big. In her mind she rifled through the emails that had been going back and forth over the preparations, but she couldn't think of any that had stated a thing about a change of actors. She would ask Olivia on Monday. But in the meantime, if what Parker was saying was true, she would be within feet of her teenage heartthrob in mere days. Good grief, she would have to be careful to remain professional and not regress into a swooning teenager if ever he spoke to her – which he probably wouldn't anyway so it was no doubt a moot point.

At only three years her senior, she had dreamed of one day meeting Zachary on set – when she was obviously cast to play opposite him – and in this make-believe scenario they would fall head over heels in love during filming and then, of course, they'd run off into the sunset together before moving into her newly purchased castle and begin filling it with beautiful children. But now he was going to be at Drumblair Castle starring as the younger brother of the male lead in *An Unlikely Inheritance*. If only her dreams of becoming an actress hadn't been thwarted by overly cautious parents, she might have had the chance to audition for the film.

Get a grip, Esme Cassidy, even if you'd taken that place at the Conservatoire there's no saying you'd have even got an audition for the film.

4

As the drinks flowed, Esme relaxed into the evening. She chatted with Paisley, the gift shop manager, and Noah, the chef from the café. The former navy chef was stocky with broad shoulders and dark hair cropped close to his scalp. He was always clean shaven and smartly presented and took great pride in his work. During the previous summer he had embarked upon a project to open the café up on an evening and it had been a great success. Lady Olivia was full of praise for her team and Noah was thought very highly of.

It was clear to Esme that Noah was besotted with Paisley. The petite blonde was quite the firecracker, and to Esme she epitomised Shakespeare's *A Midsummer Night's Dream* quote, 'Though she be but little, she is fierce' and there was no doubt that that was what attracted the tough tower of a man. He gazed at her with such longing and puppy dog eyes that Esme felt quite sorry for him. She had spent many a lunchtime chatting to Paisley since starting work as Olivia's PA and had enjoyed the feeling of a friendship beginning to blossom. On these occasions Paisley often showed Esme the new stock she had bought in before the rest of the staff saw it, insisting Esme had impeccable taste – something that no one had ever said about her before.

For the first time since drama club at school, Esme felt like she was part of something meaningful and fun. All her old drama club friends had gone off to pursue their dreams and she had sadly lost touch with them. She tried not to be envious and that was a little easier now she worked at Drumblair, but she still often wondered how different her life might have been if she'd accepted the place on that acting degree course at the Royal Conservatoire in Glasgow.

As the night wore on, Esme really was beginning to wonder why she hadn't made more of an effort to attend staff nights out, in spite of her finances. Everyone had made her feel so welcome and had insisted that she was part of the group now, so she would be expected to attend every such gathering. It felt good to have friends again; something she had never really experienced during her adulthood.

Throughout the evening, she caught Judd watching her in her periphery; not in a creepy way, however, more as if he was intrigued by her, which she found flattering but reminded herself she was off relationships for the foreseeable future. On a couple of occasions, Parker nudged her and whispered things like, 'He keeps looking at you. I think he's smitten.'

They talked about the castle and their individual roles and Esme was fascinated with Judd and his knowledge about flowers and plants.

'Did you know each flower has its own meaning? It's called the language of flowers,' he said oozing with enthusiasm. Esme had heard something about that but didn't know a great deal. Judd went on, 'Back in the Victorian era, and before that even, people used to give flowers with hidden meanings.'

Esme shook her head. 'What kind of hidden meanings?'

'Well, for example, if you loved someone you would give them red chrysanthemums. If you felt affection for someone you would give them morning glory. But a dark crimson rose would indicate feelings of grief.'

He impressed her with his knowledge, and she was quite surprised at it too. Not that she wanted to stereotype but he didn't appear the type to know about such things. 'Oh, wow. I had no idea it was all so in-depth.'

He nodded. 'Yeah, you could really use it to your advantage, either in a good way or bad.' He cringed. 'I have a tendency to go quite deep when I'm interested in something.'

'Well, I can understand how it would be interesting,' Esme replied with a smile.

The subject rolled around to DIY and their varying levels of expertise or lack thereof. Noah was renovating a flat in an old former bank in the centre of Inverness and Paisley was suffering while her landlord fitted a new kitchen to her little cottage.

Judd turned to Esme and asked, 'So where do you live, Esme? I've seen you being dropped off or walking up from the bus stop at the end of the lane so it must be a fair trek.' His words slurred ever so slightly, which was endearing in a funny way. He was definitely chattier after a few beers. She felt her cheeks warming and she chewed her lip for a moment. He frowned and then widened his eyes as he gaped around at the rest of the group. 'Shit, I'm not trying to stalk you or anything. I'm pretty rubbish at small talk to be honest, you ask Noah. I always seem to say or ask the wrong thing, sorry.'

Noah laughed and slapped him on his back. 'Aye, he's really bad at it. First time I met him he asked me why I always look so pissed off. Talk about blunt.' He shook his head and grinned at Judd, who cringed.

'Yeah... sorry about that. You're a serious-looking dude, but you're all right under the hard exterior.' Judd chuckled.

Feeling guilty, Esme shook her head. 'Oh, no, it's fine. I wasn't thinking anything bad at all. It's just a bit embarrassing. I still live with my folks.'

Judd's brow crumpled in apparent confusion. 'That's not embarrassing. It's practical. Getting on the housing ladder is no mean feat these days.'

She knew he was right in a way, but still would rather it wasn't the case. 'I was supposed to move out when I returned from travelling but... it didn't quite work out. So, a temporary thing has become a lot more permanent than I'd hoped.'

'You're looking to move out then?' he asked with a tilted head, genuine interest in his focused gaze.

She nodded. 'At some point soon, yes. My mum and dad are a little... how do I put it? Overprotective, let's say.'

Judd gave a small smile. 'But that's because you're precious to them, that's all.' His statement was so matter-of-fact and, again, she knew he was right.

'I know. I just had a lot of independence when I was...' She stopped mid-sentence, realising the untruth she was about to speak. 'Well... maybe not independence as such... It's complicated.' Esme took a large gulp of her drink, hoping that the conversation would end there.

'Don't worry, I know all about complicated.' He looked as if he was about to say more but seemed to think better of it and closed his mouth.

'Have you looked at many places yet?' Noah asked.

'Not in person. But the ones I've seen on the internet haven't been suitable so far.'

Judd huffed. 'Oh yeah, I know. I was looking for ages and the only places I saw were either shoe boxes or filthy. And I know

I'm not the tidiest person, but I refuse to live somewhere with mould growing on all the walls.'

Her eyes widened and she pointed randomly. 'Yes! And the ones that claim to have garden access have a patch of cracked concrete slabs with weeds growing in between.'

Judd laughed. 'And the ones that say open-plan living, dining, kitchen which actually means the sofa is a foot away from the sink. They really do exaggerate the features of these shiteholes. Pardon my language.'

Esme giggled. 'It's a minefield. I fear I may be stuck at my folks' for a while yet.'

'Come on, missy, taxi's here and poor Gladys will be desperate for a widdle,' Parker said as he returned to Esme's side.

Esme cringed. 'Sorry, guys, we've got to go.'

Judd smiled. 'No worries. It's been really nice to chat to you this evening. I hope you get sorted with somewhere soon. See you on Monday when the madness really starts.'

'Don't remind me. The number of menu changes I've had to make has been ridiculous,' Noah said with a shake of his head.

'I'm just hoping that Hugo Delaney falls madly in love with me and whisks me away to his penthouse in New York,' Paisley said dreamily about the actor playing the lead role opposite Ruby Locke.

A look of dismay flashed across Noah's face. 'Isn't he a bit old for you?'

'Pfft. Age is just a number when you're as gorgeous as he is.'

'It's all Botox and fillers, Pais, take it from someone who studies these things,' Parker said with a chuckle. 'Now Zachary Marchand is a different case.'

'Ooh, no, he's too pretty for my liking,' Paisley said, scrunching her nose. 'What do you think, Esme?'

'I'm saying nothing,' Esme replied, laughing. 'Anyway, see you all Monday.' They all hugged and Esme turned to follow Parker.

'Judd definitely fancies you,' Parker said as he linked arms with her.

'Even if he does, and he doesn't by the way, but even if he does it's not happening. I'm sworn off men. Well, straight men, anyway.'

They climbed into the taxi and Parker swivelled in his seat. 'Do tell. Who broke your heart? Who do I have to set Gladys on? Because she will do some serious damage to their ankles!'

Esme giggled; the fresh cool air that had hit them as they left the pub had made the alcohol whizz straight through her bloodstream, not stopping until it hit her brain. 'It'd be a bit tricky seeing as he's all the way over in Australia.'

'Oooh, did you meet him on your travels?'

She sighed. 'I did. I thought I was the love of his life but...'

'Aww, no. Did he turn out to be a total shit?'

'You could say that.' She pulled out her phone and rifled through the photos, showing her friend and, as she did so, she relayed the gory details of her failed relationship with Rhys. She knew she probably should have deleted the pictures, or at least uploaded them to the cloud and removed them from her phone so the constant reminders weren't there every time she looked at it. But the truth was she hadn't been ready to completely let go. Until the letter.

Parker looked at the photos of the supposedly loved-up couple and listened intently as Esme – surprisingly coherently, and even more surprisingly without crying, in spite of the alcohol she had consumed – regaled him with the atrocious way she had been treated. Of course, like any decent friend would do, he gasped in shock and scrunched his face in disgust in all the right places.

Once she had finished the terrible tale, he scoffed. 'You deserve so much better than that ageing pseudo-surfer boy and his stupid floppy hair. He should go and throw his head on the barbie with the shrimps! I mean, who the hell does he think he is? Jason Donovan when he was in *Neighbours*?'

Esme scrunched her nose. 'Who?'

Parker gasped. 'Don't tell me you've never watched reruns of *Neighbours*. The most famous Aussie soap of the eighties.' Considering she'd been born in the year 2000, she vaguely recalled the name but wouldn't know the man if he slapped her in the face. Her expression must have spoken volumes. Parker tapped on the screen of his own phone and held up a photo of a blond man she didn't recognise. 'No bells? *Joseph and the Amazing Technicolour Dreamcoat*? Kylie Minogue? Margot Robbie? Although, admittedly, she was added to the cast a bit later.' He shook his head. 'Anyway, never mind. Let's just say it's a good thing Rhys is a gazillion miles away because if we bumped into him his nose might have a collision with my fist.'

Esme giggled at his assertion. 'Come off it, Parker, you're the least aggressive man I know. I think your idea of setting Gladys on him was more realistic.'

He feigned shock. 'Hey, just because I'm gay doesn't mean I can't stand up for myself. I work out, you know, and it's wrong to stereotype people.'

Esme pursed her lips and tilted her head. 'Says the man who just did the exact same thing to my Australian ex.'

He held out his hand in a swiping motion and tilted back his head. 'Ugh, whatever. Anyway, hand me your phone. From now on you're going to start every day with a reminder from Mother.' Esme handed over her phone and another scrunch of her face elicited a further look of exasperation. 'Queen Taylor herself.' He shrugged as if it should have been completely obvious he was talking about his idol Taylor Swift. 'In fact...' He tapped at the screen again. 'Not only your alarm, but if that shithead *ever* calls you again, his new personalised ringtone will remind you that you're never *ever* getting back together with him. You can call me and Miss Swift the Rhys Police.' He chuckled at his own joke.

* * *

The following morning, Esme awoke in the spare room of Parker's parents' house. Her head was throbbing in time with the thumping of her heart and her mouth was as arid as the Sahara Desert. Perhaps the shots of tequila when they'd arrived back at Parker's had been the final straw because she couldn't remember much about the night after that. Although distinct snippets returned, like flashbacks of her dancing around the kitchen with Parker singing Taylor Swift's 'We Are Never Ever Getting Back Together' at the tops of their voices. She remembered it feeling like a kind of affirmation, entirely fuelled by alcohol, but it had felt good. Cathartic even. But now, in the cold light of day, she was mortified. God, his neighbours must have heard everything. It's a wonder they hadn't called the police to put in a noise complaint.

As she glanced around the room she hadn't really taken in last night, she realised she was surrounded by so much clashing floral chintz and frills that it appeared the 1980s had thrown up the contents of its interior design disasters in there. Even the box of tissues on the bedside table had a floral cover over it. The framed pictures of clowns were a little disconcerting and she was glad she hadn't noticed them last night or sleep would have definitely evaded her. She wondered if maybe she had accidentally clicked her heels together and ended up back in 1985. Perhaps Jason Donovan would walk through the door any second singing 'Especially for You', a song Parker had introduced her to the night before, and insisted on serenading her with – seriously, those poor neighbours.

There was a knock on her bedroom door, bringing her back to the present. 'Come on, sleepy head. I've made fresh coffee. And it's a bright day today so I thought we could take Gladys for a walk by the river before you head home. Blow away the cobwebs.'

Esme sat up and rubbed at her temples. 'I think my cobwebs would need a force ten gale. How can you be so fresh after the amount we drank last night?'

Parker shrugged. 'Good genes, I guess. I've made toast if you want some.'

Esme nodded but quickly regretted the action as the motion made her head swim and it took her fragile stomach along for the ride. 'I'll be down in a minute,' she said carefully, holding still so as not to shake her brain around too much.

'Okay. I've left you a bath towel in the bathroom. It's the one with the frilly lace edging,' he told her with a roll of his eyes. 'Honestly, my folks give a whole new meaning to the phrase *time warp* and sadly I don't mean the Tim Curry kind. The shower over the bath is pretty self-explanatory. See you downstairs.' He was far too jolly; annoyingly so in fact, Esme decided.

Once she had showered, she felt a little fresher and on her arrival downstairs she was greeted by Gladys's excited yips and frantic tail wagging, along with the earthy aromas of freshly brewed coffee and only slightly burnt toast. Surprisingly her stomach growled, and she sat at the little kitchen table to eat.

5

The months leading up to filming day had been quite hectic, with the cinematographer and set designer wandering around selecting the best angles and locations from which to shoot; which pieces of furniture to use and which needed to be removed, and which portraits would make the cut. There had been Zoom meeting after Zoom meeting between Olivia, Brodie and the production company, some of which Esme had attended to listen in as she would be on site for the majority of the three or four months of shooting. The director had been to the castle several times to produce a shot list and plan on site. The culmination of the previous few months was about to come good now, however.

Esme arrived early to the castle on Monday morning, the first day of the schedule, with a nervous trepidation about the months ahead. There were already people extricating huge technical-looking items from vans and slowly guiding them through the double entrance doors. As she got closer, she had to dodge official-looking types who were engrossed in conversation with very serious expressions, pointing and gesturing at parts of the castle and its grounds. Her heart leapt into her throat, knowing that today was the start of something huge for Drumblair but also, more inadvertently, for her. She had, of course, always dreamed of being the one standing in front of the camera, perhaps being directed by someone like Greta Gerwig and obviously acting opposite Zachary Marchand, but it would still be fascinating to see it all happening from the wings, so to speak, and it would be far more professional than her amateur group. And even though she adored the am dram society, it would be good to see how things were done in films rather than on a village hall stage.

Once inside she removed her coat, pleasantly surprised that it was warm for once. Brodie must have worked his magic and got someone to finally repair the ailing boiler prior to the big day. Knowing the rumours about certain members of the cast, she was relieved as no doubt there would have been hell to pay if working conditions were less than perfect. She hung her coat on the antique coat stand in the vast entrance hall and made her way to the library which she had used as her office from the very beginning of working at the castle. Only, when she arrived, she found the door propped open and inside it was overrun with a crew of people and their lighting rig with its huge bulbs and steel structures that could have been mistaken for modern sculptures; cables were strewn across the floor and people carried on about their work without noticing her.

'Are you Esme?' a tall, skinny man asked from behind her, causing her to jump.

Esme placed a hand over her heart, nodded and frowned as she glanced around the place that had been her sanctuary and workplace for months now. It was a little disconcerting to see it amidst the current chaos. 'I am,' she said with a questioning bewilderment to her tone.

'Right.' He looked up to the ceiling and said, 'Erm... okay... Lady Olivia left a message to say she's sorry for the upheaval, it was a bit last minute but could you please go to her office.'

Esme was a little perturbed by the change but nodded her agreement. 'Ah, okay. Thanks.' She left to walk along the stone-floored hallway until she reached the room that used to be Olivia's father's study but now acted as her base within the castle. It was also the room where Esme had been interviewed. She knocked.

'Come in!' Olivia called and Esme pushed through the door. Olivia had already walked across the room to meet her. 'I'm so sorry about dumping this on you at such short notice but the director decided to set up in the library first. I'm a bit frazzled, to be honest, with the early-morning feeds and all this going on. Thankfully Mirren has Freya for a few hours so I can be here at the start in case there are any major disasters.' Mirren, the housekeeper and Brodie's stepmum, had been a fixture at the castle since Olivia and her brother were wee, and she was a force to be reckoned with. What she didn't know about the castle or the family wasn't worth knowing.

'Aww, that's good. Is there anything I can do? Do you want a cup of tea or anything?'

In a surprising move, Olivia pulled Esme into a hug. 'You're so lovely. Thank you. I'm not sure what I'd do without you.' Her voice wobbled and Esme hugged her back.

'Aww it's fine, honestly. Don't get upset.'

Olivia pulled away and dabbed at her eyes. 'Ugh, look at me! I'm a blubbering wreck all the time. Who knew being a new mum would make me so emotional?' She laughed.

'I think it's a commonly known fact so please don't worry about it,' Esme replied with what she hoped was a reassuring smile. 'So, tea?'

Olivia held up a finger. 'In a while perhaps but for now, come and have a seat, I need to talk to you about something pretty big.'

Esme's heart skipped. She wasn't a fan of conversations that started this way and was trying to gauge Olivia's expression to see if it was something big *good* or something big *bad*. But obviously it was tricky due to the fact that she was still wiping at her eyes and blowing her nose.

Olivia sat and patted the sofa beside her and laughed. 'Don't look so terrified, I'm not about to fire you, or stand you in front of a firing squad.'

'Well, that's a relief,' Esme replied as she sat, trying to appear a little more relaxed than she felt.

'So, you know how you said you were looking for a place to live so you can move out of home?'

Esme narrowed her eyes. 'Yeeees?'

'Well, I may have a solution. It's not the most perfect one but it's a solution nonetheless, and it can be a stepping stone if necessary.'

Esme's interest piqued and she sat up a little straighter. 'Oh? Go on.'

'You know Judd who works for Kerr and with Dougie in the grounds?'

'I do. I hadn't spoken to him much, but he was out on Friday night with the rest of us and we had a good chat.'

Olivia beamed. 'Oh, of course! I'm so glad you went! Anyway, yes, so Judd moved into the cottage beside Dougie and Mirren after Rod and his wife retired, and a while ago he mentioned he'd like to look for a housemate. He asked my permission, bless him, he's so polite. But, of course, I said that'd be fine. And then you mentioned wanting to move out of your parents', so I had a chat with him yesterday and asked if he was still looking for someone as I might have the perfect candidate. As it happens, he's still keen so I thought I could take you across to have a look around. He said he'll be in as he has a day off today.'

Esme was a little taken back by the suggestion. 'Erm... The thing is we talked about my living situation on Friday, and Judd never mentioned anything, so maybe he doesn't want a female housemate? I don't want him to feel pressured into having me move in. And I'd have to bring Betty with me. She's my dog and I couldn't leave her behind.'

'Judd loves dogs. He's great with Wilf and Marley. They often follow him around the grounds while he's working waiting for him to throw a ball for them. And as for not mentioning it, I know him quite well now and all I can say is he probably never even thought about it. But he's a great guy. Very respectful, and I think you'd get along. Why don't you come and see the cottage? You might not like it and if not, there's your answer.'

Esme pondered briefly. It couldn't hurt to look, could it? 'Okay. Let's go over.'

'Yay!' Olivia stood and grabbed her jacket from the back of her chair and slipped her arms into the sleeves. She picked up her phone and tapped the screen. 'I'll just drop him a message and tell him I'm heading over with a potential new housemate,' she said in a sing-song voice.

Once Esme had put on her own coat, they took a steady walk across the castle grounds towards the row of former workers' cottages. The flower bulbs scattered at the edges of the grassed areas had started to push through the earth, verdant shoots just visible above the soil; and the sky overhead was pale blue with the sun, a ball of white light, hiding behind a wispy line of clouds. Their feet crunched on the gravel as they made their way along the tree-lined driveway as the castle, along with its new interlopers, receded into the distance. After a few moments, they turned off before they reached the main road, down a lane to the right. Neat hedges lined the narrow road and birds darted from amongst the foliage at one side and into the green leaves on the opposite side, as if daring each other to get close to the humans encroaching on their space.

After a few hundred yards, they reached the sage-green front door of the pretty, double-fronted stone house. A painted sign by the door read *Garden Cottage* and Esme's heart pounded in her chest. She wasn't sure why she was so nervous. Judd was a nice man, but she hadn't lived solely with a member of the opposite sex since Rhys, and although these would be different circumstances, it would be a total contrast to her current situation with her parents. And whilst that wasn't necessarily a bad thing – it was what she wanted, after all – it was that whole fear of the unknown thing. And these days, after what had happened with Rhys, Esme usually avoided the unknown at all costs.

Olivia knocked and within a few moments the door opened. Judd was standing there in light blue jeans and a cream cable-knit jumper looking fresh faced and clean again. He wiped his hands on the tea towel he was holding and smiled. Then he scrunched his brow, and then smiled again, evidently a little confused by Esme's presence.

'Hi, Judd. You already know Esme,' Olivia said, gesturing behind her. 'She's looking for a place to live so she can move out of her parents', and I suggested she should talk to you with you looking for someone to share with.'

His eyebrows lifted and he nodded. 'Of course! Hi, Esme, you must think I'm such a doofus for not saying anything on Friday.' He placed his hand on his forehead. 'I'm so sorry. I sometimes just don't put two and two together, and when I do, I often don't get four.' He chuckled. 'Why don't you come in and have a look around?'

As Esme stepped over the threshold and followed him into the hallway, Olivia said, 'I'll leave you to it. I need to get back in case I'm needed. Esme, take as long as you need though. No rush. And thanks, Judd. Good luck!'

Esme raised her hand in a nervous wave and turned to follow Judd. The stairs ascended away from them in the hallway and off to the left was a dining room with an old-fashioned dark wood table and chairs. On the right was the living room that was a little tired but cosy with a real fire roaring away in the grate. They walked through the lounge to the back of the house and off to the left was a well-kitted-out kitchen with a small white table and two chairs and opposite this, across a small tiled hallway, was a bathroom. It was all very clean – something that had concerned her – and tidy.

'And then if you follow me back to the front hallway I'll show you upstairs. The only downside is that the only bathroom is down here and gets pretty chilly at night, so I recommend a nice warm dressing gown if you don't already have one. Olivia has said I can decorate as much as I like so I'm going to start that very soon. I've only been in since January and I don't seem to have got anything done. As you can see, it's all a bit tired and nothing has been done since before Rod and Ada moved out. I don't think either of them had a knack for interiors, but the wee cottage garden is stunning. I'm quite excited about getting stuck into putting my own stamp on the place... or should I say *our* own stamp if you like the place. It's only fair that my housemate should have a say in what's done.' He shrugged.

Esme followed him back to the front door and then up the

stairs. The two bedrooms, one off to each side of the landing, were quite large. 'This is me, again it's a work in progress but I'm pretty tidy for a bloke,' he said with a smile. 'And this would be you.' He opened the door into a room with bare floorboards. A rickety old bed with a holey mattress sat in the middle of one wall and a beautiful old 1920s oak wardrobe against another. A rocking chair sat in a corner, there wasn't much wrong with it that a good clean wouldn't fix. Overall, the room was rather like something out of a Catherine Cookson TV series. But even though the room smelled quite musty and *clearly* hadn't been touched in decades, she could see the potential. It was quaint with its little open fireplace and cast-iron mantle. The floral wallpaper was probably a remnant of the sixties, and would need to be changed as soon as possible as it was falling away from the wall in places.

'You could do whatever you liked to the room. But first it needs a good airing out.' He cringed. 'Rod and Ada didn't use this room once their daughter moved out to get married, so it's in a bit of a sorry state. But Olivia says whatever major jobs need doing the estate will pay for which is good. And the rent is so reasonable. And let's face it, the commute could be a whole lot worse.'

Esme nodded thoughtfully, taking it all in. 'Oh, absolutely.'

'So... what do you think? Not that you need to rush into a decision, of course.'

Esme smiled. 'I really like it. It's got such a homely feel to it. But the thing is, I have a wee pug called Betty. Would it be okay if she comes to live here too?'

'Ah, I love dugs. That'd be grand.' He smiled. 'So, roomies?' he asked, holding out his hand to shake hers.

Esme took his hand. 'Roomies.'

6

The rest of Monday was hectic to say the least. Esme was quite distracted with thoughts of what she could do with the pretty room at Garden Cottage and furthermore how she would go about breaking it to her mum and dad that she was leaving again.

After her viewing, Olivia asked for her help with paperwork for the distillery project, and after that she was tasked with being on call for the film crew as a point of contact for local knowledge. She was able to advise on the best shopping spots, the best Indian takeaway, her favourite drinking establishments and what there was to do in Inverness, the city she had called home since birth. By the end of the day, she was exhausted but no sooner had she arrived home and showered the day off her skin than she had to leave to meet Parker in the city for drama club auditions. Her dad was staying in for the evening, so she borrowed his car and set off with only seconds to spare to ensure she would arrive on time.

Esme arrived and parked at Eden Court theatre, the venue for auditions that had been secured by Sylvia MacNab, the director. She was a stereotypically flamboyant character and a little eccentric with it – think Ms Darbus from *High School Musical*. She was strict on punctuality, loved her colourful kaftans and, even though she was in her sixties, she had long, perfect, grey-streak-free chestnut-coloured hair – 'A box dye if ever I saw one,' Parker had said on their first attendance. Sylvia tended to go overboard with the winged eyeliner and her mascara was always clumpy on her lashes and she usually had more lipstick on her teeth than on her lips. To add to her eccentricities, she spoke with a pseudo-posh English accent that only gave way to her native Scots when she was annoyed. To top it all off, she often inserted into conversation that her nephew, Charlie, was a famous actor but would never divulge his full identity, which was irritating and led most people to believe she had nothing but a vivid imagination. Esme felt a fondness for the woman in spite of her foibles, simply because of her passion for the craft and that she knew how to get the best out of her actors.

Esme had never auditioned for a main part before, feeling that as a relative newcomer to the group it would be rather presumptuous of her, but tonight she was auditioning for the role of Juliet. It was a part she had played in high school so she was already familiar with the lines. She had refreshed herself over the weekend and was going to perform the monologue scene from Act 2, Scene 2.

The modern theatre was an interesting array of angular shapes and modern materials including glass and metal, in juxtaposition to the adjacent wing, a purple granite Victorian Bishop's Palace that had once been the home of Robert Eden, the theatre's namesake. Esme had seen many a film, play and panto at the Eden Court and it held plenty of happy memories for her.

Parker was waiting outside the main entrance doors and as

she approached he placed the back of his hand on his forehead and croaked out, 'Ask for me tomorrow and you shall find me a grave man.'

Esme giggled. 'Very good. How can she not cast you?'

The two friends hugged, and Parker held her at arm's length. 'In the words of Taylor Swift, aka Mother, "Ready for it?" I mean could they have chosen a more Taylor Swiftesque play to put on? It's perfect! I think we should try and convince Sylvia to get the rights to "Love Story" to play at the end or something.'

'Hmm. I wonder if Miss Swift gets as nervous as this before she performs,' Esme replied, holding up a visibly shaking hand.

'Our mother is a strong independent woman whom nothing fazes. But if it makes you feel any better, I'm pooping my pants too. Come on before "Ms Darbus" gives us detention,' he said, making air quotes.

Esme laughed. 'She reminds you of her too?'

'Scarily so. Come on.' He linked his arm through hers and they entered the building.

Once inside, they were greeted by the other members of the group. Bryce was dressed in a frilly shirt reminiscent of something Simon Le Bon wore in the eighties – Esme knew this because her mum had been a huge fan, and still was. Parker was trying not to laugh and in doing so made Esme want to laugh too. Bryce was a bald man in his late fifties who had lost most of his teeth, allegedly when he used to be a boxer. Although to Esme he was far too skinny to have had any success, which could explain his lack of teeth, of course.

'Good evening, darlings,' Sylvia said with a flourish of her hands from her position at centre stage. 'And welcome to the Highlands home of performance. It's an honour to be treading these hallowed boards once again. The last time I acted here was in the eighties in a performance of *A Streetcar Named Desire* when I took on the role of Stella. I was quite the looker back then.' She patted her hair and paused as if waiting for a response.

'Aye and you're still a looker now, Sylvia,' Bryce piped up.

Sylvia smiled and waved her hand. 'Oh, Bryce, you're too kind. Well, we should begin. Now, who are my wannabe Romeos? Let's be having you!'

One by one the members of the group took to the stage to recite their lines. Esme was impressed by the calibre of the auditions and her nerves ramped up. She decided her main competition was a teenage girl called Chelsea who had just left school and was trying to make a living as a TikTok influencer. She had clearly studied the play for her exams too and had selected Juliet's death scene.

Esme had her turn and then Parker, and before she knew it Esme was returning to her car.

Parker walked beside her. 'You've got it in the bag. You smashed it, Esme,' he told her.

'Thank you but I get the feeling Chelsea is a firm favourite with Sylvia.'

'Hmm, I think it would be a bit creepy to cast her if Bryce is going to be Romeo.' He stopped in his tracks and grabbed her arm. 'Or maybe... *maybe* Sylvia's famous nephew "Charlie" will make an appearance and take the part.' He put the name in air quotes and rolled his eyes, a clear indication that he didn't exist.

Esme pursed her lips. 'Yeah, but if he exists and he's that famous why would he come and take a role in an am dram show?'

Parker's face crumpled and his lips curled downwards. 'I suppose. If he exists... which I'm almost sure he doesn't.' He started walking again.

Esme was the one to grab Parker's arm for a change this time. 'I almost forgot. I have exciting news.'

Parker tapped his chin. 'Let me guess, you've been having a secret affair with Kerr MacBain and you're carrying his love child?'

Esme scoffed. 'Er, nope! You know that I've been looking for a place to live?'

'You're moving into the castle!' he blurted.

'I wish. No, I'm moving into Garden Cottage in the castle grounds though, so not far off the mark.'

Parker stopped again. 'Since when? And where is Judd moving to? I thought that's where he lives.'

'He isn't going anywhere. Olivia suggested me as a housemate for him and he agreed to me moving in.'

Parker's eyes widened. 'You're moving in with *Judd*?'

Esme began walking again and smiled. 'I am. Although I have to tell my folks and I'm not sure what they'll make of it.'

'But Esme, it's clear he fancies you. Do you think it's a good idea?'

She rolled her eyes. 'He does *not* fancy me. And as I said before, even if he did, I'm sworn off relationships. I want some independence and it'll be good to stand on my own two feet for once.'

'Well, I suppose it reduces your commute,' Parker said. 'And if someday you fall in love with each other you're already living together.'

Esme laughed. 'You don't give up, do you?'

Parker twirled on the spot. 'What can I say? I'm a sucker for a love story.'

'You're something. Anyway, see you at work tomorrow. Maybe we can meet at lunch and I can tell you how my announcement went.'

Parker cringed. 'You're telling them tonight then?'

Esme opened her car door and paused. 'I think it's probably just better to rip off the band aid.'

Parker hugged her. 'Happy ripping. Call if you need me.'

* * *

'How was the audition, pet?' Colm asked as he walked into the kitchen where Esme was sitting on the floor with Betty, giving her a belly rub.

'It was good, I think.'

'Did you get the part, sweetie?' Sally asked as she joined them.

'I won't know for a few days. Sylvia is going to look back at the videos she took and make a decision. She takes these things very seriously. And with it being something as complex as Shakespeare she wants to get it right,' Esme replied without looking up. Her stomach was already churning with guilt about telling them her news.

'Oh, well, I'm sure you've got as good a chance as any of them.' Her mother's reply was a little dismissive and proved that they still didn't take her love of acting seriously.

She got up from the floor and pulled out a chair at the table. Betty jumped up, begging to sit on her lap, so she scooped up the pug and stroked her. It had a calming effect, and the nerves began to dissipate a little.

'Guys, could you sit down for a minute? I have something I want to talk to you about.'

Colm chuckled. 'Now that doesn't sound ominous at all.' They both pulled out chairs and sat.

'What is it, love?' Sally asked, a crumple of concern etching her brow.

Esme took a deep breath and released it slowly. 'The thing is... I'm... I'm going to be moving out.'

Both of her parents widened their eyes and leaned back in their chairs simultaneously. They had been together so long, Esme joked that they shared a brain.

'I just think it's the right time. And I've found somewhere perfect. Well... it's not quite perfect yet but it will be.'

Sally's eyes welled with tears. 'Oh... right, I see.'

Colm reached for his wife's hand. 'It's okay, pet, we knew this day was coming. So, where's the place you've found?'

Esme straightened her back. 'It's a cottage in the castle grounds. Very pretty and obviously handy for work. Means I won't have to rely on lifts so much. I'll save up for a car too once I'm settled. I'll need to decorate as it hasn't been done in a long time but maybe you guys could help?' she said in a hopeful tone. 'The wee garden is something extra special. It used to belong to a couple who worked on the grounds and the garden was their pride and joy.' When neither of her parents spoke, she added, 'I'm excited about this. I hope you can be too, for me.'

'How can you afford to live in the castle grounds? Surely you don't earn enough for a whole house to yourself?' Sally said in a wobbly voice.

'I'm moving in with a colleague,' Esme replied, giving as little information as possible.

Colm smiled. 'Oh, aye? That's nice. Is it that Paisley lass?'

Oh, good grief. 'Erm... no, it's Judd. He's one of the groundskeepers.'

Her mother gasped. 'A man? You're moving in with a *man*? But... how do you know he's safe? He could be a monster. He could have a criminal—'

'Sally, it's fine. You have to remember our Esme is a smart young woman. She'll know what's best for herself.' Her dad turned his attention back on Esme. 'And I'm presuming you do know this man? How... how old is he? Are you and he...?' Colm waved his hand around.

Esme widened her eyes. 'No! We're just colleagues. Not even friends, really. But he's a nice man. Very kind and respectful.' She heard Olivia's words falling from her lips and hoped they convinced her parents as they had convinced her.

Colm smiled at his wife and then at Esme. 'Aye, that's good.'

'You didn't say how old he is,' Sally snapped.

Esme couldn't help the sigh that escaped. 'Mum, please stop worrying. I'm an adult. You have to let me go and make a life for myself sometime. And he's around my age. Maybe a little older but not much. Not that it makes a difference as we're *just* going to be housemates.'

'Right, well, I think I'm going to have an early night,' Sally said as she stood abruptly and left the room. It was only 9.30 p.m.

Esme was relieved that there hadn't been more protesting but wished her mum would loosen the apron strings a little. It was stifling being so overprotected.

'Don't mind your mum, pet. She's just worried about you. She only wants your happiness and doesn't want you to get hurt again.'

Esme carried on stroking Betty. 'But the thing is, Dad, you can't protect me from hurt forever. Sometimes to be hurt is to learn. And I've learned so much about myself, and relationships in general for that matter, from my situation with Rhys. Not all great but I now know I have to not leap headfirst into relationships like I did with him.'

Colm smiled. 'You're a wise one, Esme Cassidy. Your mum'll come around. And I think she'd probably love to help you with the decorating. She's far better at wallpapering than I am, as you already know.'

Esme smiled. 'Thanks, Dad. I *will* be okay, you know.'

He nodded. 'Aye, I know, pet. Come on, there's a rerun of *Monty Python and the Holy Grail* showing. We always loved watching that together when you were younger. What do you say?'

She placed Betty on the floor and they both followed her dad into the living room.

7

'So, Esme, Olivia tells me you had an audition last night. How did it go?' Brodie asked as he accompanied her and Olivia back from grabbing pastries at the café. He was pushing a sleeping baby Freya in her pram.

The film crew were in the café eating breakfast and Olivia had wanted to check in to make sure they were all happy and had everything they needed. It was a dull spring morning, and a mist hung low over the loch in the distance. But even on days like this, the place was stunning and so atmospheric.

'I think it went well,' Esme replied.

'Exciting stuff,' Brodie replied.

Olivia said, 'I saw Parker earlier and he said you were amazing. In fact, he said you're wasted working as my PA.'

Esme cringed and placed her hand on her forehead. 'Oh, heck, trust Parker. I'm so sorry he said that.'

Olivia laughed. 'It's fine. I got what he meant.'

'I think it's great that you're indulging in your passion again. We're not quite ourselves when we avoid what we love, eh, Olivia?' Brodie said with a wink.

'He's right,' Olivia said. 'Take it from someone who knows. That's why I've started designing again.' Before inheriting Drumblair, Olivia was a designer for New York fashion house Nina Picarro and had only recently returned to her drawing board.

Brodie said, 'Aye, you'll be so glad you did it when you're up there on that stage.'

Esme laughed. 'I haven't got the part yet.'

Olivia smiled. 'I really think you'll get it. I have a feeling.'

'Did you speak to your mum and dad about Garden Cottage? Judd's a top bloke. I reckon you and he will get on great as housemates,' Brodie said as he reached in to pull Freya's blanket up a little.

Esme nodded. 'I did. My dad was great about it but Mum...'

'Struggling to let you go?'

Esme sighed. 'She really is. It seems worse now than when I went travelling. I don't get it.'

Olivia reached out and patted her arm. 'Don't take this the wrong way, Esme, but I think it's intrinsically woven into the very soul of being a parent. We're only just realising this now, aren't we, Brodie?'

He nodded his agreement and widened his eyes. 'Oh, aye, totally.'

Olivia continued, 'I remember when I relocated to New York to work for Nina. Mum was distraught, but she eventually came around. I'm guessing your mum will do the same.'

Esme sighed. 'It's not as if I'm going all that far. It's a mile up the road, if that.'

They reached the castle and Olivia opened the doors so Brodie could push the pram inside. 'I don't think the distance is the only factor. I think it's the fact that you're an adult now and she has to accept that she won't know where you are or what you're doing every minute of the day. It's not about control though, it's about protection.'

'I agree,' Brodie said. 'They just want you to be safe, that's all.'

'I suppose so.' Esme wanted to change the subject as thinking about her mum's face last night made her stomach churn. 'Anyway, I was wondering if I could make a start on decorating my room at Garden Cottage this weekend. I think it might be better to do that before I move in so I don't have to sleep amongst the dust and mess. Is that okay with you both?'

'It's absolutely fine with us,' Olivia said with a smile. 'Judd knows you both have free rein to do whatever you want. Within reason, of course.' She laughed.

'Aye, don't go all Laurence Llewelyn-Bowen on us and paint everything fuchsia pink, will you?' Brodie gave a deep laugh. 'And maybe steer clear of leopard print too, eh?'

Esme feigned sadness, sticking out her bottom lip like a petulant toddler. 'What's wrong with leopard print? And fuchsia's my absolute favourite colour.'

Olivia laughed. 'Well, in that case you'll definitely need to curb your design choices.'

Esme saluted. 'Aye, cap'n. Creams and neutral tones it is.'

'Right, my darlin', I'll be off to the kitchen to see Granny Mirren,' Brodie said as he leaned to kiss his wife. 'Love you.'

Olivia gazed up at him with eyes filled with adoration. 'Love you too. Bye, my precious girl, be good for Daddy,' she said, reaching in to stroke Freya's cheek. Brodie turned and headed in the direction of the castle kitchen and Esme and Olivia continued on.

When they reached the study, a voice called from the other end of the corridor. 'Lady Olivia!' They stopped as Eilidh, the production coordinator from the film crew, approached them in a hurry, her long blonde hair bouncing as she jogged. 'Sorry to bother you. I just wanted to let you know that the actors will be on set from tomorrow. This means the security team will be here too, and at times there'll be restrictions on where people can and can't go within the building. I just wanted to check that you're happy with everything.'

Olivia gave a strained smile. 'Oh, yes. Everything's fine. It's quite exciting. Oh, and I've finished up the Georgian ballgown for Ruby if you want to send her to me for a fitting when she arrives.'

Eilidh's face lit up. 'Oh, my word, I can't wait to see it. Thank you for agreeing to take such a huge task on when you have a baby to look after. I don't know how you do it. How is the wee princess today?'

'She's fine. Her daddy has just taken her to see her Granny Mirren for a few hours. Then Brodie and I are taking the afternoon off to have a drive out and get some fresh air.'

Eilidh tilted her head and made that dreamy face people made when thinking about babies, puppies or kittens. 'Aww, how lovely. Right, well, I'll let you get on. Bye just now.'

'Bye, Eilidh,' Olivia and Esme said in unison.

* * *

The following morning, Esme was woken before her alarm clock by her phone ringing. She rubbed at her eyes and reached for it, squinting through blurry morning vision to see Sylvia McNab, the drama club director's number highlighted on the screen. Betty woke up from her slumber too and gave an annoyed sneeze then stretched, yawning with a loud grumble to show her displeasure.

'I know how you feel, Betty Boo. It's a bit early to be having an am dram emergency.' She noticed the time and groaned. 'Ugh, it's only 6 a.m. I didn't have to be up for another hour.' She sat up and cleared her throat, then, trying to mimic the bright and breezy voice of someone who had been awake for hours, she answered the call. 'Hello, Sylvia, how are you?'

'Esmerelda, darling! I'm so glad I caught you.' *Caught me? Where did you think I'd be at this time?* 'Are you well?'

Apart from being half asleep and rudely awoken, I'm great. 'I'm good, thanks. What can I do for you at this early hour?'

There was a pause. '*Early* hour? I've been up since four!' Esme fought the words *more fool you* to stop them escaping from her lips and wondered if perhaps the woman had been drinking espressos since she rose, on account of her unusually high-pitched, squeaky voice. Sylvia continued, 'Anyway, I thought you would be happy to know *you* are my Juliet!'

Esme's heart skipped and she gasped. 'Really? Oh, that's wonderful! Thank you so much!' She jiggled about in bed, waving her free arm around, punching the air and simultaneously silent screaming with her eyes closed as Betty looked on with a tilted head.

'Have I interrupted you while you're out for a jog?'

Esme ceased her movements and sat stock still. 'No, why?'

'Nothing, it just sounded like you were jogging. Bryce will be your Romeo.' She followed this with an almost inaudible mumble of, 'He's no Leonardo DiCaprio, that's for sure, but he's the best of who we have. Right, I'd better go and make the rest of my calls. Rehearsals begin next week so get preparing. Ciao, ciao.'

'Ciao, erm, I mean bye, Sylvia, and thanks again.' She hit the end call button and immediately texted Parker.

> I ONLY GOT THE BLOODY PART DIDN'T I?!!!!!

Within seconds he responded:

> Can u please not shout at me this early in the day (insert winky face) Srlsy tho, I knew u wd! Well done! See you in a cpl hrs. P xx

No mention of his own call from Sylvia so she would have to wait to hear if he had secured the part of Mercutio.

Esme almost floated off the bus and up the lane towards the castle but as she reached the gravel area in front of the castle she stopped in her tracks. A fancy black car was parked outside and a tall dark-haired man that she would recognise anywhere was climbing out of it. Her mouth went dry, and her heart began pounding at her ribs.

It's him... it's really him, in the flesh, all six feet two of him. Zachary Marchand... Oh, my word, he is beautiful...

He was wearing dark-coloured jeans and a black leather jacket; a little reminiscent of a 1950s bad boy. His hair was a little longer than the last time she had seen him on screen, and he had a distinct five o'clock shadow gracing his angular jawline. He was as dreamy as she remembered, if not more so.

'Caught you!' Parker said as he slammed his hands down on her shoulders, causing her to squeal loudly.

Much to her horror, Zachary Marchand stopped and turned in her direction. She covered her mouth with her hand with such force she bashed her lips into her teeth and her eyes watered. 'Bloody hell, Parker, you scared me half to death!' she hissed.

Zachary simply smiled that heart-stopping smile he used in his movies, and for the cameras on the red carpet, and her insides turned to jelly. Then he turned and walked into the castle, followed closely by his security guard.

'My God, he is *so* gorgeous it should be illegal,' Parker said dreamily.

'I can't believe you made me squeal like that in front of him,' Esme said with a whack to his arm.

'Well, at least he's noticed you.'

'Yes, for all the wrong reasons. He probably thinks I'm some stupid fan girl who squealed because I saw him. Oh, God, I'll never be able to face him now.'

Parker linked his arm through hers and began to lead her towards the castle. 'Don't be daft. You're Juliet. If you can face losing Romeo, you can face anything.'

* * *

Parker popped in to see her mid-morning to share the news that he had got the part as Mercutio.

'I can't believe it!' Parker said, fanning his face. 'Me, on stage in a serious role! I wonder what the costume will be like. I hope it's not tights as I haven't been concentrating on my legs at the gym and I just know I'll look like a turkey.'

Esme laughed as she pictured him on stage dressed as poultry. 'Oh, heck, I hadn't even thought about what we'll be wearing.'

'It's all I can think about! Look, I know we were going to do lunch together, but would you mind if I take a rain check? I want to call Benoit and tell him all about it.'

Esme hugged him. 'I don't mind at all. He'll be so excited for you. Maybe he'll come to see the show.'

Parker sighed. 'I just wish he'd come over for good. We've been saving towards a deposit for our own flat for ages now and I'm ready to move out of my parents'. We just need him to find a job over here. Anyway, enough of me moaning, I'd better get back to work.'

At lunchtime, Paisley was in a meeting with Olivia, meaning Esme was alone for her break. She grabbed her lunch bag, lovingly prepared for her by her mum, and wandered out into the grounds to find a quiet spot in the fresh air to eat and decompress after the morning of phone calls from local and national press wanting the scoop on the castle's latest guests. She walked across the gravel to a little bench that had been crafted from rustic logs and sat amongst the trees and took a seat. She opened her lunch bag and found a note in her mum's handwriting:

You won't get this treatment when you move out. I bet you'll miss my lunches as much as I'll miss you. Love Mum

Esme sighed and pulled out the greaseproof paper, unwrapping it to find a chicken salad sandwich on crusty homemade bread. Her stomach growled in anticipation, and she took a much-needed bite and began to chew, eyes closed and head tilted slightly back, letting the fresh air tousle her waves.

'Oh, hi,' said a male voice from behind her.

She opened her eyes, swivelled in her seat and locked gazes with none other than Zachary Marchand. Her pulse rate increased and all the red blood cells in her body seemed to decide that precise moment would be a good time to have a meeting. In her face. She knew she must be the same colour Olivia and Brodie had insisted she *not* paint her room.

With her mouth full of half-masticated lettuce and roast chicken, she smiled and swallowed then made a weird noise that was supposed to be, 'Hi, Mr Marchand,' but came out garbled and squeaky due to the food.

Zachary chuckled and said, 'Oh, goodness, please, it's just Zach. And I'm sorry to interrupt your lunch. It looks good. I was just trying to find a peaceful spot to go over my lines and I'd spotted this bench earlier and thought how peaceful it looked so... here I am.' He glanced around and then in a theatrical whisper said, 'Between you and me, I should know my lines already, but...' He shrugged and cringed.

Esme swallowed the rest of her mouthful and took a long swig of her water. 'Oh, it's no bother. You're fine.'

He pointed at the bench. 'Do you mind...?'

She cleared her throat and croaked, 'Not at all. Mi bench es su bench.' Then mentally slapped herself for the utterly stupid reply.

He smiled and held out his hand. 'I'm Zach, by the way.'

She nodded. 'I know.' She shook his hand and kept her disbelieving gaze on him.

He narrowed his eyes. 'And you are...?'

'Oh, yes, sorry.' She giggled and immediately felt even more ridiculous – if that was even possible. 'Esme. I'm Esme Cassidy. PA to Lady Olivia.'

'Ah, yes, she mentioned that we should speak to you in her absence if we needed anything. Her baby is the sweetest little thing I've ever seen. The prettiest eyes.'

Esme smiled. 'Oh, yes, Freya is lovely. And they're such good parents. Completely natural.'

'I'm a bit of a sap when it comes to babies. Just love them. My younger sister has a one-year-old boy and he's a real character. A stocky little bruiser with these vivid blue eyes and a mop of brown curls like his mum. Calls me Yak.' He laughed and his eyes crinkled at the corners. He shook his head, and his smile faltered. 'I miss seeing him when I'm on location.'

Esme felt sad for him. 'I bet it's hard to be away from your family so much.'

He nodded. 'It is but... this is the life I chose so...' He stared off into the distance for a few moments. 'Anyway, don't let me interrupt your lunch. I'll just sit here quietly and read for the next scene rehearsal. Next time you see me, I may have on a very fetching wig and satin breeches.' He wiggled his eyebrows, and she laughed.

He opened his script and began to read. She wanted to continue with her lunch. It had that delicious mayonnaise stuff on it that her mum made by mixing... *something* with it. But her stomach was now too full of butterflies to accommodate a sandwich as well. She watched Zach in her periphery as he silently mouthed the words on the page before him.

He sighed deeply and Esme's heart leapt. Had he caught her watching him and got annoyed about it? *Shit*. Maybe she should get up and leave.

'Look, I know you're on your lunch break but—'

She immediately stood. 'Oh, heck, I'm so sorry, am I distracting you by being here? I-I can move.' She gestured back towards the castle.

He held up a halting hand. 'No, no, not at all, I was going to ask a favour actually.'

She widened her eyes. 'Oh?'

'Could you maybe read Lucille's lines for me? I think it would be easier to reply to someone rather than imagine it.' The statuesque blonde American actress Lucille Delgado was playing his betrothed. She was the epitome of stunning. If you looked up the word beautiful online there would no doubt be a picture of her face.

Esme grinned. 'Well, they do say acting is reacting.' *Oh, God, why am I so geeky?*

Instead of the expected snide or sarcastic retort, Zach said, 'Exactly! And I always find it easier to work with someone when I'm practising lines. Could you be my someone?'

Her heart melted and she almost disintegrated into a pile of mush. All that was missing was a halo of hearts around him and some soft, dreamy music. Realising she hadn't replied, she straightened her back and cleared her throat. 'Okay, I'd be happy to help.' She sat again and couldn't help the beaming smile that spread across her face as she hoped to goodness she didn't appear possessed.

'Right, we're starting here.' He pointed to the script and scooted a little closer to her. She could smell his cologne and wondered which one it was. It was fresh and expensive, that one thing was certain. 'Good day, Miss Robertson. I trust you're feeling recovered.'

Esme narrowed her eyes momentarily until she realised he had started. She looked at the next line. 'You trust I'm feeling recovered? Who are you to speak of trust? Do you not know of the heartache you have caused me?'

For a moment, Zach was silent and simply fixed his eyes on her. And then, as if he too had forgotten he was supposed to speak, he shook his head. 'S-sorry. Erm... I can assure you I didn't mean to cause pain to you, my dearest. Your happiness is all that I crave.'

Esme scoffed, getting into character. 'I am no longer your dearest, Lord Christoph, that much is clear to all. You have made a fool out of me. And I dare not enquire as to your brother's wellbeing. I only know that there should no doubt be a duel ahead. And then I shall lose you all over again.' Esme's voice wavered as she expressed the emotion she expected her character to be feeling.

Zach stared at her again for a moment and then he smiled.

He shook his head and straightened his features. 'Miss Robertson... *Amelia*... I'm leaving tonight for that very reason. I do not wish to fight my brother for I know I shall kill him. I want to ask your forgiveness before I go. I wish I hadn't fallen for Lady Eleanor. It was not meant to happen but who can help the path their heart decides upon? And you're right, my brother is baying for my blood. But I swear that causing pain to you was the furthest thing from my mind. All you have ever been is gracious.' He reached out and took her hand, fixing his chocolate-brown gaze on her.

Esme glanced down at the line and then returned her attention to him. 'I was gracious to a fault and that fault has now caused my heart to break irrevocably. I shall not forgive you, Christoph. Not while I have breath in my body.' She snatched her hand away and turned sharply to face the opposite direction.

'Bloody hell, you're quite good at this, aren't you?' Zach said, breaking character and grinning.

She wanted to say, 'Yes, I was supposed to be doing what you're doing, in fact I could've been Lucille Delgado but instead my parents convinced me I would be mad to pursue an acting career so here I am!' but instead she felt her cheeks warming again and simply replied, 'Thank you.'

They went through a few more scenes and Esme suddenly glanced at her watch. 'Oh, shit, I should've been back at my desk ten minutes ago. I'm sorry but I'm going to have to head back.'

Zach nodded. 'Of course, absolutely. I really appreciate your help, thanks.'

Esme smiled. 'No bother. It's been fun.' Her heart skipped in her chest with a rush of adrenaline.

Zach ran his hands over his hair and opened and closed his mouth a few times before saying, 'Look, I know it's really cheeky, and a hell of a lot to ask, but is there any chance you could help me again tomorrow lunchtime? I mean if you don't usually get a lunch break that's fine. Or if you've got other things to do...'

'No, I'd be happy to help. Same time and place?'

That handsome smile appeared on his face. 'Same time and place. Thanks, Esme.' She tried not to swoon at how her name sounded coming from his luscious mouth but was pretty sure the colour of her face by now must have given the game away.

She turned and headed back towards the castle, almost floating on an invisible cloud. She pinched herself and when she didn't wake up, she grinned. It really did happen. She glanced once over her shoulder to find him watching her.

8

For the next two days, Esme waited at the bench as Zach had requested but he didn't show up. She felt rather foolish and wondered if it had been a joke when he had asked for her help. She was, after all, only a PA, not an award-winning actress like Lucille Delgado. Maybe he was watching her from a distance with his cast mates and having a good giggle at her expense as she hung around the wooden bench in the cold. He probably remembered her from that incident when he arrived and decided to play a joke on a silly squealing fangirl.

Even though she didn't see Zach for the next couple of weeks, Esme repeatedly replayed their short conversation over and over in her mind. He had seemed genuine but then again so had Rhys. And add to that the fact Zach was also an award-winning actor and you had the perfect recipe for a great prank. Maybe she had expected a little too much from someone she had literally just met.

Luckily she was rather busy at work and with planning the décor for her new home. Her mum had agreed to help her with the wallpapering, but this had been delayed due to an urgent edit she'd received, so Esme dragged Parker on trips to B&Q, Homebase and TK Maxx to pick out accessories and paint colours. Although Parker was as excited as she was and spent much of the time picking out things for his own, hitherto non-existent, future abode.

On a Saturday morning towards the end of March, Esme awoke to Taylor Swift's 'We Are Never Ever Getting Back Together' blaring from her phone, dragging her from a fever dream in which Rhys had been parading a new woman in front of her. When her eyes sprang open, in her half-asleep state of mind, panic washed over her at the thought her ex was calling. However, when she lifted the phone she realised that of course it was just the alarm tone Parker had set on her handset on the staff night out. She'd heard it may times before but following such a vivid dream Rhys had been her first, albeit unwelcome, thought.

Esme had been a fan of Miss Swift since she was a barely known country and western singer and had followed her career through to adulthood. Recently she had found her lyrics held a much deeper resonance and the tracks she had heard from the upcoming *Tortured Poets Department* already sounded like they were based on her own story and what had happened with Rhys.

Her dad – an avid nineties grunge fan – had always ribbed her about her musical tastes, but she steadfastly defended the American singer-songwriter's talent for perfectly expressing emotions that many people couldn't put into words. She was a voice for the people, and contrary to what her dad thought, Taylor didn't only write break-up songs.

She was looking forward to having her own space to listen to her favourite songs and sing along without her dad mocking her, even though she knew he was only teasing good-naturedly.

There had been countless times when they'd been listening to their family playlist on Spotify in the kitchen at home and something like the intro to 'Cruel Summer' began and her dad would grab the dish brush and sing, badly, into it, 'He broke up with me, so I don't like him any more, he's a bad, bad man and I'm telling my mom!' On these occasions, Esme would whack him with a tea towel and return the favour when Soundgarden or Nirvana began to play, 'Everything is dumb, the sky is black and I can't play my guitar, so I'll scream myself sick…' Her dad simply chuckled, shook his head and said, 'Touché.'

As Freya June MacLeod had arrived a fortnight earlier than anticipated and had captured everyone's hearts with her bright blue eyes and wispy dark curls, the film crew were in catch-up mode and were working weekends and evenings. Esme knew that when she went to the cottage to start the wallpapering they would all be there at the castle, including Zach, and she wasn't sure how to act around him now if she saw him; she could only hope she didn't.

It was the end of March now and there had been a slight improvement in the weather. The sun was out, and Esme loved the fact that snowdrops were in full bloom around the entrance to the castle. When she arrived in the grounds of Drumblair with her mum it was as if spring had arrived in an uncharacteristically warm and sunny outfit adorned with a rainbow of spring flowers leading along the driveway towards the castle.

They turned off onto the lane and parked outside Garden Cottage. Once out of the car, her mum peered up at the building. 'It's very pretty, darling. I can see why you like it. I'm looking forward to seeing inside.' This was progress and Esme relaxed a little.

'Why don't we have a walk up to the castle first and say hello? I messaged Olivia to say we would.'

Her mum nodded and her face lit up. 'Ooh, yes, I'd love to see baby Freya.'

They walked in silence, listening to the birdsong and enjoying the fresh air. The outside was bustling when they arrived and everyone on site seemed to be smiling. Esme almost expected people to burst into song and dance routines, but the film wasn't actually a musical; rather a serious period romance story about a woman who had, also uncharacteristically, inherited a castle; something virtually unheard of in the Georgian era in which the movie was set. The similarity of the main character's story arc hadn't been lost on anyone, and even though the author of the original book on which the film was based had never met Lady Olivia MacLeod nor did she know the Clan MacBain story, people still gossiped about the parallels and wondered if the writer had some insider information.

Kerr's old Land Rover was parked outside, meaning he was there too, probably with his teenage son Will and Charlotte, the boy's mother and Olivia's former PA, as it was the weekend. The pair were coparenting and from the Drumblair rumour mill Esme had heard that they were dancing around each other romantically, neither really daring to make that big step of turning it into something more. Esme hoped that after all they had been through they might make a go of their little family. She loved a happy ever after.

Once inside they passed the usual people with clipboards, walkie talkies and equipment but thankfully Zach was nowhere to be seen, so that was one less thing to worry about.

Olivia and Brodie were in the drawing room with Kerr, Charlotte and Will. Will was holding baby Freya in his arms, clearly besotted by his baby cousin.

'We won't stay long,' Esme insisted. 'We've got decorating to do and I'm excited to get stuck in but like I said when I messaged you, Mum wanted to come and meet Freya.'

'Of course, hi, Mrs Cassidy, lovely to see you again,' Olivia said with a smile.

'Oh, please, it's Sally.'

Freya snuffled and rubbed her face before letting out a single cry. Will's eyes widened and he looked over to Olivia. 'Do you want to take her?'

Olivia laughed lightly. 'Of course, Will. She's only cranky because she's just woken up. She adores her cousin though, don't you, Freya?' she said as she scooped up the infant and walked across to where Esme and her mum stood.

'Oh, my word, she's absolutely precious,' Sally gushed, stroking the wispy curls on the baby's head. 'She's the image of you both. Her dad's hair colour and your eyes, Lady Olivia. Just beautiful.'

Olivia's cheeks coloured pink, and she smiled. 'Thank you, I think so too. And it's just *Olivia*.'

* * *

True to Esme's word, they left the family to their day after a short visit and her mum linked arms with her as they walked back to Garden Cottage.

As they reached the cottage, Judd was leaving. 'Morning, guys.' He wore a tight t-shirt that was covered in mud where he had wiped his dirty hands down himself.

'Hi, Judd,' Esme said. 'This is my mum, Sally. We're here to make a start on my room.'

Judd wiped his hand down a clean spot on his t-shirt and held out his hand. 'Good to meet you. I promise to be a good housemate so you've nothing to worry about.'

Her mum beamed. 'That's good to know. Nice to meet you, Judd.'

Esme pointed at his t-shirt. 'Are you working today?'

Judd nodded and gestured in the direction of the castle. 'Just helping out with some planting for the film set. They're a friendly bunch, aren't they? Can't believe the actors are so down to earth.'

Esme's heart tumbled. 'Which actors have you been chatting to?' she asked with intrigue whilst trying to appear nonchalant.

Judd cringed and scratched his head. 'I'm not really a movie buff but mainly the woman with the red hair who's playing the main character. She's really sweet. And the guy who plays the younger brother of the main guy. Zach, I think he said his name was. He seems really nice. There's a pretty blonde woman too but she hasn't spoken to me. I think she seems a bit shy.'

Esme had a feeling the blonde he mentioned was Lucille Delgado, Zach's ex, and from rumours she'd heard she was aloof rather than shy. She smiled. 'Ah, yes, you've been chatting to Ruby Locke and Zachary Marchand,' Esme informed him.

Judd grinned and shrugged. 'Oh, well, I talk to everyone. We're all human,' he said very matter-of-factly. He had a point but clearly wasn't fazed by their fame at all, unlike Esme.

'Esme used to have a huge crush on Zachary Marchand, didn't you, Esme? She still has a poster on the inside of her wardrobe door,' Sally said. 'Ooh, maybe Judd can put in a good word and get you an autograph.'

'Muuum,' Esme hissed as she felt her face blazing into colour, and all at once she was back to that shy, gawky teenager with braces.

'I can ask him for a signed photo or something if you like but you could just ask him yourself. He's really nice,' Judd said.

Esme shook her head vehemently. 'Och, no. Don't be daft. I was a teenager when I had a crush on him. I'm over that now. Just forgot to take the poster down, that's all.' She knew very well her furnace of a face was giving her away.

'Away with you,' her mum said, giving her a nudge. 'I saw your face when you told us he was going to be in the film. All starry eyed again you were.' Esme wanted the ground to open up and swallow her whole.

Judd seemed oblivious to her embarrassment. 'Why don't you just come and say hi at lunch time? They usually all just sit around out the back. I have to say, it looks really boring being an actor. I thought it'd be all action and excitement, but they seem to do a lot of sitting around waiting in silly costumes,' he said with a laugh. 'You wouldn't catch me wearing those white tights and fancy shoes.'

'We might just pop along,' Esme's mum said.

'Great! Well, I'd better be off. Those plants won't bury themselves. See yous later,' Judd replied as he walked away, raising his hand in a wave.

Once he was out of earshot, her mum said, 'He seems nice. If a bit blunt. Handsome though.'

'Is he? I hadn't noticed,' Esme lied. He was a very attractive man on the surface, but she had learned that meant very little in the great scheme of things. She was yet to get to know him properly and she certainly didn't need her mum trying to set her up with her soon-to-be housemate; how awkward would that be?

'And I didn't think you'd be allowed to approach the stars, but Judd seems to be doing that and hasn't been told off so there's nothing stopping you.'

Esme crumpled her brow. 'Honestly, Mum, you didn't have

to say all that about my poster. He'll think I'm a total silly fangirl. And anyway, I'm not sure the actors will want to be bothered by hordes of people on their lunch break.' She hadn't mentioned her accidental meeting with Zach to her parents.

Her mum snorted. 'Pfft, you heard what Judd said. They're sitting around bored in between takes. Look, all we can do is go and see. If we get sent away then... well, so be it.'

Esme tilted her head and narrowed her eyes. 'Anyone would think it was you with the crush.'

'Don't be daft, you bampot. I'm very happy with your father, thank you. And Zachary is young enough to be my son. I'm thinking of you. He might be able to offer you some acting tips for your play, that's all. Or he might fall head over heels in love with you and sweep you off your feet.'

Esme shook her head. 'That only happens in movies, Mum. And talking of sweeping, we'd better crack on with this decorating.'

'So, we're not going up at lunchtime?' her mum asked with a disappointed pout.

Esme sighed. 'I don't think we'll have time. And I don't want us to make a nuisance of ourselves. I could get fired and I need this job if I'm going to be independent.' Ready for the conversation to be over, Esme turned and walked into the cottage.

'Ugh, spoilsport,' her mum said as she followed her.

* * *

Judd had kindly cleared the old bed out of the room and had moved the wardrobe and rocking chair into the middle so they could access all the walls, and so they cracked on right away. Luckily the old wallpaper peeled off easily and after they had cleaned away the cobwebs, Sally began to put up the new paper while Esme washed down the fireplace, the chair and the wardrobe. The paper went up relatively quickly and already the room was looking brighter. They had paused for a couple of drinks and a lunch break but hadn't left to go see the movie actors after all. Thankfully her mum had dropped the subject, and they had happily sung along to Esme's Spotify playlist as they worked.

At around six that evening, Esme and her mum stood peering around at the almost completed walls of Esme's soon-to-be bedroom. They only had a few pieces of the pretty sage-green and cream 'leaf trail' wallpaper to apply but had decided to call it a day and finish off on Sunday. Her dad had picked up a Chinese takeaway and had messaged their family WhatsApp group to say he was on his way home with it.

'It's going to be so beautiful,' Esme said dreamily. 'I'm having gold-coloured accessories and I've seen some gorgeous sage-green textured bedding and curtains that will go really well.'

Her mum wiped her hands on a towel. 'It's very grown up. Unlike your room at home. What are you going to do about a bed? You can bring your one from home if you like.'

'Thanks, Mum, but I think I'm going to get a double bed from one of the charity shops in Inverness. I have a day booked off on Tuesday, so I'll go and have a look.'

Her mum nodded. 'Ah, yes, of course you'll want a double bed. And you've always loved charity shopping. But what will you do about a mattress? And a rug? Floorboards will be cold in winter and—'

'Mum, stop worrying. I'll get it all sorted. I'll be fine.'

Her mum slipped her arm around Esme and kissed the side of her head. 'I know you will, darling. I just want to help as much as possible to make this transition easy for you.'

'And I just want you to trust me, Mum. Trust that I know what I'm doing.'

Her mum nodded and her eyes welled with tears. 'I do, sweetheart. I do.'

9

Esme had taken the following Tuesday off work and had a fun day planned. First she would take the bus into Inverness to go shopping for the last bits for her new room, then she was going to start packing up the things from her room at home that she wanted to take with her to Garden Cottage. Following all that, the evening would see the first *Romeo and Juliet* rehearsal of a fairly gruelling three evenings a week for the foreseeable future.

It seemed that Sylvia had acquired friends in high places as she had miraculously secured a room at the Eden Court theatre for their rehearsals going forward, and there had even been talk of them using one of the stages at the place to put on the play in the late spring or early summer, depending on how things went. Esme couldn't quite believe that she could soon be treading the boards at the theatre she had visited as a child. It was all a little surreal but probably the closest thing to achieving her childhood dream that was ever likely to happen.

She stepped off the bus in Inverness and was happy to see that the sun had made an appearance into what had started off as a dull and damp day. She walked through the doors of the first charity shop and made a beeline for the bedroom furniture. The first thing she spotted, as if a spotlight shone down on it just for her, was a stunning old brass double bedstead that reminded her of the film *Bedknobs and Broomsticks* that she had watched a couple of times at Christmas as a child. The bed wasn't to everyone's taste admittedly, but to Esme it was just what she wanted, fitting perfectly into the 'cottagecore' aesthetic she had planned. She checked all around it for a sold sticker and when she couldn't find one she couldn't believe her luck. She was so giddy she was tempted to do cartwheels along the aisle but managed to curb her excitement and instead she hurried to the cash desk to enquire about it before anyone could beat her to it.

The woman behind the counter, wearing a navy-blue polo shirt and gilet emblazoned with the Salvation Army logo, smiled when Esme told her what she was after. 'Well, I never. This must be one of those strange, kismetty, *meant to be* occasions you hear about,' the short, dark-haired woman said with a disbelieving shake of her head. 'We *had* sold it, but the buyer rang when we opened today to say they had changed their mind.'

Esme widened her eyes. 'Oh, my word, that's amazing. I'm so glad they decided they didn't want it because it's absolutely perfect for me.' After she had paid for, and arranged delivery of, the bed for later in the week, she wandered around the rest of the shop with a trolley, adding things she liked. It was so exciting to be buying things for her new place even if it wasn't entirely her own.

On Olivia's advice, she had checked out the website of her best friend, and very first PA, Bella Douglas. Bella had relocated with her Granny Isla to move in with her boyfriend and was now working as an interior designer based at her home on the

Isle of Skye. As Olivia had suggested, the website was filled with tons of inspiration.

Using the ideas from one of Bella's blogs titled *The Thrifted Home*, Esme selected some lovely pieces to purchase: a tiffany-style lamp – obviously a copy though – with a green and cream glass shade and a brass base, a couple of gold picture frames, a patchwork quilt in varying shades of green, some pretty China mugs, a set of white dinner plates, and a pretty old painting of a highland glen carpeted with heather that reminded her of holidays she'd had with her mum and dad. At another charity shop in the city, she found a wicker bedside table and a couple more pictures. She was getting more excited by the minute and couldn't wait to pull it all together.

When she arrived home, her dad helped her unload the taxi and then she was greeted by a very excited pug.

'Have you missed me? I haven't been gone that long,' Esme said as she crouched to scoop up her little dog. 'Guess who has got a new bed for the new place?' she asked in a high-pitched voice that made Betty wriggle with excitement. 'You have! It's like a little sofa and it's all for you. Yes, it is.'

'You've bought her a sofa?' her mum asked, a glimmer of amusement in her eyes.

'It's so cute, Mum. It's the same green as the bedding I bought for my bed, and it looks so comfy. She's going to love it.'

Her mum laughed and shook her head. 'That dog is spoiled rotten. Anyway, come on, I've made an early dinner so you're not late for your first rehearsal.'

They sat at the kitchen table and Betty curled up on Esme's feet. The spicy aroma of her mum's signature dish, slow cooker chicken curry, filled her senses and her stomach growled.

As they ate, Esme told them about the brass bed and that all she needed now was a mattress. Her dad told her, 'Me and your ma have been talking and we've decided we'd like to get you a new mattress. We were going to get you a bed frame too but seeing as that's sorted we'll get you a rug for your new place.'

'Oh, that's so lovely, thank you but you don't have to do that, honestly.'

Her mum reached out and squeezed her arm. 'No, we want to, sweetheart. Sleep is so important, and we'd prefer you to have a good one. And I think you may struggle to find a rug at a charity shop that will go with your scheme so have a look online and find something you like. Our treat.'

Esme's stomach flipped with excitement. Her mum was coming around and that was all she had wanted.

* * *

At seven o'clock that evening, Esme and Parker walked into the rehearsal space that Sylvia had arranged for them. It wasn't a huge room but there was a proper stage at one end and tiered seating for around fifty people. Esme's heart felt as though it was trying to escape from her body and return back home. It was a nervous excitement though, not one born of fear. The rest of the cast were already there, that is, apart from Bryce.

'Good evening, all, let's get started, shall we?' Sylvia's voice bellowed out from the low stage. 'Now we have a little issue in that Bryce has poisoned himself with some out-of-date salmon.' She rolled her eyes in evident exasperation. 'The timing couldn't have been much worse. He's under strict instructions to check the use-by dates on things before he consumes them from now on. Anyway, this means that, just for this evening, I shall be reading Romeo.'

'Or I could stand in, Aunty Syl,' came a voice from the back of the room.

Sylvia spun around. 'Charlie! My dear, dear boy! How marvellous to see you! I didn't think you'd have the time!'

Esme and everyone turned around to see the owner of the voice and a collective gasp traversed the group. Esme widened her eyes and Parker gripped her arm, giving it a hard squeeze.

'She wasn't lying after all about her famous nephew,' Parker hissed.

Confusion boggled Esme's mind. Charlie? *Why is she calling him Charlie? His name is Zachary Marchand.*

'My dears, I would like to finally introduce you to my wonderfully talented nephew, Charles Zachariah MacNab!' She began to applaud and after a split second of stunned silence everyone else joined in.

Okay, that doesn't really explain anything.

'Now you will all no doubt know Charlie by his stage name Zachary Marchand, which is made up of his middle name and his mother's maiden name, but to me he is my younger brother Angus's son, whom I have always affectionately known as Charlie Chuckles.'

A rumble of laughter travelled the group this time and Zach crumpled his brow and covered his face in embarrassment. 'Come on, Aunty Syl, don't go giving away all my secrets. Leave me a wee bit of mystery.'

Sylvia walked across the room to hug her nephew. 'I genuinely wasn't expecting you to show up when I invited you, but I'm so glad you have. This is a special treat.'

Zach hugged her back tightly. 'How could I turn down an offer of watching *Romeo and Juliet* taking shape? And to have the opportunity to play Romeo again, even if it's just for one night, well, I can't pass that up.'

Sylvia led Zach over to Esme, a wide, beaming smile across

her face. 'Esmerelda, my dear, meet your one-night-only Romeo.'

Zach's eyes locked on Esme's, and his face flushed the deep pink of what Esme guessed to be awkwardness. 'Esme. Hi. It's so good to see you again.' He held out his hand.

'Hi, Zach,' she said, and as she slipped her hand into his, a shiver travelled her spine. 'Good to see you too.' She felt her own cheeks warming.

Sylvia clapped. 'So, you *have* met! I did wonder with you working at the castle, Esme, but of course my lips were sealed about my nephew's identity. I'm not one to hang on the coattails of my nephew's fame.'

'Yeah, Esme helped me rehearse my lines one day when I was struggling,' Zach said without taking his gaze from hers.

Sylvia put an arm around them both and gave them a squeeze. 'Wonderful, wonderful! And now you can return the favour. Right, let's begin! Places, everyone!'

Halfway through the rehearsal, Sylvia called for a coffee break, and everyone began to disperse into the corridor where there were vending machines. 'Just a short one, my dears! We have plenty to get through this evening!'

Parker walked over to stand by Esme. 'You didn't tell me you'd been helping him with his lines,' he whispered. 'You dark horse.'

Esme shrugged. 'It was no big deal.'

Parker gasped and placed a hand on his chest. 'No big deal? How can you say that? No big deal indeed. It's a very big deal, Esmerelda Cassidy. It's the deal of all deals. In fact, it's the deal of the decade. I can't believe you didn't tell me.'

Before she could explain herself further, Zach appeared in front of them. He cleared his throat and shoved his hands into the pockets of his jeans. 'Ahem, Esme, could I have a quick word?'

Parker stared for a moment until he realised Zach meant a *private* word. He gestured to the door. 'I'll go and get a hot body...' His eyes widened in shock and he placed a hand on each side of his own face. 'Shit, I mean a hot *chocolate*. Hot *chocolate* is what I'll be getting. From the vending machine where the d-drinks are,' he stuttered and dashed for the door and Esme watched him with a smirk.

She turned her attention to Zach. 'So, how come you don't go by your actual name? That was so confusing,' she blurted.

'Ah that, yeah, it's to do with SAG-AFTRA,' he replied as if it was common knowledge.

She narrowed her eyes. 'With a what now?'

'Sorry, it's an acronym for Screen Actors Guild and American Federation of Television and Radio Artists. The rule is that you can't register with a name that's similar or the same as another registered actor. There was already an American actor called Charlie MacNab so I had to come up with something new.'

Esme raised her eyebrows. 'Oh! That seems a bit mean, making you change your name like that.'

He shrugged. 'It is what it is and I don't really mind. It means I get to pretend to be someone else even when I'm not acting.' He chuckled.

She shook her head. 'Anyway, sorry, you wanted to talk to me?' she asked, trying her best to appear nonchalant and to remember Judd's words, *'We're all human.'*

Zach fixed her with those delicious dark brown eyes. 'Look, I owe you a huge apology.'

Esme feigned ignorance and gave a shake of her head. 'For what?'

'For asking you to help me with my lines and then not showing up.'

Esme brushed invisible lint from her sleeve. 'Oh, that, it's no problem. Don't worry.' She added a shrug for good measure.

'No, Esme, it wasn't nice of me to not turn up like that. And I'm really sorry. The thing is...' He rubbed his chin. 'The thing is Lucille is still jealous when I talk to other women. So when I mentioned I was meeting someone called Esme to run lines she decided we needed to practise a scene that *she* was apparently having trouble with. Utter rubbish. She doesn't have trouble with scenes. She doesn't want me, but doesn't want anyone else to have me either.'

Esme scoffed. 'But I don't *have* you. We met briefly for one lunchtime. It hardly constitutes an affair, does it?' *Whoops, that sounded catty and rather bitter. Rein it in, Cassidy.* 'What I mean is she has nothing to be jealous about. It was just lines.'

He pulled his lips into a line and nodded. 'You're right. I know. And I shouldn't even care what she thinks any more but she's a horror to work with if she's not getting her own way and we end up bickering and then scenes take twice as long. So, I just take the easy route. Just while we're filming. Then afterwards we can get back to avoiding each other like the plague.'

Esme raised her eyebrows. 'Sounds like a good plan.'

'Anyway. I wanted to tell you that I enjoyed running lines with you. And... I have to say, I'm very impressed with your Shakespeare. There aren't many people without training who get the gist of it right away with the language being so complicated, but you...'

Esme scowled. 'A mere PA? Is that what you were going to say?' She gave a wry smile.

His eyes widened and he held up his hands. 'God, no, not at all, I just meant Shakespeare is notoriously hard to grasp even for trained actors so to be as good at it as you are with no training is pretty incredible.'

Esme cringed. 'I'm not technically untrained. The truth is I was offered a place at the Royal Conservatoire in Glasgow but... I couldn't accept it... for... personal reasons that I won't go into.'

Zach shook his head and narrowed his eyes in what appeared to be disbelief. 'You turned down a place at the Conservatoire? Seriously?'

She nodded. 'Seriously. Crazy, I know. And although I love my job at Drumblair, I do sometimes wonder what might have happened if I'd accepted it. But hey-ho, too late to be regretting it now.'

'Hey, it's never too late. You could always get back into acting properly. Not that this isn't proper acting but... well, you get what I mean. You really do have talent.'

Esme tucked her hair behind her ear and glanced at the floor, finding it difficult to accept a compliment from someone so well known for his own talent. 'That's very kind of you but I'm okay with my life as it is.'

'But you could have so much more.'

Esme shrugged. 'I'm grateful for what I do have. I know it probably seems a bit boring to someone like you but—'

Zach's eyes widened. 'No, that's not what I...' People began filtering back into the room again. Zach rubbed his hands over his hair and lowered his voice. 'You've got me wrong. I didn't mean—'

Sylvia clapped her hands, cutting him off. 'Right, everyone, let's continue! You'll have plenty of time for chatting after rehearsal. Come along!' Everyone quickly took their positions once more.

* * *

At the end of the evening, Zach's security guard appeared at the doorway and stood there in his black clothing looking like a night club bouncer, with a serious expression on his face and his bulky arms folded across his broad chest. He was a giant of a man, and not someone you would want to meet in a dark alleyway, not least because you'd never be able to pass him; he was almost as wide as he was tall.

'Thank you for your efforts this evening, everyone. Please get learning those lines though. The sooner we can get down to acting rather than reading from the script the better. And I hope you will all join me in saying a huge thank you to our special guest. I'm sure you'll all agree that he is the epitome of Romeo.' Sylvia began to clap and this time everyone quickly joined in with the applause.

As some people left, other members of the drama group gathered around Zach to shake his hand. He signed scripts and t-shirts and posed for selfies.

'Oh, to be so adored,' Parker said as he joined Esme. 'I think the only time I feel that amount of adoration is when I get home to Gladys.'

'What about Benoit? He adores you, doesn't he?' Esme asked.

'He does but sadly I don't see him as often as I would like so I have to cuddle my grumpy chihuahua.' He began to chuckle. 'That sounds like a euphemism.'

They stood and watched as Zach said his goodbyes and headed for the door. As he reached his security guard, he glanced back over his shoulder and gave Esme a sad smile that she wasn't sure how to interpret.

10

Even after all Zach had said at the first *Romeo and Juliet* rehearsal, nothing changed. He didn't come to any more and Esme only saw him from a distance for the rest of the week. On one of those occasions, it was post-lunch and he was heading back into the castle with Lucille who wore a stunning, if rather wide, bejewelled satin gown in pale blue, cinched in at the waist and with a fitted bodice that gave her the appearance of a heaving bosom, synonymous with Georgian-era fashion. Her hair was covered by an ornate white-powdered wig that stood so high atop her head she seemed to be having difficulty keeping herself upright. Zach was holding onto her arm, and she clung to his. He released himself from her grip momentarily to wave and he smiled when he spotted her. Esme waved back but this resulted in a sour glare from the usually dark blonde actress walking beside him. From that one glance, Esme now clearly understood what he'd meant about the issues they had as a former couple working together.

Esme had seen interviews with the famous actress where she had come across as sickly sweet and most people adored her, but where Ruby Locke seemed genuine, Lucille Delgado lacked the sincerity in her eyes. To Esme, who had been fascinated by actors and their interactions with people for many years, she always seemed to be on TV shows or meeting fans under duress, glancing around for an exit, and her smiles were fake, never quite reaching her eyes. Esme thought it must be exhausting to be so filled with disdain, especially for those people who had helped to get her to where she was. After all, she had everything she could possibly want handed to her on a platter. She'd even had Zach but had dumped him for someone else, so she clearly was crazy.

* * *

Bryce, aka Romeo, made a full recovery from his bout of food poisoning and attended the rest of the rehearsals. He did so sporting two *delightful* (and not at all amusing) new additions; a chestnut-coloured toupee – that reminded Esme of some poor creature that had been run over and discovered at the side of a road – and ill-fitting false teeth that dropped from his top jaw every time he moved his mouth to recite a line. This resulted in a constant smacking of his lips as he tried to keep them in place or, alternatively, soliloquising through clenched teeth, meaning he appeared angry every time he spoke, regardless of the content of his speech – both very disconcerting situations. His delivery of the lines was a little clunky to begin with but he soon relaxed into the part and even paid Esme a compliment at the end of one of the rehearsals.

'I'm taking all my cues from your acting, you know, Esme. You make it so easy to understand the gobbledegook that Shakespeare wrote, and I can almost understand it. I mean, talk about *why use three words when thirty-three will do.*'

'That's very kind of you, Bryce, thank you,' Esme replied.

'By the way, I'm sorry about these things.' He pointed to his mouth. 'I'm having Turkey teeth soon.'

A bizarre image popped into Esme's head of a dark grey winged bird with broad tail feathers, a pink jowly neck and a full set of pearly whites, shouting '*Gobbleobble!*' as its teeth fell from its top jaw like Bryce's did. Her expression must have shown her utter confusion because he added, 'Aye, you know, I was hoping I'd have my op in Turkey for my implant dentures before we opened but my flight was changed so I had to rearrange things, which means I'm stuck with these things until afterwards.' He jabbed a finger towards his falsies again and rolled his eyes.

Ah, that makes more sense! Esme thought as she stifled a giggle.

On the final rehearsal of that week, Sylvia made an unwelcome and devastating announcement that due to scheduling conflicts – she didn't say whose – their performance had been brought forward by a couple of months and would now be a 'one-date-only' thing, which horrified Esme. This meant that they had only had three weeks of rehearsals that would culminate in a single day of performances; a matinee and an evening. Gone was the prospect of months to prepare and instead the whole cast was thrust into a frenzy of learning lines, trying on countless hired costumes, dodging the volunteer set builders and endeavouring not to leg each other up on stage as they learned their marks. Their play now possessed most of the ingredients for a comedy of errors, even though that wasn't old Will Shakespeare's initial intention.

From that point on, the rehearsals were gruelling, and Sylvia lost her temper on more than one occasion, stating that she 'wouldn't have to put up with this level of amateurism in the

West End'. Parker responded, albeit under his breath, that in the West End they'd 'all be getting paid astronomical amounts for this shit so would probably try much harder' and Esme tried not to laugh – he did have a point.

* * *

April arrived and along with it there seemed to be an indubitable air of spring about the place. The sun was a frequent guest in the sky and the mood on site at the castle was buzzing. She had met Judd for coffee breaks a few times in a bid to get to know her soon-to-be new housemate. They chatted easily and Esme began to wonder why she'd been so anxious. The more she got to know him, the more she really liked him. He made her laugh and was so incredibly kind and thoughtful. But for reasons she had tried to ignore she had been putting off moving in with him. For all the initial desperation to be independent, she was nervous about stepping out on her own again, especially after the disaster her first time living away from home had ended up being.

'So, do you cook? I love cooking but I'm not the best,' he said as he placed his mug down.

Esme rolled her eyes. 'I do like to cook but my mum always beats me to it. She's a freelance book editor so she works from home.'

'That must be nice, to be so well looked after. Are you sure you want to move out?' He smiled and his eyes lit up. He had such bright, happy eyes. *Ugh, I make him sound like a puppy.*

'As lovely as it is, it can be quite stifling. So yes, I'm sure.'

'So, when are you moving in? Not that I'm rushing you. I'm just looking forward to having some company,' he told her with a shy smile.

'Ugh, sorry, I'm almost ready. Just a few more bits to get,' she lied. She'd had everything she'd needed for ages. Right there on the spot, however, she made a decision. 'In fact, I think I'll move in on Friday night, if that's okay with you?'

A wide, handsome smile spread across Judd's face. 'Perfect.'

On Thursday afternoon, when they met to go over the bookings for the art space and to collate some other castle admin, Olivia told Esme that she had been chatting to Eilidh and that the shoot was back on schedule and going really well. 'They're so happy with the castle as their location, Esme, and to be honest there hasn't been as much disruption as I'd expected,' Olivia said. 'And I want you to know I'm so grateful to you for all the hours you've been putting in to make sure it's all running smoothly; it hasn't gone unnoticed.' Esme loved the fact that she was appreciated. 'Oh, and I had coffee with Ruby and Lucille yesterday lunchtime. They're both so lovely,' she gushed.

'First name basis already, huh?' Esme replied. 'That's really good to hear.' She didn't mention the fact that Lucille would have happily killed her with a stare à la a Georgian Darth Vader when she had seen her earlier in the day.

Olivia's smile disappeared and a look of concern crumpled her brow and then came something she had hoped not to hear. 'The only problem that's occurred, or that that they made me aware of at least, is something Lucille mentioned.'

Esme swallowed a lump of discomfort that had lodged in her throat. 'Oh? W-what was that?'

'She said one of the staff had offered to help Zach rehearse his lines a couple of times and he had tried to let them down gently, but she said they'd kept bothering him. Apparently they were quite insistent. She said he hadn't had the heart to tell them how irritating it was and that they should leave him to it. After that he just had to stop going to that part of the castle grounds to avoid them. I don't suppose there's any point asking the team who it was because they usually all stick together. They're all friends, which is great, of course; however, on this occasion I could do with knowing. I have to be honest that I'm a little annoyed a member of my team is bothering the actor when everyone was warned at the start of this whole thing to get on with their work and not make a fuss, so I'm not sure which part of that instruction someone has misunderstood. I don't think I could have been much clearer. Anyway, I apologised, and she was really sweet about it, thankfully, but I think I might get you to send an email to all staff members to reiterate to everyone that this is currently a working film set and that they shouldn't get in the way.'

Esme felt her face heating and her heart played a drum solo worthy of Roger Taylor from Queen. So, Lucille was now trying to drop her in it, was she? She had never even spoken to the woman, but it was clear that the green-eyed monster was at play.

Esme was on the verge of confessing when Brodie appeared in the doorway with Freya. 'Look, there's your beautiful mummy,' he said, pointing at Olivia. 'I'm sure she must've almost finished work, and that means we get her to ourselves for the whole evening,' he said with a wink at Olivia.

She stood and crossed the room to kiss her husband and her daughter. 'What a lovely surprise. And yes, I think we're all done here, aren't we, Esme? Can I leave you to send the email about what we discussed?'

Esme nodded. 'Sure, I'll get to it before I head home.'

Olivia waved a hand. 'Oh, no, do it tomorrow. It'll be fine then. Get yourself off home.'

* * *

On Friday morning, Esme got to work early and caught Parker as he was making himself a coffee in the castle kitchen – one of the few rooms that wasn't being used for filming. As she made a drink for herself, she explained about the lies Lucille had told Olivia.

'The cheeky bitch!' Parker whispered, albeit a little too loudly. 'I knew she was a nasty piece of work. She could give Rachel McAdams and Amanda Seyfried from *Mean Girls* a run for their money.' Esme stifled a smile at his ability to once again mix up the actor with the character they played, as he continued, 'The ones who look like *her* always tend to be like that; never a hair out of place, pristine makeup, perfect clothing, gleaming white teeth. They're always false just like their boobs. And bitchy to boot.' His eyebrows shot up. 'You didn't admit that it was you who had been helping him, did you?'

Esme glanced over her shoulder to check the coast was clear. 'I didn't get a chance,' she whispered. 'She wants me to send out the email this morning, but I feel like I'm getting everyone in trouble for something I did.'

Parker reached out and squeezed her arm. 'Just send it. Don't go admitting to anything when you did nothing wrong. Lucille's version is bull, and she knows it. And okay, people will no doubt play detective, and try to figure out who the culprit is, so prepare yourself to be asked twenty questions, but they won't hear anything from me, I can assure you.'

Esme smiled. 'Thanks, Parker. I really appreciate that. I mean, it's not like it'll happen again anyway. Zach hinted as much when he apologised for not turning up the day after, when we'd agreed to meet up to go through his lines again.'

Parker narrowed his eyes and pursed his lips while crossing his arms over his chest. 'And all because of Lucille, I bet.' Esme simply nodded so he added, 'That conniving cow. Who the hell does she think she is?'

'A rich, beautiful actor who can get any man she wants and who everyone thinks is wonderful?' Esme replied with a shrug.

'Yeah, well, I wouldn't touch her with someone else's, even if I was straight. Just because someone's beautiful on the outside and portrays a sweet and innocent persona doesn't mean they're the same on the inside.'

He had a point. And later that morning, with no small amount of trepidation, Esme hit send on the email. She was as tactful as possible, but the guilt made her stomach do somersaults and eventually stole her appetite too. She knew that, at some point, she would have to tell Olivia she was the culprit in question, even if it didn't go down exactly as Lucille had explained it. She just hoped she didn't get into too much trouble or worse still, get fired.

* * *

After work on Friday, Esme, along with her mum and dad, loaded up both of their cars with her belongings and once Betty was secured into her car seat they set off for Garden Cottage. It was finally happening; Esme was moving out and couldn't have been happier.

The drive from Dores to Drumblair was as picturesque as ever. The hedgerows were alive with butterflies fluttering hurriedly about their work, and birds collecting twigs to build their nests, and the sky overhead was the kind of blue you usually saw in places like Spain in the summer months. *There's one in the eye to all those who think it rains all the time in Scotland*, Esme thought. In a small way she was going to miss this short commute to the castle but in so many others she was happy that she wouldn't need to make it unless she was visiting her parents.

Judd met them at the door of Garden Cottage. 'Hey, Mr and Mrs Cassidy, good to see you both. Evening, roomie!' he called out with a wave, his attention focused on Betty. 'Oh, and hi to you too, Esme,' he added with a wink.

'Very funny, Judd,' Esme replied as she lifted Betty down to the ground. 'Betty's excited about her new house, aren't you, princess?' The little dog ran towards Judd with her curly tail wagging a wild rhythm all of its own.

'Aye, it'll be great to have a wee dug around the place,' Judd said as he helped them carry the boxes inside and up to Esme's new room. As they worked, Betty sniffed her way around the place, familiarising herself with her new surroundings.

'This sofa's a bit too small though. Not sure we'll both fit on it,' Judd said with a chuckle as he carried Betty's new bed under his arm. He still was a little hit and miss with his eye contact, but Esme put it down to him being shy and the fact that they didn't yet really know one another that well.

'I'm not sure Betty will want to share anyway,' Esme replied, laughing.

A new mattress and a rug had been delivered to her room so all she needed to do now was unpack, make her bed with the new dark green forest creatures bedding she had found – it was rather special with its fox, rabbit, stag and toadstool print – and settle in.

On the window ledge of her room stood a simple glass vase filled with sunny yellow roses; their sweet fragrance filled the cosy space. She hadn't seen either of her parents bring them in so that could only mean one thing. She smiled as she turned to face Judd. He was placing a pile of boxes on the floor in the corner of the room by the fireplace.

She pointed to the vase. 'Did you get these for me?'

His face coloured pink and he nodded, scratching his chin. 'I did, aye. Yellow roses for friendship,' he stated matter-of-factly, before he turned and headed back down the stairs with no further comment.

'What a thoughtful young man,' her mum said, a hint of surprise to her voice.

Esme tilted her head with intrigue as she watched Judd walk away. 'He is. And what he doesn't know about flowers isn't worth knowing.'

Once the boxes were in situ, she walked down the stairs with her parents.

Judd was waiting in the hallway. 'I'll make a cuppa, shall I?' he said, gesturing to the kitchen.

'Thanks, Judd, but not for us,' Esme's dad said before turning his attention to his daughter. 'We'll get going and let you unpack, pet. You know where we are if you need us.' He hugged her tightly.

'Thanks, Dad,' she said as she hugged him back.

Then her mum wrapped her arms around her. 'You can always come home if it doesn't work out. You'll always have a place to live with us, sweetheart,' she said as her voice wavered.

Esme held her mum at arm's length. 'I know, thank you. But remember I'm only up the road this time. Not in a whole other country thousands of miles away.'

Her mum laughed and swiped at tears that had escaped and trickled down her cheeks. 'I know, I know. I'm being ridiculous. I'll just miss your grumpy face at breakfast,' she teased.

'Charming!' Esme said, laughing. 'I can't help not being a morning person.'

'Ooh, noted!' Judd said as he walked back through to the

lounge from the kitchen. 'I'll be sure to avoid you until you've had coffee.'

Esme laughed and called after him, 'I'm not that bad, honestly.'

Her mum hugged her again and kissed the side of her head. 'I'll message you tomorrow and we'll come and see you after the weekend to check out your room once it's all sorted. Love you.'

'Love you too. And you, Dad.'

Once both her parents' vehicles were out of sight, Esme closed the front door and a wave of sadness tugged at her insides, but she mentally shrugged it off. This was a whole new, very positive chapter to her life.

Judd called through from the lounge, 'Come and have a break. I've made fresh coffee, and I even got some nice biscuits in honour of you moving in. You can sort your stuff later.'

When she walked into the room, she was surprised to find Betty snuggled up beside Judd on the sofa. 'Looks like you've got a new friend,' she said, nodding towards the snoozing pug.

He laughed. 'Aye, I seem to have an affinity with dugs,' he said as he gently stroked Betty. 'I was on the verge of getting a golden retriever pup from the same mother as Brodie's dog, Wilf, seeing as she's had a new litter. But when you decided to move in with Betty I changed my plans.'

Esme felt a little bad. 'Oh, no, you should get a pup if that's what you want. Please don't let us stop you.'

'No, don't worry, you didn't stop me, it's not like that. I just felt like it was the kind of thing we should maybe agree on.'

His words didn't help to ease her guilty conscience. 'But I have Betty, and we didn't agree on her, so...'

'Yeah but you already had her and anyway, I wasn't sure if she liked other dogs, so I thought it best to wait. But she's a wee sweetie, aren't you, Betty?' he said as the pug rolled onto her back, and he rubbed her belly.

'I'm just glad you didn't mind me bringing her. She's my little saviour.'

Judd crumpled his brow. 'Oh? How so?'

Esme picked up her mug and took a sip of the steaming aromatic coffee. 'Oh... I don't want to bore you with my problems on night one. Surely that's a night seven topic.' She laughed, trying to make light of things.

Judd shrugged. 'Hey, sorry, I don't mean to pry. You don't have to tell me anything you don't feel comfortable with. I just think if we're going to share a house it would be good to get to know each other a bit. And I'd like us to be friends. If-if you're comfortable with that, of course.'

Says the man who won't make eye contact, she thought but didn't say it aloud. 'Oh, absolutely. Me too.' She pursed her lips and pondered for a moment. 'Let's just say I experienced a pretty rough heartbreak and when my dad brought Betty home for me, I finally started to heal.'

Judd nodded but didn't speak for a few moments, he simply stared straight ahead and tapped his fingernails on his mug, a rhythmic drumming sound but not one to any tune she could recognise. After a pause, he said, 'I was never allowed a pet when I was younger because we spent a lot of time moving around. Dad was in the army, and Brigadier General Fergus Alec Cowan was of the opinion that dogs were akin to vermin. The only dog he tolerated were the ones trained to sniff out bombs and even then he wouldn't have one in the house. Plus, we moved back and forth overseas a fair bit, so I suppose it wouldn't have been fair... or easy. The houses we lived in were always spotless just the way he liked it and even since Dad died my mum has kept her place as pristine as when he was alive, so

I didn't bother suggesting we got a dug before I left, even though I think it would have been excellent company for her. I worry about her being alone.'

'Was he quite strict then, your dad?'

Judd huffed. 'And then some. I'm an only child, even though they tried for years for more kids after me. Probably because I was a disappointing son for my dad.'

Esme was shocked at this admission. 'How?'

He sighed. 'I had loads of issues with settling in at all those different schools when we moved around, and as a result I didn't have many friends.' He laughed without humour. 'I got in trouble a lot too and Dad said I wasn't disciplined enough, which was totally untrue if you'd witnessed my homelife growing up. Everything was so regimented. Get up at this time, eat at this time, go to bed at this time, repeat, ad infinitum.' He stared off as if he was talking to himself and scratched his chin. 'I knew from early on there was something different about me and I spent a lot of time googling when I was younger, heard about ADHD and autism and thought, "Ooh, maybe that's me," because there were so many similar traits I recognised in myself back then. In fact, I'm still convinced now, but back then things like that were just weaknesses and made-up conditions to my dad, so when I mentioned it he refused to have me tested, telling me I was looking for excuses to behave badly. His answer to the whole thing was more discipline and even more shouting, like I was one of his subordinates. And it didn't matter who was around so there's no wonder I couldn't keep friends really, when he was at home, when you think about it.'

Esme's heart sank at the apparently lonely childhood Judd must have experienced. But now some of his little foibles made a lot more sense. 'I'm so sorry to hear that, Judd. Have you thought about seeing someone now about a diagnosis? Would it help?'

He sighed. 'Nah. There's not a lot of point trying to get diagnosed these days. It takes so long to even be seen for consultation unless you can afford to go private, and who has that kind of money? And anyway, sadly, folks seem to think it's some trendy bandwagon that people like me jump on, so I fear they would take me even less seriously than they already do.' He chuckled but, again, there was no humour visible in his stoic expression. 'I would've loved a canine companion so much, and I actually think it would've helped me to no end. You hear about people having dugs for anxiety and other health issues, so I'm sure it would have been great company and comfort. No judgement, you know? Just unconditional love. Anyway, I always swore I'd get one when I moved out.'

When Esme didn't speak, he chewed his lip and covered his face with one hand, rubbing roughly before giving a deep sigh. 'Shit, sorry. That was what you'd call a *serious* unintentional info dump, eh? In case you hadn't noticed, I have a tendency to overshare too.'

Esme smiled. 'Not at all.' She wasn't sure what she could say to ease his mind but went with, 'And you're not alone with the dog thing. I always wanted one when I was little, but my mum was never a fan either. After I arrived back home from travelling, Dad got me Betty without even consulting her when I was living at home, so I'm guessing he got in plenty of trouble about that. You should have seen her face.'

Judd laughed. 'I do love a rebel.' He took a gulp of his coffee and munched on a fancy biscuit for a moment. 'So... you're single now then?'

Esme almost choked on the mouthful she had just drunk. 'Pfft, come right out with it, why don't you?'

Judd cringed. 'Sorry. I really don't have a filter, do I? Feel free to tell me to get lost if I ever ask things out of turn.'

She found she couldn't be annoyed at him. He was pretty straightforward kind of guy. 'No, you're fine. And yes. I'm single. I've sworn off men, actually. At least for a while anyway.'

'Can't say I blame you. We can be a shitty and unpredictable bunch.' He picked up another biscuit and took a big bite.

'What about you? Are you seeing anyone?'

Judd chewed for a moment then sighed. 'Alas, no. I get the impression women think I'm a bit odd. But come to think of it, in all honesty I don't think I'd know if someone fancied me even if they came and danced naked in front of me.'

Esme giggled. 'I think in *that* particular case it may be pretty obvious, depending on where you were, of course.'

He laughed. 'Actually, I think I may wait until that really happens. The last time I took the plunge and asked someone out was an utter debacle involving one of the waitresses in the café. She was so pretty, and I really liked her. We'd been chatting and she was super friendly and did that tucking her hair behind her ear thing loads, and she touched my arm a few times which, according to what you see on YouTube, means someone fancies you, apparently. So of course, I stupidly, and very wrongly as it happens, thought that meant she was flirting with me, so I asked her if she fancied going out some time. After she'd finished looking at me like I'd suddenly grown a second head she declined and never spoke to me again. Then she left a week later, and I haven't seen her since.'

'Aww. I'm sure that was just a coincidence.'

He shrugged. 'Who the hell knows? Although, I suppose it would help if I could read people better. I don't know.'

As they chatted, Esme warmed to Judd more and more. He was quirky and had a wicked sense of humour but was quite blunt in some ways too. If he wondered it, he asked it. It was weirdly refreshing. And at least, she figured, she'd always know where she stood with him. She could definitely see them being friends as well as housemates.

'What type of music do you like?' she asked.

'A bit of everything, to be honest. Mostly rock music though. I like Queen, Kiss, you know, all the older stuff where people actually played their instruments. You?'

'I do like Queen and Kiss. My dad loves all that kind of thing so it's what I was brought up on, but I'm more of a Taylor Swift kind of girl.'

Judd stood abruptly and pointed to the door. 'Right, that's it, get out!'

Esme gasped and for a split second she thought he was being serious, and she felt the colour drain from her face. She made to stand up, but he burst out laughing.

'Oh, God, Esme, I'm joking, you wee dafty! Sit down!' She slumped quickly back onto the sofa and relief flooded her body. He leaned forward, resting his elbows on his knees, his expression a mask of seriousness again. 'Now, what I'm going to say can go no further, okay?' She nodded so he continued, 'Don't tell anyone but I'm a bit of a closet Swiftie myself. I arrived late to the party, but she impresses me. Not just her music but her business acumen and her charitable works. And her lyrics are pretty poetical which is cool. But,' he wagged his finger at her, 'if word gets out about any of this I'll tell everyone you have false teeth. I have a reputation to uphold as a mean and moody type.'

Esme laughed. 'I wouldn't call you mean or moody, and I don't have false teeth.'

'No, that's as may be but I'll still tell people you do. And you've seen how convincing I can be with the whole *get out* thing.' He grinned.

Esme stood and walked over to him, her hand held out. 'My lips are sealed, and my teeth are real. Deal?'

Judd shook it. 'Deal. Blimey, with poetry like that you could give Miss Swift a run for her money.' He laughed. 'So, what's your favourite Swift era?' he asked.

She sat again and pursed her lips. 'Oh, I love them all but honestly I think I'm a *Folklore* girl. You?'

He shrugged. 'Hate them all. Remember?' He gave a theatrical wink.

Esme tapped her nose. 'Got it.'

* * *

Sleeping in a new room shouldn't have been so strange considering her travels but Esme found herself lying awake for what felt like hours. And every time she began to nod off, a noise would startle her awake. The house was old and of course this meant it creaked a little as the wood expanded and contracted in the changing temperature. Betty didn't have any such problems and snuggled up on her new sofa, snoring her little head off.

Esme glanced at the screen of her phone to find it was half three in the morning and rather than fighting with herself she decided to go down to the kitchen and get a drink of milk or tea; anything so she wouldn't associate her bed with insomnia. As she closed her bedroom door and turned, she almost jumped out of her skin as she came face to bare chest with someone in the hallway.

She stifled a squeal and covered her mouth. 'Oof!'

'Oh, shit, sorry! Are you okay?' Judd asked, grabbing onto her arms to steady her. The second time this had happened.

In the dim moonlight coming through the landing window,

she could see the striations of the taut muscles of his body. The skin of his biceps and his stomach was smooth and flawless, and she realised she was staring. She shook her head to dislodge the wave of whatever the heck had just washed over her. 'I'm fine, yes, sorry about that. I was just going to get a drink.'

'Can't sleep?' he asked.

'No. Maybe the new mattress, I don't know.'

'I can't sleep either but my insomnia's a fairly common occurrence. I tend to be a bit of a night owl, but I made an effort to try and sleep tonight. Didn't want to be clanging around when you were sleeping. Come on, I'll make us some hot chocolate, that might help.' He flicked on the light, and she was greeted by the clear sight of his muscular torso and thick, bare thighs that were barely covered by the tight-fitting boxers he wore. 'Nice PJs,' he said and when she didn't reply he glanced down at his body and state of undress, and his face coloured a similar shade to what she was wearing. 'I'll, erm, go stick some clothes on first.' He disappeared back into his room and Esme made her way down the stairs to the kitchen. Thankfully the cottage was toasty warm, and she sat at the little bistro table in her cerise satin pyjamas waiting for Judd.

When he reappeared, he was wearing joggers and a t-shirt. 'Sorry about that. Didn't mean to scare you half to death with my pasty flesh.' He chuckled.

'No, it's fine. I think we both may take a while to adjust to this situation.'

'I'm just glad I remembered to put some boxers on. I'm a naked sleeper.' He closed his eyes briefly. 'Not that you needed that mental image. You'll never sleep now.'

She laughed and shook her head. 'Honestly, it's fine.'

He set about making their drinks with hot milk in a pan. 'I'm guessing your wee pal is sleeping well in her new bed.'

'Oh, yes. Betty can sleep through most things. I was expecting her to be a little disconcerted by the move but she's obviously tougher than me.'

'You've lived away from home before, though, haven't you? Didn't you say you'd been travelling?'

'I did. I sort of lived with someone though, as in the same bedroom, so it's a bit different.'

He raised his eyebrows. 'The heartbreaker?'

She nodded. 'The very same,' she replied dramatically, trying to make light of things.

'I'm so sorry that happened to you.' She lifted her face to find his gaze fixed on her and sincerity in his kind eyes.

She smiled and looked away. Sympathy had a way of making her emotional usually but coming from Judd it was different. Her heart skipped. 'Thank you but I'm getting over it now.'

'Good. Anyway, here's your drink.' He placed a mug before her on the table. 'I'm pretty bloody good at hot chocolate if I do say so myself.'

She took a tentative sip of the steaming liquid and inhaled the sweet aroma. 'Mmm... delicious.'

'Told you, didn't I?'

'You weren't wrong.'

Eventually Esme went back to bed and, before sleep took her, Judd's body and his smile whirred around her mind in a repetitive loop. His smooth skin, angular jaw with a smattering of stubble, his smiling eyes, his smooth skin, angular jaw...

Nope. Stop it. You're not going to find him attractive, Esme Cassidy. You can't. Stop it now.

11

The following morning, Esme was woken by Betty snuffling at her face and whining. Esme rubbed at her eyes and reached for her phone. It was past 9 a.m. After a brief bout of insomnia, she had settled into restful sleep. As well as being delicious, the hot chocolate Judd made must have been some kind of magic elixir.

'Oh, heck, Betty, I'm so sorry! You must be desperate to go out.' She leapt from the bed and dashed to the door, the little pug following closely behind.

As they reached the kitchen, Judd was sitting at the table drinking coffee. 'Afternoon, sleepy head!' he said as she lurched for the back door.

'*Morning*. Poor Betty. I never sleep this late.'

He laughed. 'You needed it after being wide awake most of the night. And there's nothing spoiling. Well, apart from your new rug, I suppose.'

Esme glanced over her shoulder to see him smirking. 'She's housetrained, don't worry, and very good, bless her heart. She woke me up to tell me, actually. No accidents thankfully. I'm going to take her out for a bit of a walk around the grounds once I've had a shower. I think the fresh air will do us both good.'

'Mind if I join you?' Judd asked as he placed down his mug. 'It's quite nice out.'

'Not at all. The human company would be nice.'

'Human I can offer, although it's a good thing you didn't say adult.' He laughed.

Once she had showered and dressed, Esme slipped on Betty's harness, grabbed a jacket and met Judd in the hallway.

He had on khaki cargo pants and a navy-blue hoodie with a slogan that read *Gardeners Like it Dirty*. There was a cartoonish picture of shovels and plant pots beneath the lettering. She sniggered and shook her head.

'You like?' he asked as he held out his arms and performed a twirl on the spot, a cheeky grin curling his mouth upwards. 'Personally, I think it's rather rude, but you appear to appreciate it, which says quite a lot, I think.' He chuckled and she rolled her eyes. She couldn't help liking him and was relieved they were already clicking. He inhaled a deep breath as they left the cottage. 'It really is a nice day for a walk. You've gotta love living here.'

It was fresh and there was an aroma of earth and damp grass in the air. 'I totally agree,' she said with a smile as she watched Betty snuffling and sniffing the ground, like she was reading the newspaper and catching up on all the gossip of the castle wildlife. Esme loved spring and the new life it brought in abundance. It made her think of new beginnings and starting over, which she was, of course, doing herself.

They walked along the lane and towards the castle. The sky provided a pretty cornflower-blue backdrop to the ancient building and the sun glinted off the stonework, highlighting the tiny particles of natural glitter therein.

Esme spotted Olivia and Brodie by the castle. Olivia was pushing baby Freya in her pram and together they were the picture of family bliss. Marley wandered along beside them as Wilf, the younger dog, covered twice as much distance running back and forth, back and forth, his tail wagging frantically and his tongue lolling around out of his mouth. They strolled away from the castle towards the loch. Brodie was carrying a picnic basket in one hand and had a tartan blanket under his other arm.

Esme and Judd chatted as they walked, and it felt easy. Betty ran to the full extent of her retractable lead and continued to investigate everything and anything, pausing every so often to sniff the air and listen to sounds carried on the breeze that were imperceptible to the human ear. Esme smiled to herself, a feeling of contentment settling over her. This move had been the best decision.

As they reached the entry to the stable block apartments, Esme glanced over and spotted Zach sitting on a bench outside his accommodation. He wore a navy track suit with chunky designer trainers, and a band t-shirt she couldn't quite make out. In his hand was an iPad that had evidently wronged him in some way judging by the way he was scowling at it and chewing his lip. As if he sensed them walking close by, he lifted his chin and waved. Esme did the same and Judd followed suit.

'Nice guy, that Zach. Although did you hear about one of the staff supposedly bothering him?' He slapped his forehead. 'Of course you did.'

Esme snapped her attention to him. 'What do you mean *of course I did*?'

Judd frowned. 'Erm... You sent the email out on behalf of Lady O?'

Relief flooded her. 'Oh, yes. I did. *Of course*.' She gave a light laugh and her stomach twinged with embarrassment as her guilt almost gave her away.

He paused for a moment and lowered his voice. 'Between you and me, I think I might know who it was.'

Esme's stomach flipped and she swallowed hard. 'Oh?'

He chewed his thumbnail for a moment. 'Yeah. I'm a bit worried that I'm the culprit. I was chatting to him one day last week. Although I was working, and technically he was the one standing talking to me. But... I know I can be a bit full on, so maybe I got on his nerves. I always worry that I talk too much... although sometimes I could be accused of not talking enough.' He gave a heavy sigh. 'Life's a bloody minefield sometimes.'

There was that guilt again, chip, chip, chipping away at Esme's mind. 'Oh, no, I'm sure it wasn't you. And you talk just the right amount so don't worry.'

'Judd! Excuse me, Judd!' They stopped walking and turned to see Eilidh from the film crew waving from across the gravelled area.

'Aye, what can I do for yous?' Judd replied.

'Sorry to be a nuisance but could you come and give us a hand to move one of the planters in the picture gallery, please? We're just going through the shot list for tomorrow and it's in the way, but it's one of the antique ones so we didn't want to move it ourselves.'

'Sure, no bother.' He turned to Esme. 'See you back at home?'

Esme smiled. 'See you there.' She carried on walking but heard the gravel crunching hurriedly behind her.

'Esme, wait up.' It was Zach.

She stopped and turned. 'Oh, hi.'

'Hey. How are you doing?' he asked, thrusting his hands into his pockets as usual. For someone who oozed confidence on screen, off screen he appeared to be strangely shy. She could now make out the t-shirt he was wearing was from The Darkness's latest tour. He smelled fresh like high-end shower gel, and he had the shadow of stubble across his jaw. She imagined what it would feel like to run her fingertips over it and an involuntary shiver trickled down her spine.

She realised she may have stared a moment longer than was acceptable and nodded a little too vigorously to make up for it. 'Oh, me? Yeah, yeah, I'm good. You?'

'Meh, you know. Anyway, who's this cute little fella?' he asked, crouching to say hello to Betty, whose little curled tail wagged at his soft tone.

'Erm, this little *fella* is a girl. She's called Betty.'

'Whoops, sorry, Betty. Of course you're a girl. You're the cutest girl, aren't you?' He scratched the little dog behind her ears and her tongue lolled out.

He stood and they began walking again along a path that would eventually lead to the nursery within the castle grounds. Zach huffed. 'I'm glad you walked by because I was desperately in need of a break.'

'How come?'

He ran a hand roughly over his head and shrugged. 'I've been going over the lines for one of my most terrifying scenes of the whole movie.'

Esme's interest was piqued. 'So that's why you were glaring at your iPad as if you'd happily stamp on it. Why is it so terrifying? Don't you have a stunt double?'

He laughed. 'It's not that kind of terrifying. It's one of the scenes with Ruby. A love scene, actually. I hate filming those because, contrary to what people think, there's nothing sexy about making out with someone you barely know, with fifty people standing around watching.'

Esme gasped. 'There'll be *fifty* people watching you?'

'Okay, so maybe that was an exaggeration. But that's not even the scary bit. She is *so* incredibly talented, and I...' He sighed and shook his head. 'I feel so inferior and unworthy.'

'Is this you fishing for compliments? Am I supposed to tell you how incredibly talented *you* are?' she teased.

He grinned. 'You can if you like, I'm an actor so obviously I'm all for the ego stroking.'

She rolled her eyes and laughed. 'I don't understand why you'd feel inferior though. You've been in way more movies than she has. And you're far more well known.'

'Doesn't seem to change anything on this occasion. I'm so nervous which is frustrating because I never get nervous.'

Esme stopped walking. 'Lucky you. I'm terrified about my play. I'm scared I'll freeze or make a total fool of myself.'

He turned to face her. 'You really have no need. From what I've seen you're amazing. And yes, this may sound cliché, but you're a real natural. You're believable and your emotions really do shine through, like you feel every line as if you wrote it. And that's saying something for Shakespeare,' he held up a hand, 'and before you jump to conclusions again, I'm not insulting you. I'm saying you deliver the Bard's words ridiculously well for someone with no professional training. In short, I'm saying you're really very good. Take a compliment for once.' He laughed and Esme joined in.

She felt her face heating. 'Okay, that's very kind. Thank you.' She had never been any good at accepting praise, always her own worst critic, but hearing it from Zach Marchand was bizarre to say the least. She felt like she had stepped into the Twilight Zone or some parallel universe where they happened to be friends. How the hell was this her life all of a sudden?

'I mean it. You really should get an agent. I could put you in touch with some of my contacts.'

Esme's eyebrows shot up at the mere suggestion. 'What? Me? Oh, gosh, thanks but I really think I'm past all that, like I said before I'm happy with my life. Am dram is about my level these days.'

'I think my aunt Sylvia would say *there is nothing am about this dram, darling.*' His impersonation of his aunty was spot on and made Esme giggle uncontrollably. Zach laughed along and added, 'She was quite the star back in the seventies and eighties, you know.'

'So I understand. She likes to tell us about her on-stage exploits.'

Zach grinned. 'Oh, I can imagine. She's certainly a character.' Their laughter subsided and they carried on walking until they reached the boundary hedge of the nursery. Off in the distance, Kerr and his son were busy tending the plants and singing along to the radio that was perched on a bench just outside the little wooden shack on the lot. Will paused what he was doing to play a guitar solo on the rake he'd been using, and Kerr threw his head back, laughing before ruffling his son's hair.

'Those guys are always together, and they seem to have such a fun relationship. Are they related?'

Esme nodded. 'Father and son. Only recently connected, so Olivia told me, and under quite difficult circumstances too. Kerr has quite a history if you listen to the castle gossip.'

Zach tilted his head. 'And you don't?'

Esme shrugged. 'I like to hear things straight from the horse's mouth personally. Gossip can get you into all kinds of trouble.'

'How about Judd? Is he as diplomatic as you?'

What a weird question. 'He seems to be.'

Zach nodded. 'I got that feeling about him. And I bet he's massively supportive of you pursuing your dreams again.'

Esme frowned. 'Erm... I suppose. Although we haven't really discussed it.'

Zach was no longer making eye contact. 'He seems a great guy. I hear you both live in one of the pretty cottages along the lane.'

She absent-mindedly wondered who he had been talking about her with. 'Yeah. I've only just moved in but it's lovely. Judd has been keeping up with the garden and he really has a knack for it.'

Zach nodded and gave a brief smile. 'That's great. Really great. Congratulations.'

Esme was a bit confused. 'It's no big deal really, but thanks.'

'Oh, I don't know. I always think if you love someone enough to move in with them it's a pretty big deal.'

'Sorry? Love...?' She realised what he had mistakenly thought. 'Oh... you think Judd and I...? We aren't... I mean we're just housemates. I wanted to move out of home, and he had a spare room and it's so convenient for work, so...'

Zach's eyes widened. 'Oh! Right! Sorry. I thought you were together because you seem... I don't know. My bad.'

Esme shrugged. 'No harm done. He's a really nice guy but we're just sort of getting to know one another.'

'I get you, of course. So... are you single or is there someone else?'

Esme felt her face warming again and wondered why on earth Zach Marchand would be asking her, plain old Esme Cassidy, if she was single. 'I'm very much single.' She cringed, *as opposed to only slightly single*? 'That is, I... erm... had my heart broken not too long back so I've sworn off relationships for a while.' *Why did I say that?* She clenched her jaw, but it was too late, the words were out there.

He nodded. 'You too? I'm sorry to hear that.'

'Thanks. It's not fun, eh?'

He gave a small smile tinged with sadness. 'You're not wrong.'

A heavy silence fell between them for a few moments and Esme could've kicked herself. Maybe he was going to ask her out and she had ruined it by oversharing. Although how ridiculous did she have to be to imagine such a scenario where a famous actor asked her out? Especially one as handsome as Zach. She silently shook her head and glanced off into the distance.

He glanced at his watch. 'Shit, I suppose I should be getting back. That scene isn't going to rehearse itself.'

'Well, if you need any help I'd be happy to... *help*.' Her face warmed again. Why couldn't she get her words out around him?

'Are you free now?' he asked, his eyes filled with evident hope.

'Oh, I mean yeah, I'm not busy. I was just taking Betty for a walk and then doing laundry so...' *And you have your own lines to learn, you muppet, don't let professionalism stand in the way of you helping a heartthrob.*

'Amazing! Let's go back to mine and I'll put the kettle on.'

* * *

The stable apartment where Zach was staying was so cosy with a real fire and exposed stone walls. Esme had heard that Olivia's friend Bella had designed the apartments and from what she had seen they were beautiful; worthy of a magazine spread, in fact. Zach made coffee in the kitchen as Esme admired the artwork on the walls of the living room and Betty curled up on the rug in front of the fire, tired from her walk.

Once Zach had brought two steaming mugs of earthy-smelling liquid and placed them on the hearth, he handed Esme a paper script and he retrieved his iPad then he slid the coffee table to one end, and they stood in the centre of the lounge.

'Okay, so this scene is the first time Lady Eleanor and Lord Christoph are actually alone together. Up to this point they have been sharing glances and very brief skin-to-skin touches, erm, a hand, an arm. They're both nervous and on edge because this thing between them is so clandestine but it's consuming them both and they know they feel the same. Lady Eleanor is having second thoughts now that she is set to inherit the castle but Lord Christoph can't bear to think of not being with her.' He paused and closed his eyes for a moment, then when he opened them it was clear from his shift in stance he was in character. He waited for Esme to deliver her line, his eyes were intently fixed on her, searing deeply into her soul and for a moment she forgot to speak. He was mesmerising without uttering a single word.

She managed to break his gaze briefly to glance at the highlighted part on the paper. 'We... we can't do this, my lord. If we are found out I stand to lose everything,' Esme said in a breathy voice that was only partly acted. 'The castle, my reputation... and my heart.'

Zach stepped closer and he reached out his hand to cup her cheek. 'But I can't move away. Can't you see? I'm drawn to you. You fill my mind during my waking hours and my dreams when I'm in slumber. If this is so wrong, why would I gladly be caught just to have another moment alone with you?' He clenched his jaw and spoke with such passion he took her breath away.

She pressed her hand to his chest, glanced down at the script briefly and then back up to Zach. 'You must stop. You must. You're my betrothed's brother. There is no positive outcome for this tryst.' Her heart pounded as she locked her gaze on his. 'It will surely be the death of us both, Christoph,' she whispered his character's name as she felt Lady Eleanor would have, being so personal for the first time.

He lowered his face and took another step closer; his chest was heaving now. 'Then I will die for this. I would die for you, sweet Eleanor,' he growled, and she felt her legs weakening as his chest rumbled beneath her hand.

She almost forgot to read her next line. 'Don't say such things. You will surely break my heart. You must leave.'

He rested his forehead on hers. 'Then push me away. Make me leave your presence. Tell me to go,' he whispered.

Esme closed her eyes for a moment. 'Please be strong for both of us and don't make me say the words... *please.*'

'If I must leave, I wish for one kiss. I wish to feel your lips against mine, just once, Eleanor. That is all I ask.'

As she opened her eyes again, she watched in what felt like slow motion as he lowered his face until she could feel his warm breath on her skin. His lips were millimetres from hers. *Oh my God, he's actually going to kiss me. It's only acting, Cassidy, remember that. It means nothing. But he's actually going to practise the kiss on me!* Her eyes fluttered closed again and she waited...

The door burst open. 'Oh, there you are, Zachy! I've been looking everywhere,' Lucille said without so much as a hello.

Zach stepped back quickly as if he'd been slapped. 'Luce, ever heard of knocking?'

She snorted. 'Oh, please. I've practically been sharing this place with you since we arrived. The tabloids would have a field day if they knew what's been going on.' She laughed but there was no humour, just a sinister tinkling to her voice that reminded Esme of the Wicked Witch from *The Wizard of Oz*. 'What on earth are you doing in here with a staff member anyway?' she asked with a curled lip as if the words had a bitter taste. 'You could get into serious trouble, you know. *Both* of you.'

Esme's stomach knotted. She imagined Lucille would be telling Lady Olivia about this discovery as soon as possible, meaning her job and her reputation would be on the line, and the rest of the staff would know *exactly* who had been the topic of complaint in the email she had sent on behalf of her boss.

'I should get going,' Esme said, her face burning at furnace-level proportions now. 'Come on, Betty.'

Lucille appeared confused for a moment and glanced around. 'Betty? Who on earth is... oh!' She recoiled, grimaced and placed a hand on her chest. 'Eeugh, what an ugly little creature.'

'Hey, there's no reason to be cruel about the dog, Lucille,' Zach said, stepping protectively in front of the pug.

'Who says I was referring to the dog?' Lucille chuntered, her voice barely audible but Esme heard everything.

Zach's brow crumpled, and he took a step towards her, jaw clenched. 'What did you say?'

Lucille waved a dismissive hand. 'Oh, nothing. Anyway, I've come to run lines. I'm guessing you're panicking about the love scene again like you were when I helped you yesterday.' She fanned herself with her hands. 'That kiss was pretty hot, though, wouldn't you say? Really, Zachy, you should stick to the professionals to help you, otherwise you'll be completely knocked off your game. Run along now, Doris.' She waved her hand in Esme's direction. 'I'm sure you've got something to clean somewhere. Don't let us keep you.'

Esme clenched her jaw, and her nostrils flared. 'How dare—'

Lucille stepped forward and with a sly smile she said, 'Oh, I dare, and I'd be mindful about coming into the actors' accommodation again if I were you. I'd hate to see you acquiring the reputation of floozy, or getting fired for interfering with a working film set.'

'Lucille, that's enough,' Zach said, his face also beet red now.

'It's okay, Zach, I do have to go. I'll see you later,' Esme said, glaring at Lucille. She clipped Betty's lead on, grabbed her coat and dashed for the door, her pulse rate thundering around her body as she fought to contain her anger, both at herself for being caught in Zach's apartment and at Lucille for thinking everyone was beneath her.

12

On Monday morning, Esme awoke after a fitful night, filled with a sense of dread. She needed to plan what she would say if Lucille had got to Olivia first. Although she hoped that Zach might stand up for her in that situation. But she hadn't had a chance to speak to him.

She had spent an hour on the phone on Sunday evening talking to Parker about everything but unfortunately he had been unable to ease her mind.

'She's such a jealous bitch. She can see that Zach likes you and she's determined to sabotage it. I wouldn't mind but she clearly doesn't even want him. I can't stand people like that. I heard that they split up because she was always off having flings with other famous people and then turning it back on him and accusing him of doing that. You can see why he'd had enough. But she had the audacity to dump him for being a cheater. Ridiculous! And now he likes you she is back to her old ways. If she ever even changed. What is it they say about leopards?'

Esme was under no illusions about her friendship with Zach. It was farfetched, to say the least, to even consider he might be attracted to her. But if Lucille was as paranoid as she appeared to be, that fact wouldn't help her at all. 'I don't think he likes me like that. But she clearly thinks something is going on, which puts me in a tricky situation. I feel like I should say something to Olivia first. Make sure she hears everything from me before Lucille gets to sensationalise everything.'

Parker had huffed. 'I would ordinarily say you didn't need to do that, but we can both see what Lucille is like. You might be best to cover yourself and make a pre-emptive strike.'

When the call had ended, she had gone downstairs to find Betty asleep in Judd's lap. He was watching Monty Python on TV and chuckling to himself as the man on screen was waving around a fake parrot.

He lifted his chin, and his brow crumpled. 'Oh, hey. Is everything okay? You seem out of sorts.'

She nodded and forced a smile. 'Oh, yeah, I'm good, don't worry. Just nervous about my rehearsals for the play.' It wasn't a complete lie. 'I haven't really had much time to practise my lines, and Sylvia is a stickler for that kind of thing, and to add to the stress the performance has been brought forward so I have even less time now.'

'I'd be happy to run through them with you, if it'd help. Although I have to warn you I'm a bit lost when it comes to Shakespeare. Give me the Monty Python Parrot Sketch any day.' He gestured at the screen. 'But I'd be happy to help if you need me?'

'That's really kind, thank you. Maybe later.'

'I've just made a fresh pot of coffee, want me to get you one?' he asked as he stroked his hand down the sleeping dog.

'Oh, no, it's okay. I'll get some. Betty looks far too peaceful on your lap to be disturbed.'

He grinned. 'Yeah, sorry about that. I think she likes me.'

'I think she does.' *She's not the only one.*

He laughed lightly. 'Aye and I have to make the most of the female attention, it doesn't happen to me often.'

He was so self-deprecating, unnecessarily so in Esme's opinion. He was funny, handsome, had a pretty spectacular physique from what she had witnessed, so she couldn't understand it at all. Perhaps she needed to enlist Parker's matchmaking help to find him someone.

* * *

A short while later, when she had arrived at work, Esme paused outside Olivia's office. Her palms were clammy and her heart racing. It was now or never. If Lucille had got to her first, no doubt there would have been embellishments to the story. Perhaps by now her story would be that she had walked in on Esme with Zach naked and in the throes of passion. She wouldn't put anything past her. She swallowed hard and turned the handle. She walked in to find her boss sitting at her desk with Freya in her arms. 'Oh, hi, Esme. I've been meaning to talk to you. Come and have a seat,' she whispered so as not to wake the sleeping infant.

Esme's heart flipped over in her chest. Was this it? Was she too late? Was this where she got fired for fraternising with the actors? She did as requested and sat in the chair opposite.

'How is it going with you and Judd at the cottage?' Olivia asked with a smile.

Esme beamed, more than a little relieved, although knowing it could be short-lived. 'Oh, it's wonderful. Thank you so much. I can't tell you how good it feels to have my own place.'

'And you and Judd are getting on okay?'

Esme grinned and nodded. 'So far, so good. He's really nice

and Betty clearly adores him. She spends most of her time snuggled up in his lap.'

'Have you heard from Rhys again at all?' Olivia asked with a concerned tilt of her head.

Esme straightened her spine. 'Nothing at all. Although that's a good thing. The letter hurt and I can do without more reminders of him. It's not like we can be friends because that's definitely not something I could cope with. A clean break was what I needed and even though I can't say it was clean, it was definitely a break. Anyway, I need to talk to you about something if you have the time?'

Olivia winced. 'Oh, heck, can it wait? I really need to head out. I have a meeting with Eilidh from the film crew, they are wanting to rummage in the attic space for more Georgian pieces and I don't want them to go unsupervised.'

As much as Esme knew time was of the essence, she nodded. 'Sure, it can wait. Don't worry.'

* * *

For the rest of the day, Esme walked around as if on eggshells. Paranoia had whipped her up into a frenzy and with every task she completed she was reminded that she hadn't come clean to Olivia. Surely it was only a matter of time now before she was called back in and handed her P45. She had tried to own up to her misdemeanour, but Olivia had bombarded her with a list of jobs for the day, meaning she hadn't had a chance. Then Brodie had arrived to take Freya for a few hours while Olivia and her Uncle Innes met with someone who was allegedly very important that couldn't be rescheduled. She was being decidedly cagey and hadn't imparted any information to Esme about the meeting, which was odd. By the end of the day, she resolved to go visit her parents and ask for their advice. It would mean admitting to them that she had been secretly meeting with the actor, but she had to do something.

* * *

After work Esme disembarked the bus and walked along the road towards her family home. She was surprised to find her dad's car already in the driveway.

As she walked through the front door, she called out, 'Hey, it's only me!'

'We're in the kitchen, pet,' came her dad's voice. He sounded different. Low.

She hugged them both and realised her mum had been crying. 'What's happened? What's going on?'

'Your dad's had some bad news, love,' her mum replied, dabbing at her nose.

Esme filled with dread and slumped into chair. 'Dad? What is it?'

Her dad sighed deeply. 'McIver has been diagnosed with cancer. He's really quite poorly so I'm, erm... I'm being made redundant. The distillery is closing down.' He shook his head. 'I'm heartbroken for him and his poor wife but I'm also worried about our future. When I was younger you got a job, and you stuck with it until retirement. Now here I am, fifty-five years old. Who's going to employ me? I'm no graduate. I'm unskilled. I've worked at the distillery since I met your mum.' He ran his hands through his hair and his shoulders rounded. 'I know this is incredibly selfish and I'm racked with guilt for feeling this way but I'm worried we may have to sell the house.'

Esme's stomach plunged. 'Oh, no, Dad, I'm so sorry. Poor Mr and Mrs McIver. But surely they can sell it on as a going concern? It's a successful business and part of Inverness's heritage.'

He shook his head. 'Unfortunately, he's been trying that route behind the scenes for months since his diagnosis but there was no interest. He and his wife have been going through this alone for fear of worrying us all. It's sold now but the new owner is turning the distillery into a swanky place full of independent shops. McIver's just started really intense chemotherapy, bless him, so he needs to just draw a line under it all. I do understand it all but we had a union rep in today and a guy from the employment service talking about retraining.' He laughed without a single ounce of humour. 'Bloody retraining at my age. Absolutely ridiculous.'

Esme's insides knotted. She had never seen her dad like this; so despondent. 'Would it help if I move back home? I could contribute to the mortgage, help with bills—'

Her dad shook his head vehemently. 'Absolutely not. This isn't your mess to clear up, pet. You're settled in your new place, and I refuse to stop you from living your own life. I have so many regrets about doing that before, so I won't do it again.'

* * *

The next few days were a blur of rehearsals and work but in the back of Esme's mind was the worry over her dad's redundancy. By Friday she had plucked up enough courage to speak to Olivia about it all.

'How long will it be before the distillery is licensed and up and running?' she asked as casually as possible.

Olivia sighed. 'Not too long at all if my uncle has anything to say about it. But in reality a couple of months because Brodie is determined to make sure it's done right. He's having to curb my uncle's enthusiasm but we feel that after the shoot has finished will be best for the launch. Why do you ask?'

Esme frowned and picked at a hangnail she had caught when taking Betty out for a walk the night before. 'Oh, it's just that the McIver distillery in Inverness is closing down so I suppose the competition will be reduced.' She forced a smile.

'Oh, yes, Innes did mention that he'd heard whisperings about that. Doesn't your dad work there?' she asked with a crumple of her brow.

Esme nodded. 'He does.'

Olivia leaned forward. 'I'm so sorry, Esme. It must be a very worrying time for your parents. I'd say tell him not to worry but of course that won't help.'

'When will you be advertising for staff? Not that I'm asking for any special treatment or anything. I just want to make sure he doesn't miss out on applying.'

'I'm sure it'll be quite soon. Brodie and Innes are dealing with most things connected to the new distillery but I'll definitely keep you posted.' She gave an encouraging smile, but it dissipated all too soon. 'Look, now that I've got you, there's something important I want to talk to you about,' Olivia said, fixing her with a stern gaze.

'Oh, yes?'

Olivia nodded. 'Yes. Not great news or an easy topic I'm afraid.' Esme's mouth was quickly sapped of moisture and her heart rate picked up. Olivia sighed. 'I've been made aware of who the culprit was in the whole Zach being bothered situation.'

Esme's eyes widened. 'Oh. Right. I see. But perhaps can I explain and maybe give my side of the—'

Olivia's brow crumpled. 'There's no need, Esme. You don't have anything to explain. I know you and Judd are housemates now and you've clearly become friends but that doesn't mean you're responsible for him, nor do you need to make excuses for his behaviour.'

Esme opened and closed her mouth a few times as confusion washed over her brain. 'I'm sorry, what?'

Olivia straightened her spine. 'Judd is a great guy, and he's so knowledgeable about the plants on site, so he's incredibly valuable to my team. And I've recently discovered there's a high possibility that he's on the spectrum, but that doesn't excuse him for defying the rules. He has to realise that the actors aren't here to make friends. They're here to work and to get a job done. Just as he is. So, I wanted to let you know he's now on a warning.'

Esme shook her head. 'A warning? But—'

Olivia held up a hand to halt her reply, something Esme had never seen her do before. 'I'm aware that you may want to defend him which is very noble, and I do understand that. You're a very loyal person so it's just what I would expect from you. But my advice is that if you get the impression he's going to try and talk to the actors while they're on the set again, remind him he shouldn't. I don't want to fire him, Esme. He's such a good worker, but I can't have employees that completely contradict the instructions they're given. As you know, everyone was made aware of the importance of keeping their distance from the actors and crew while the film is in production, and everyone else seems to be managing to follow that rule.'

Esme's heart thumped at her ribs and her stomach churned around what little breakfast she had managed to eat like a faulty washing machine on an erratic spin cycle. 'Olivia, can I just say something, please?'

There was a knock on the door. 'One second, Esme. Yes? Come in!'

Uncle Innes walked into the room. 'Ah, hello, Esme, lovely to see you. Sorry to intrude but I need to speak to my niece on an urgent matter. Olivia darling, can I have a word?'

'I'm sorry, Esme, we can continue this later,' Olivia said. 'But there's nothing for you, personally, to worry about.'

Esme nodded and stood but before she left she tried once more. 'But it won't take a moment, if I can just—'

Uncle Innes interjected. 'I'm so sorry, dear, but time really is of the essence.'

Esme chewed her cheek as tears threatened. 'Okay, no worries. I'll leave you to it.' She left the office and closed the door just as tears spilled over and a sob escaped her chest. Judd was on a warning, and it was all her fault. She had to speak to him and explain. She didn't want to be the reason he lost his job, and then in turn his home.

13

'Hey, what's up, Esme?' Parker asked as he approached her from the direction of his own office space further along the corridor. 'You look awful, what's happened?'

'Are you free for a minute? I really need a friendly ear,' she said, and he nodded, concern etched into a crease in his brow.

He linked his arm through hers and walked her into the kitchen. 'Come on, let's get whatever this is sorted.'

Once inside the room with the door closed, Parker got her a glass of water and she sat at the old, battered table as she explained what had happened with her dad, and now with Judd. Parker sat beside her and held her hand.

More tears slipped down her face, leaving warm, damp trails in their wake. 'I feel absolutely awful. This is my fault entirely.' She wanted to go home and crawl under her duvet to forget the last two days. 'He shouldn't be on a warning, Parker, *I* should. I tried to tell Olivia, but Innes came in with something urgent he needed to speak to her about and I had to leave so I didn't get a chance to explain.'

Parker squeezed her hand. 'Oh, honey, this is awful. I hate to see you in this state when it's not your fault. It's been blown out of all proportion by that sour-faced witch of an actress. I'd bet money she's behind all this.'

Esme shook her head. 'She can't be. Surely she would have grassed on *me*, not Judd. Someone else must have told her it was him, but who? Poor Judd. He's so lovely, he really doesn't deserve any of this. Maybe I should just send Olivia an email explaining it all.'

Parker cringed and sucked air through his teeth. 'Don't do that. It's the kind of conversation that comes across better in person. If she sees your face and how sorry you are she'll be more inclined to be lenient. But why don't you go over to the nursery and talk to Judd? Ask him what's happened. I'll cover for you if Olivia comes looking.'

Esme nodded and placed down the glass of water. 'Yes, good idea. Thank you.'

As Parker left the kitchen, Esme ran from the castle and into the grounds just as the sky above darkened and rain began to pour. Instead of heading back inside to grab her coat, she set off sprinting, figuring the rain wasn't forecast so would most likely pass over. Unfortunately, however, the tiny droplets turned into ice-cold hail stones that felt like needles on the bare skin of her arms and she cursed the choice to wear a short-sleeved dress. *Ah, the joys of the unpredictable Scottish weather.* She ran towards the nursery as fast as she could in her heels and swiped the wetness from her face in a bid to clear her blurry vision. It had been sunny only an hour before but now it was as if spring had gone on lunch break, leaving winter to step into the breach. The frigid air burned her lungs, and she regretted the decision to run. Out of breath and with a pounding heart, she stopped to pull in air. *Good grief, I'm so unfit.* She was doubled forward, resting her hands on her knees, the rain soaking through to what felt like the bones beneath her skin now, and didn't see anyone approaching.

'Hey! Esme, are you okay?'

Startled, she straightened a little too quickly and blood drained from her head so fast that her head began to spin, and her legs weakened as she heard a loud whooshing in her ears. Knowing of old that she was probably about to faint as her body lurched forwards and the space before her seemed to be sapped of colour, her hands shot out automatically to brace for impact, but instead arms grabbed for her, and she was quickly hoisted from the ground and either floating or being carried; in her fuzzy state of mind it was hard to tell. For a brief moment, she relished the feeling of being in someone's arms and rested her head on the damp shoulder by her ear as the rain pounded down onto the exposed side of her face. Her senses were filled with petrichor and alongside this she could smell leaves, earth and soap all mingled together. It was a heady cocktail. Then, before she knew it, she was sitting in a chair in the small shed in the boundary of the nursery and a warm fleece was placed around her shoulders. The temperature increased minimally, yet she still shivered.

'What the hell happened? Why are you out without a jacket in this weather? Are you okay? Do you want some water? Should I call anyone?' Judd bombarded her with questions as he crouched before her.

She lifted her face and was met with a deep look of concern that matched his strained tone. His eyes were actually looking right into hers for the first time, and it took her completely off guard. 'Th-thank you but no, I'm okay. I just stood up too quickly, that's all. It happens sometimes. It's a low blood pressure thing, I think.' She shook her head. 'Anyway, I was looking for you. I need to explain something.' He handed her some paper towels, and she dabbed at her face.

He placed a hand on both of her arms and kept his eyes locked on hers. It was strange and tugged at something deep inside of her that she couldn't quite grasp the meaning of.

'Okay, Esme, what is it? You're worrying me.'

Her chin trembled again as she took in his worry-filled expression. 'It's my fault, Judd. I should be the one on a warning, not you.'

A furrow appeared between his eyebrows. 'Who told you?'

'Sorry?'

Judd's nostrils flared and he asked again. 'Who told you I'm on a warning?'

Esme swiped tears from her cheeks. 'It's fine, it was Olivia. But the thing is... it was me; I was the one fraternising with the actors. Well, *one* actor to be exact. Zach.' She felt her cheeks flaming as if admitting something far more salacious than the innocent meeting she'd had with him. 'I was helping him with his lines, that's all. Just lines.'

The furrow disappeared and Judd smiled. 'Oh, that. Yeah, I know about that.'

It was Esme's turn to be confused now. 'What do you mean you know?'

He released his grip from her arms and sat back on his haunches. 'I saw you and Zach a while ago on that bench in the trees with the scripts. You looked like you were both concentrating so I didn't come to say hi in case I was interrupting.'

Esme closed her eyes for a moment. 'Hang on, so how come you're on a warning? None of this makes sense.'

He sighed and rubbed his hands over his face. 'Because I overheard that blonde actress, the one who always looks like she has a bad smell up her nose, you know the one I mean? I thought she was sweet at first but I soon realised the truth. Lucille, I think her name is. Anyway, like I said, she was talking to one of the other actors and telling them that she'd walked in on you and Zach kissing and undressing each other, walking towards his bedroom in his apartment, and that she was going to make sure you lost your job because of it.'

Esme gasped. She knew the lies would be piled on like some twisted game of Jenga, but this was ridiculous.

Judd continued, 'Apparently she and Zach were,' he made inverted commas in the air, '*on the verge of getting back together*, and you swooped in and ruined it all,' he said dramatically. 'Pfft, total bull, I've seen how he looks at her as if everything she says is utter mince. So, I went to see Olivia and told her it was me who'd been chatting to the actors when they were on set. I made sure to explain what I'd overheard, and that the blonde one clearly has it in for you but that it was all crap, so she wouldn't believe anything that sour-faced bint said. I asked her not to tell you I'd spoken to her though, so that's annoying.'

Esme widened her eyes and shook her head. 'But... why did you do that?'

He shrugged and the eye contact disappeared again. 'Because I don't like liars. And I don't like people dropping others in the shit for no reason.'

Esme shook her head. 'But I *was* in the wrong, Judd. And you admitted to something you didn't do.'

He looked at her again, albeit briefly. 'You helped him with his lines. I saw it for myself so it was hardly fraternising. And Parker mentioned that Zach had turned up at your Shakespeare rehearsal and seemed to like you so... I don't like people trying to hurt my friends, that's all.'

She reached out and took his hand. 'Oh, Judd, you're so

sweet. But you've put yourself in a tricky position now. I'm going to speak to Olivia and explain everything. You shouldn't be getting in trouble for something I did.'

He shook his head. 'You did nothing wrong, either. And I *did* talk to Zach when we were both supposed to be working so it wasn't a lie. And I know we haven't known each other that long but I think I know you well enough to see what that Lucille person said about you and Zach dashing off to his room is a load of crap. You're a very respectable person and that's just not something I could imagine you doing even if you do like him. And I didn't want other people muddying your reputation.'

Esme sighed. 'I didn't kiss him, you're right about that. But I did go into his apartment, which in hindsight was silly. We were rehearsing a scene he was worried about and there was supposed to be a kiss at the end of it, but we didn't practise that part. She burst in and was clearly not happy about finding me there with him.'

'Exactly, and that's why I wanted to speak to Olivia first. That actress wanted to get you fired and I wasn't having that. Anyway, I've seen how you look at Zach, so I can see you really do like him. You deserve a chance to see where it goes without her jealousy spoiling that for you.'

Esme flung her arms around Judd's neck. 'You really are the loveliest man. Thank you so much for trying to protect me. But I *will* have to go and speak to Olivia. I can't have you being on a warning because of me.'

He peered up at her from under his eyelids like a scolded puppy. 'I'd rather you didn't do that. You'll put yourself in the frame for discipline and she's already lost two PAs. She really likes you and is always saying how good you are at your job.'

'Well, then maybe she'll listen to me.' She stood and removed his fleece from her shoulders, and he stood too. She looked up at him, he was a good four inches taller than she was, so she had to tiptoe to kiss his cheek. 'Thank you, Judd. You're a real friend.'

He smiled shyly but didn't speak and she left. The rain and hail had stopped as quickly as it started, and the clouds overhead had cleared now. She walked back to the office in search of Olivia.

* * *

When Esme finally got Olivia alone, she closed the door. 'I need to tell you something so could you please just let me speak before I lose courage and run for the hills?'

Olivia frowned. 'If it's about Judd and the actors, you should know—'

'Please, Olivia, I'm sorry to interrupt you but I really just need to get this off my chest.' She then blurted out the somewhat garbled confession she had tried, but failed, to plan fully. 'And I can assure you it won't happen again, Olivia, but if you feel the need to let me go I totally understand.' Her chest heaved as if she had just admitted to capital murder.

Olivia held up her hands. 'Esme, I didn't say anything about letting anyone go. I was just initially concerned about the situation, and felt it needed nipping in the bud, but now, from what I've been told, just a few minutes before you got here as it happens, it seems there wasn't even a sit—' A knock on the door cut Olivia off.

For goodness' sake, can't I just admit to my crimes, get my P45 and be done with it? Esme thought as she closed her eyes and let her head roll back.

'Yes, who is it?' Olivia called out tersely, evidently just as annoyed for the intrusion.

The door opened. 'Erm, hi, sorry to bother you but I felt I needed to come and defend Esme,' came a familiar voice.

Esme watched as Olivia's eyebrows raised. 'Oh, hi, Zach, nice outfit. There really isn't any need to defend Esme but come on in,' Olivia replied.

Zach stepped forward and smiled down at Esme where she sat opposite Olivia. It was then that she noticed his clothing. He was wearing rust-coloured breeches with white stockings and black shoes adorned with large silver buckles. On his top half was a tailcoat with brass buttons that matched his knee-length trousers, and beneath that, a frilly white high-necked shirt poked out above the collar. His own hair was hidden beneath a powdered white wig that had two tube-like curls resting above his ears, giving the appearance that he had forgotten to remove his rollers. Esme tried not to smile as it felt inappropriate under the circumstances, but he looked so strange standing there juxtaposed by the two modern women.

He began to speak. 'I just wanted to let you know that this whole thing has been blown out of proportion and, if anyone is, I'm the one responsible for the mix-up.' Olivia opened her mouth to speak but he continued. 'The thing is, I knew that Esme was a skilled actor, and *I* asked *her* for help with some scenes I was worried about. I didn't want to go to any of the crew because, as you can imagine, I would've ruined my reputation as a cool cucumber when it comes to stage fright.' He chuckled nervously.

'My ex, Lucille, heard that Esme had been helping me and the green-eyed monster reared its ugly head. And then a few days later she barged into my apartment without knocking and walked in on Esme and me rehearsing another scene. Admittedly it was a more intimate scene, but we kept things strictly PG. I wasn't about to put her in that situation. But afterwards,

Lucille was allegedly overheard telling other actors what she supposedly saw, although that was all lies, I can assure you, and she was heard saying she would be getting Esme fired. I've just heard about this from Judd and wanted to come here immediately and let you know that I was the one to seek help from Esme, she in no way bothered me, so she absolutely does *not* need to be fired. She should be promoted if anything because she's gone above and beyond as far as I'm concerned, and has shown herself to be discreet, supportive and an incredible actor but that's by the by. So please release Judd from his warning because he was defending his friend, and let Esme keep her job.'

Olivia paused, open mouthed and wide eyed for a moment, and then started to giggle, her hand over her mouth. Esme and Zach shared a confused glance until Olivia spoke. 'Goodness, I had no idea this whole thing would be so blown up. Lucille is definitely someone to watch, and take with a pinch of salt by the sound of it. And Esme, you have some incredible friends willing to put themselves in the way of you getting into hot water. But that's just the thing. I'd just found out the whole thing was rubbish. Eilidh came to see me because she'd heard the rumours and wanted to let me know what Lucille can be like. So, I was going to be letting you, and Judd, know that the whole thing was to be forgotten.'

Esme was flooded with relief and grinned. 'That's brilliant news.'

'Thank goodness for that,' Zach said as he stepped forward to shake Olivia's hand. 'Thank you, and my sincere apologies for storming in here guns blazing like that.'

Olivia held up her hands. 'No harm done. It's good to see that my staff are appreciated.'

'Right, I'll get going. I'm supposed to be on set as you can probably tell.'

Esme glanced at Olivia and said, 'Really? We figured you were simply setting a new trend.' Zach stuck out his tongue like a petulant child and they shared a laugh.

As he left, Esme followed Zach out of the office. 'Thank you for doing that, Zach. I really appreciate it,' she told him.

He shrugged. 'I may have a reputation for being a bit of a rogue but the one thing I won't do is let someone else take the blame for something they didn't do.'

'Well, I'm grateful to you.'

He smiled. 'It's me who's grateful. You really helped me and I appreciate that. I stick by what I said about you getting an agent.'

Esme felt her face heating and she tucked her hair behind her ears. 'Thank you but there are so many better and more deserving actors out there.'

He stepped a little closer. 'How are the rehearsals going?'

Esme sighed. 'Intense. The play is on in just over a week which is absolutely ridiculous. The cast are all spitting chips about the scheduling conflict that's forced us to have so little time to prepare. But Sylvia is as annoyed as the rest of us.'

'Yeah, she was so upset. She feels she has let you all down, but it really wasn't her fault. She wasn't prepared to cancel because she had made a commitment to you all, so I hope the others can cut her some slack.'

'Don't worry, they are. Well, I'd better get back to work if I'm going to finish on time. I've another rehearsal tonight and it's exhausting. I don't know how you professionals do it.'

'See you later, Esme,' he said with a smile that did funny things to her insides and he turned to go but then stopped. 'Oh, hey, listen, the crew are having a barbecue at the weekend.

Filming is quite intense so every so often we like to have a night off to just chill. And don't worry, we've cleared the staff's attendance with Lady Olivia, and she says it's fine to cook down by the loch. On Sunday evening – why don't you and Judd come along? I think most of the staff have said they'll come.'

'Sounds like fun. I'll mention it, thanks.'

14

After the rehearsal, Esme stood outside the theatre with Parker and filled him in on all the events of her day.

'Thank fudge it's all sorted. I was going to go bald with the stress and it wasn't even me going through it,' he said as he hugged Esme. 'And believe me, bald is not something that would look good on this.' He gestures to his body and Esme giggled.

'I know, I'm so relieved to still have a job. Anyway, how are you feeling about the play now?'

Parker huffed and dropped his shoulders. 'Terrified. You?'

Esme laughed. 'About the same. I just don't see how we're going to be ready.'

Parker glanced over his shoulder towards the theatre as more people filtered out. He lowered his voice. 'I know. And I worry about poor Sylvia having a heart attack or something, she seems so stressed with the whole thing. Anyway, at least your costume is nice. Zach and Judd will be fighting over you when they see you in it.'

Esme grinned and shook her head. 'I doubt either of them

will come. And how many times do I need to tell you that Judd is just a friend and Zach is out of my league?'

'Oh, stop it. You can't really think that? I'd say you're out of his league.' He looked at his watch. 'Dammit, I'd better go. Poor Gladys will think I've moved out without her.'

'Pfft. Betty won't even realise I've gone. She'll be sat on her new bestie getting belly rubs.'

Parker pursed his lips. 'Ooh, belly rubs from Judd, now that does sound nice, where do I sign up for that treatment?' He burst into cackling laughter and jogged off towards his car. 'Come on, I'll drop you home.'

* * *

On Sunday afternoon, the day of the barbecue, Judd placed a mug of coffee on the table in front of Esme. 'I've checked the weather on my app, and it's supposed to be quite nice this evening. Not much of a breeze, dry and not too chilly either. Although you might want to take a jacket in case we get another surprise rainstorm. These predictions can never be trusted 100 per cent.'

'Thanks, Dad,' Esme teased with a grin.

He appeared to ignore her. 'Did you know, on average Scotland gets the most rain out of all the countries in the UK? More than 1,500 millimetres of rain per year! And that, depending on where you live, you can expect anywhere between 170 and 265 days with rain each year?'

'I did *not* know that.' *So, the weather must have been a past hyperfixation*, Esme guessed. She had done a little research of her own into autism and ADHD in a bid to understand her housemate a little more. Things were making so much more sense now.

He narrowed his eyes. 'Yeah, smart arse, so you're always better to take a jacket to be on the safe side.'

Esme laughed. 'Oooh, handbags at dawn. I'll be sure to take my brolly too.'

'And wear some sensible shoes so I don't have to carry you again,' he said with a playful nudge to her shoulder.

* * *

At around eight o'clock on Sunday evening, Esme and Judd walked across the castle grounds, heading for the loch. Esme had opted for jeans and a sweater under a padded jacket with her umbrella tucked under her arm and a Drumblair tartan scarf hanging loosely around her neck. Judd was in jeans, a hoodie from a shop called Saltrock and a gilet. He looked good, Esme observed, and as always he smelled so fresh and woodsy; a smell all of his own that she was growing to really like.

As Judd had predicted, with the help of the weather app on his phone of course, there was little to no breeze and the sky overhead was a deep inky blue with pinpricks of light twinkling like scattered sequins. The more Esme stared and relaxed her eyes, the more dots of light became visible in the vast darkness.

A shooting star shot from left to right in her periphery. 'Oh, wow!'

'Yeah, I saw that too. Not only are they shooting stars on the film set but we're getting a display in the sky. Funny, eh?'

'Ooh, another one!' Esme gasped as she pointed. 'It's quite romantic, isn't it?' she said aloud without meaning to let her thoughts escape.

'I love the sky around here,' Judd said with a deep, contented sigh as they stopped for a moment and stared up at the starlit canopy above. 'Not a bit of light pollution.' He smiled. 'Makes it easier to see all the different constellations.'

'Are you into astronomy?' she asked, intrigued by the little snippets she had been finding out lately about her housemate and his knowledge of the most surprising things. 'I bet you know all the constellations, don't you?'

He laughed lightly and draped an arm around her shoulder. 'Oh, yeah... for example...' He pointed off into the distance. 'Over there you can see the big... erm... pizza dish, and beside it is the tiny cactus. And let's not forget the falling man over there, and beside him is the great, pointed, lesser... erm... spotted spangle.'

Esme giggled. 'I'll take that as a no then.' She gazed up at him and his attention was now focused on her. They were so close she could feel the warmth of his body. Something in the air crackled between them and her smile disappeared. Her heartrate picked up and she glanced briefly at his mouth. What would it be like to kiss those lips? The question in her mind seemed to come out of nowhere and took her a little by surprise. She watched as he swallowed, clearly feeling whatever it was too. He leaned forward as if it was an involuntary action, like she was a magnet and he was being drawn in.

But all too soon he seemed to snap out of it and removed his arm from her shoulder before rubbing a hand over his stubbled chin. 'Och, you caught me. I know nothing but I wish I knew more though to be honest. I'd love a telescope, and I don't really know why I've never bought one.' He appeared to be rambling now whereas Esme was still trying to process the feeling she had just experienced and stood in a stunned silence. 'Aye,' he continued, 'maybe that way I could attract more girls by pointing out all the proper names of the constellations like that Yorkshire sciencey bloke with the perfect teeth.'

'Professor Brian Cox?' Esme asked with a wide smile.

'All right, show off,' he said with a nudge. 'I bet he has women queuing up to date him though.'

Esme narrowed her eyes. 'Erm... I believe he's happily married actually.'

Judd lifted his arms and let them flop to his sides. 'Ugh, you see. That's what I mean. You know loads of stuff about the universe and women can't keep their hands off you. I know lots about plants and... well, enough said.' He gestured around him as if to exaggerate the lack of female attention he was in receipt of.

'In all honesty I think knowing about plants is pretty special. It shows you can care for other living organisms which is a good quality.'

'If you say so. Although thankfully plants can't verbally complain if you forget to water them, nor can they report you to social services. Don't you fancy the professor then?' Judd asked, his eyes glinting in the dimming light.

She scrunched her nose. 'He's not really my type.'

'What is your type?' His gaze was all at once locked on her again and a crease had appeared between his eyebrows. As if he too had spoken his innermost thoughts aloud without intending to, he wagged a finger at her. 'Hang on... let me guess... you only have eyes for Zach Marchand.' He followed his comment with an eye roll, but it was clear he was teasing.

Esme was glad for the cover of darkness because her face had flamed. She shrugged. 'He's very handsome but he's not likely to want to date someone like me, is he?'

As if the moment had been imagined, their conversation returned to normal. Judd frowned. 'Why not? He always seems to want to talk to you, and anyway you're equally as attractive as someone like Lucille Delgado. In fact, we've both discovered she's anything but beautiful on the inside, remember? And you can't tell me that's even her real name. It's probably Lucy Johnson or something equally prosaic. I don't know why famous people can't just use their given names.'

Esme thought back to Zach's explanation. 'It's something to do with... ugh, I can't remember the acronym but it's to do with no two famous people being allowed to have the same name.'

'Oh, right. So why do they choose such flashy-sounding *noms de geurre*?'

Esme laughed. 'All right, Inspector Clouseau, swallow a French dictionary, did we?'

'*Peut-être oui.*' He pretended to twiddle an invisible moustache. 'I mean it though. What's wrong with Lucy Johnson? It's a solid-sounding name.'

'Says the man with a movie-star name, *Judd Cowan*.'

Judd scoffed. 'Oh, yeah, because names with bovine connections are so cool.'

'It hasn't done Simon *Cow*ell any harm.'

'Great example, Esme,' he teased. 'Anyway, how did you get your name? It's not exactly common, is it?'

'Ugh. My mum was obsessed with *The Hunchback of Notre Dame* and the female lead character Esmerelda. I hate it.'

Judd grinned. 'At least she didn't call you Hunchy, or worse still Quasimodo.' He threw his head back and guffawed. 'I may have just found your new nickname. Come on, Quasi.'

Esme whacked him playfully. 'Get lost. Okay, so now we're on the subject, how did you get your name? Was your mum an eighties Brat Pack fan?'

Judd crumpled his brow. 'A what?'

'Judd Nelson. He was one of the Brat Pack. He was in St Elmo's Fire, among other things.'

'Nah. Nothing as exciting as that. My given name is actually

George, but when I was born, my cousin, who was around two at the time, couldn't say that and used to call me Jug. Then it progressed to Judd and sort of... stuck.'

'Oh, yeah? And what's wrong with George Cowan? *It's a very solid-sounding name.*' Esme used his own words against him in a voice that mimicked his.

He rolled his eyes. 'Okay, okay, it's a fair cop.' He waved a hand. 'Anyway, we're already late so we should be going.' They set off walking again until Judd stopped once more. 'All joking aside, don't you think the sky is such a romantic thing to be gazing up at and discussing, and yet here we are, both single. It's a shame, really. Our looks and talent are being wasted; wouldn't you agree?'

Esme smirked. 'You speak for yourself. I'm playing Juliet opposite the hottest man am dram has ever encountered.' She immediately felt cruel for making fun of Bryce. 'Bless him, Bryce's so nice though.'

'I've heard about his new hair piece. Poor guy. There's nothing wrong with growing old gracefully.' They walked a little further and Judd blurted, 'Hey, did you know that we're all getting invites to the red-carpet event for the movie? Eilidh has sorted it as a bit of a thank you.'

This was the first Esme had heard of such a thing. 'No! Are we? The film premiere? Seriously?' Her heart skipped at the thought.

He nodded. 'Seriously. Kerr was telling me on Friday. It won't be for a year, give or take, but how exciting is that?'

'Crazy exciting. I have no clue what to wear.'

'You've ages to plan that. Anyway, you and I should make a pact. By the time the film premieres, if we're still both single we should go together.'

Esme crumpled her brow and her heart skipped as she

thought back to the moment they had shared in the not too distant past. 'Do you mean as a date?'

He shrugged and was clearly trying to appear nonchalant. 'Why not?'

Esme knew first hand how much could happen in twelve months. 'It's a long time though, a year.'

'Aye and you'll no doubt be married or something. I've seen how Zach looks at you.'

'Oh, stop it. You and Parker obviously see things that aren't really there.'

'Ahhh, so, the Parkernator thinks he likes you too, eh?'

Esme burst into laughter. 'The Parkernator? Does he know you call him that?'

She wondered why Judd didn't reply but when she looked up at him she realised he was peering straight ahead and a wide smile spread across his face. 'Well, I think the sky gods are out to impress tonight. First shooting stars and now this!'

Esme had her back to the direction of his gaze, so she turned around and was met with the most incredible sight. Above the loch danced a moving wave of green and purple lights and she gasped.

As if without thinking, Judd's arm slipped around her shoulder again and he squeezed her into his side. 'Isn't that spectacular?'

'It's absolutely stunning,' Esme replied as tears welled in her eyes. She had only ever witnessed the aurora borealis in photographs and it was a strange time of year for it to be visible, but it was the most magical thing she had ever seen. It really was as if someone were putting on a light show just for them.

It felt nice to have his arm around her too. She was a little concerned by the way her heart responded to his touch because they were housemates and any detour from simple friendship could potentially make things tricky.

As if reading her mind, he stepped away and cleared his throat. 'Come on, we really should get down there.'

* * *

By the time they arrived at the loch side, everyone else was already there. Music was playing from an iPhone linked up to a speaker and 'Shiver' by Coldplay was the current track – Esme knew the song and the lyrics and couldn't help but wonder if the universe was trying to tell her something after the shooting stars and the northern lights, and now this song. Judd had gone over to say hi to Noah but he turned to look at her and smiled. Was she imagining things or was his smile tinged with sadness?

She tried her best to stop thinking about it and instead took in her surroundings. There was a pop-up gazebo strung with fairy lights, and torchieres had been stuck into the shingle, their light casting an amber glow of moving shadows over the faces of the people in attendance. Folding chairs had been brought down from the boathouse where the outdoor café furniture was stored, and a few tables too. It looked amazing. There was a group of people at the water's edge gazing up at the impromptu light show while some danced, holding their drinks aloft as the track changed to something with a dance beat from the mid-2000s. The smell of cooking wafted through the air and made Esme's stomach growl. She had forgotten to eat lunch again; something Judd had badgered her about earlier on.

'That's the kind of thing I do. I think my habits are becoming yours and we haven't even been living together that long,' he'd said and she had resisted the urge to sarcastically call him 'Dad' again. But now she was watching him in her periphery, like some love-struck teenager with a secret crush she couldn't, and wouldn't, voice.

Parker spotted her and came jogging over, singing along to 'I Gotta a Feeling' by the Black Eyed Peas. He spun her around as he serenaded her.

Judd came back over as someone, presumably a film crew member, walked over with a large plastic tote filled with ice and bottles of beer. Judd grabbed two, removed the lids with a twist and handed one to Esme.

'We should have been having loch-side parties long before now!' Parker said. His eyes glistened in the torch light, and it was clear he'd had a few drinks already.

The Black Eyed Peas faded and were replaced by Bon Jovi and 'You Give Love a Bad Name'. Another band Esme's dad loved.

Parker curled his lip. 'Ooh, a song about Rhys. Booooooo! Anyway, what's with the old folks' music?' he shouted at no one in particular.

Judd laughed. 'Erm, some of us young folk, with discerning taste I might add, happen to like this stuff. Jon Bon Jovi is a legend. He does all sorts for charity, you know.'

Parker rolled his eyes. 'Ugh, not you too. That's it, Esme, you definitely can't date him now.' He jogged off to chase the guy with the drinks.

Esme widened her eyes and opened her mouth to protest but it was too late. Parker had disappeared into the crowd.

'So, you've discussed dating me with the Parkernator, have you?' Judd asked with a smile and a glint in his eyes.

'Actually, no, I have absolutely no idea why he said that.'

A look of disappointment flashed over Judd's face. 'No, course not. I was only kidding around. I'm going to go grab a burger. Want one?'

Esme shook her head, and a twinge of guilt tugged at her and tightened her stomach, so her appetite vanished. 'No, I'm okay just now, thanks.'

'No worries.' He wandered off in the direction of the barbecue. Moments later she spotted him chatting animatedly to a brunette with her hair in two fashionably scruffy pigtails. Her arms and legs were covered with tattoos and her piercings glinted in the light of the torchieres. Esme recognised her as one of the runners from the set. She was laughing at whatever Judd was saying and kept touching his arm. Judd seemed smitten too. *No need for the naked dance this time, eh, Judd?* Esme thought to herself as a tiny twinge of sadness caught her off guard again.

She spotted Zach walking towards her. 'Hey, I'm so glad you came.' He kissed her cheek and lingered a little longer than she expected.

'I wouldn't have missed it for anything,' she replied, hoping he couldn't see the colour of her face.

He glanced towards her feet. 'No Betty?'

Esme laughed. 'Oh, no, she was happily snuggled up in front of the log burner and didn't want to budge.'

He smiled briefly. 'Sensible pooch. You didn't see Lucille on your way down, did you?' He glanced around nervously, and then back to Esme.

She shook her head. 'No, sorry. Has she not come?'

Still checking out the area, he chewed his thumbnail and said, 'Yeah, she was here but we had a falling out, again.' He rolled his eyes and shook his head. 'She stormed off and hasn't come back. She'd started drinking at lunch time and was already pissed when we arrived. I'm just concerned about her. She's not in a good headspace right now.'

'Oh? How come?'

Zach pursed his lips and squinted. 'I probably shouldn't say... but... she got a telling off about the whole situation with you and how she had lied to get you in trouble.'

Esme made an O with her lips but didn't know what to say.

'Yeah, she's her own worst enemy. I think I should go look for her.'

'Want some help?' Esme asked, feeling bad that she had been the reason for Lucille's mood.

Zach perked up. 'Would you mind? I'd really appreciate it. I know she and I are no longer... you know... but I still feel responsible for her, for some reason.'

'She is an adult, though, Zach. You shouldn't have to babysit her.'

He cringed. 'Yeah, I know. But when she drinks she gets... well, you can guess.'

She nodded. 'I'll go get Judd and maybe he can help too. What about asking some of the crew to join us?'

Zach's eyes widened. 'Oh, God, no. They can't know she's gone off like this again. They'll fire her. She always causes some kind of drama, no matter what set she's on, and there are so many directors who won't sign her now.'

Interesting. Esme nodded. 'Okay. Just us three then?'

Zach nodded. 'Thanks.'

15

Esme, Judd and Zach sloped off without their escape being noticed and when they reached the chapel they swapped phone numbers for ease of communication and split up. Zach headed back to the apartments to see if she had returned there, Judd headed towards the nursery and Esme made her way to the kids' play area. If she was being honest, she'd chosen *that* particular location because it seemed the place she would be *least* likely to locate the sulking actor, who also happened to be her arch nemesis.

If only she had been right.

Lucille was on the highest point of the wooden climbing fort when Esme arrived. *Of course I found her, why the hell wouldn't I?* she thought, inwardly cursing her luck, or lack thereof. Lucille had a bottle of wine in one hand and was precariously balanced, clinging on with the other hand to the wooden frame. The security lights were on, casting a daylight-bright glow over the play area. The temperature seemed to have dropped in the short amount of time the search had been ongoing, and Esme shivered, wrapping her jacket a little tighter around her.

'Lucille, could you come down, please? Zach's worried sick about you. He's off looking for you right now,' Esme snapped, annoyed that her plan to avoid Lucille had somehow failed.

'Oh, God, it's you. Why the hell did he send you, of all people, to look for me?' Lucille slurred.

'Probably because I work here and know the place. But I offered to help, actually. Like I said, he's really worried about you.' As she spoke, she fired off a quick text to Judd and Zach to let them know she had found the errant actor.

'Pfft. He wasn't worried when he was undressing you and taking you to his bed, was he?'

Esme scrunched her face in incredulity. 'You know very well that didn't even happen, Lucille. But thanks to you and your fertile imagination, I almost lost my job.'

Lucille swung out over the drop where the climbing rope was supposed to help the occupants of the fort – usually children – to reach the ground safely, but she still had one hand on the wine and one on the post and Esme covered her mouth with her hand as her heart leapt into her throat. *This can't be happening. It just can't.*

Lucille took a swig of the wine and scoffed, 'Oh, sod off, you prissy cow. It's not like you do anything important. You type memos and make phone calls and coffee all day. Whoop dee bloody doo. It's hardly rocket science. I'm pretty sure you could find the same job elsewhere easy enough.' She took another, longer, gulp from the wine bottle and slipped a little, causing Esme to gasp. Lucille seemed to get off on her fear and began to laugh. 'Ooh, I might fall, ooh, can you catch me?' The ground was covered in rubberised safety tiles and bark chippings but that would no doubt be of little help if Lucille was to fall with a glass bottle in her hand.

Just keep her chatting, Esme. Keep her focused on you. 'Well, I don't want to work somewhere else. I happen to like my job here, thank you very much, and I don't need you causing problems for me,' Esme replied through gritted teeth. 'Now please come down from there. You're going to get hurt.'

Lucille cackled and swung out again, deliberately this time. 'Ooooooh, is that a threat, *Esmerelda*? Are you going to hurt me, *Esmerelda*? Can you hear the bells, *Esmerelda*?' she said, mimicking the Hunchback himself. 'I mean, who in their right mind gives their kid such a stupid name anyway? Because it really is stupid, *Ethmerelduh*.' She mocked her again.

And you look a little like Quasimodo up there right now but I'm not throwing that in your face. Esme sighed. 'Look, Lucille, we're all subject to what our parents call us, and few of us have any say in the matter so drop the insults and just come on down, please.'

Lucille pointed the bottle in her direction. 'I chose my *own* stage name *actually*, Miss Prissy Pants. And not because of SAG-AFTRA if that's what you're thinking. Nooo, I just didn't want to be called Hilda Smethurst any longer. Even if I was named after my dear grandma. It just wasn't very *award-winning actory*,' she chuntered, almost to herself. 'I mean, Hilda went out of fashion with the sodding ark. My gran was in the bloody war, for goodness' sake. Why did my sister get such a nice name but not me? Sadie's a really pretty name. It's hardly fair.'

Esme widened her eyes. 'Well, bang goes Judd's *Lucy Johnson* theory,' she whispered.

Lucille continued with her barrage. 'You don't realise how delusional you are, do you? Do you honestly think Zach is capable of having feelings for a normy?'

Esme narrowed her eyes. 'A what?'

'Ugh. Are you dumb? A normy. Someone boring and normal

like you, who does a mundane job for a living. No real prospects, you know?'

'Oh, right. Gee, thanks. Actually, for your information I have no delusions about Zach at all. He's a nice man but I'm very much aware I'm no award-winning actor.'

'No, you're not.' Her expression changed for a second and there seemed to be a little clarity in her eyes. 'But I've heard about your am dram efforts. If I didn't hate you with every fibre of my being, I'd say good on you for at least trying. And with Shakespeare, no less. Very brave girl.' She chuckled and hiccupped, the clarity gone again.

'Gee, thanks *again*,' Esme replied. 'You're pretty handy with the compliments as usual as I see. And how can you hate someone you don't even know? How is that fair?'

'It's nothing personal, you know. I'm sure you're a fairly decent person.' The curled lip that accompanied the backhanded compliment wasn't at all convincing.

'Nothing personal? I think hating someone for no reason is pretty damn personal, actually. And if you got to know me, you'd see that I am a decent person.'

'You just don't get it, do you? Zach and I have hisssstory. Lotsssss of history. He loves me and only me. But you're blurring the lines just by being around. It's not really your fault. You're not that bad, I suppose. You're just in the way, that's all.' Her slurring was worsening with every passing second and the breeze blew her hair in front of her eyes, causing her to flail and Esme's stomach to lurch in response.

She didn't need a dead celebrity on her conscience. 'Not that bad? Charming. And, correct me if I'm wrong, but you just said you hate me with, and I quote, "every fibre of your being". I'd say that was the opposite of not that bad, wouldn't you?'

Lucille burst into a fit of giggles. 'Oh, yeah! I suppose it is. Durrrr.'

Just keep her talking. While she's talking, she's not falling. 'And also, didn't you dump him?'

'Aww, you poor thing. He's not as nice as people think, you know. He uses people too. Just like the rest of us. But you're obiv... obili... beliv...' She shook her head and growled. 'You just can't see it, can you? You really have got it bad for him, haven't you?' She pouted, her bottom lip protruding like a chastised toddler. 'Admit it and I'll come down.'

Esme took a few steps towards the fort. 'Yes, Lucille, I've adored Zach since I was a starry-eyed teenager, okay? I had his posters on my wall and dreamed I'd marry him one day, and we'd live in a castle, but I was stupid to ever think he could like a *normy* like me. Happy now? Now could you please just come down from there?'

'Okay, but only because I'm cold and want to go to bed,' Lucille replied with a sigh. She glanced around. 'Erm... I'm not actually sure how I got up here in the first place.' She twisted her head this way and that. 'I think I'm a stit buck. I mean... a stit buck. Ugh, I just said that. You know what I mean, *normy*.'

Esme took another step closer but made sure to keep Lucille in her eyeline. 'You're not a *bit stuck*, Lucille. You can do it. Just pull yourself back onto the fort and head for the ladder at the opposite side.'

Lucille peered over in the direction of the ladder and curled her lip. 'Erm... no, I don't think so. I can't be bothered with that. It's too far. I'll just jump.'

Esme screamed, 'No!' but before the word had fully left her mouth there was a resounding thud and the 'Oof' of air being expelled from Lucille's lungs.

* * *

'The ambulance is on its way, Lucille. Just stay still, okay?' Esme said as she sat on the damp ground by the injured actor, holding her hand. 'Zach has called them, so you'll be fine.'

Judd removed his gilet and hoodie. 'Here, she needs to be kept warm.' He placed the hoodie on top of Lucille. 'And we should support her head,' he said as he rolled up the gilet and placed it at the base of her neck.

'My arm's all tingly and I can't feel my leg,' Lucille said with a smile. 'It feels funny.' She giggled. Adrenaline was clearly kicking in, but Esme pitied her when it eventually wore off.

Judd gently lifted the hem of her dress and recoiled. 'Oh, shit,' he mumbled.

'What's wrong?' Esme asked in a hissed whisper.

'I can, erm...' He baulked. 'I can see bone.'

Esme widened her eyes. 'Oh, no.'

'I've got an important scene to film tomorrow so the ambulance had better hurry up,' Lucille slurred. 'I want to go to bed. I'm really sleepy.' Her eyes drifted closed.

'Stay awake, Lucille,' Judd said in a stern voice. 'Talk to me. Tell me what it's like to be famous.'

Her eyes snapped open. 'Why do *you* want to know? It's not likely to happen to you, is it, plant man? You're a bit weird really. No offence.'

Judd glanced up at Esme and rolled his eyes. 'Oh, don't worry, absolutely none taken. I'm just trying to make small talk to keep you awake.'

Esme was struck by how well Judd was handling the situation. Zach, on the other hand, had run off to supposedly wait for the ambulance and direct them, but Esme realised he had left because he couldn't quite handle things.

'What does it mean if I can't move my hand?' Lucille asked. Her wrist did look to be at a strange angle but Esme didn't like to comment and make a bad situation worse.

'Stop trying to move, Lucille,' Esme said. 'Just relax but stay with us okay? No drifting off to sleep. You probably have a concussion.'

A look of confusion flashed across Lucille's features. 'But I can't play drums,' she replied in a slurred whisper.

'*Con*cussion, not *per*cussion,' Esme told her with a slight smile.

Suddenly Lucille's eyes were wide, and she gripped Esme's arm with her uninjured hand. 'Am I going to die?' Her question was sincere and there was genuine fear visible in her pallid expression.

Esme smiled in what she hoped was a reassuring way. 'No, of course not. You're going to be absolutely fine. You've just had a fall so we need to get you checked out, that's all.'

Lucille pulled Esme down, so she was closer. 'But if I do die, please promise me one thing,' the actor whispered.

Esme nodded but grimaced. 'Okay, but like I said, you're going to be fine.'

Lucille narrowed her eyes. 'Come on, normy, promise me, please?'

'Normy? We're sticking with that, are we?' Esme asked but then shook her head. 'Promise you what?'

'Don't let them put Hilda on my gravestone, will you? No one can know that's my real name.'

A crew of paramedics with a stretcher arrived and began to fire off questions as they prepared Lucille for the ambulance: What happened? What has she taken? Where did she fall from? Is she allergic to anything? Have you notified next of kin? Are any of *you* next of kin? What medications is she taking? Etc, etc, etc.

As Esme stood to give the paramedics room, Lucille called out in a pained voice, 'Promise me, normy!'

Esme rolled her eyes. 'It's Esme, and yes, I'll see what I can do.'

* * *

At 11 p.m. Esme, Zach and Judd sat in the castle kitchen drinking coffee with a shot of whisky in, prepared by Brodie. Judd drummed on his cup and clenched his jaw off and on, the ticking visible under his skin.

'Are you guys sure you don't need anything else?' Brodie asked, running his hands back through his hair. 'It's been quite a night.'

Zach sat there, staring into his mug, hardly moving. He was pale and clearly feeling traumatised by the whole situation. Out of the blue, he mumbled, 'Her wrist was all... and the bone in her leg...'

Esme reached out to squeeze his arm. She didn't wish to relive it any more than the others, but Zach appeared to be struggling with what had played out. 'She'll be fine, Zach, try not to worry.'

'I think we're good, thanks, Brodie. Cheers, mate,' Judd said, looking to Esme who nodded in agreement. He continued to tap his fingers on his mug.

Brodie placed his hands on his hips and huffed the air from his lungs. 'Without wishing to sound patronising, you did great work tonight. Eilidh said so too. It's good that she was able to go to the hospital with Lucille and she promised to update us. I just hope the breaks aren't too severe or the shoot could be compromised,' Brodie told them. His phone pinged and he picked it up from the worktop. 'Olivia's feeding Freya, but she'll be down soon.'

Esme shook her head and frowned. 'Oh, no, please tell her she doesn't need to come down. We're fine, honestly, in fact we probably should be getting home. It's been a long night and I'm sure I'm not the only one who's exhausted.'

'Aye, Esme's right,' Judd added as he pushed himself up from the table. 'You'll all be worn out especially with having the bairn.' He lifted his mug and swigged the last of his coffee. 'That was good stuff, cheers, Brodie.'

Esme sipped at hers but had nowhere near finished it; it was a little too strong for her liking. She stood too. 'We'll let you get to bed. I'm sure there won't be much to report until tomorrow anyway. Zach, do you want us to walk you back to your apartment?'

Zach lifted his chin as if only just realising he was in a room with other people. 'Oh, erm, no, no. Thanks but I'm sure I'll be fine. Just need to sleep, I think.'

Esme squeezed his shoulder. 'Okay, well, you have both our numbers if you need anything. It must have been really difficult seeing your... erm... friend in that state.'

He nodded and his eyes widened. 'Yeah... I'm not great with... with trauma.' He smiled. 'Thanks again, guys. I can't express how grateful I am to you both.' He glanced at Brodie. 'To all of you.' He stood from the table and the three of them left the castle together.

Once they were outside, Esme hugged Zach. 'Just call or message if you need anything, okay?'

He nodded, still appearing a little spaced out, and turned to head off towards the stable block apartments. Judd and Esme turned in the opposite direction.

'Zach looked terrible. I hope he'll be okay,' Judd said eventually after they'd been walking for a minute or so in silence.

'Hmm, I was surprised at how much it affected him. I suppose when you've loved someone, seeing them in pain hurts you too.'

'Poor guy. Anyway, what was Lucille asking you to promise her? It sounded serious.'

Esme tried to stifle her grin as she remembered *Hilda's* pleas. 'My lips are sealed.'

'Spoilsport. Come on, let's get home. Betty will be thinking we've abandoned her.'

His use of the word 'we' made Esme smile. 'So, you and the tattooed brunette?' she asked without needing to elaborate.

He waved his phone. 'I have Selina's number!' he replied in a sing-song voice.

There was that little twinge of sadness tugging at Esme's heart again.

16

The following morning was the Monday Esme had been excited about and dreading simultaneously. It was the week of the show and she awoke at six feeling anything but refreshed. She immediately checked her phone.

Nothing.

She sent a quick text to Zach:

> Any news? Hope you're ok.

She went down the stairs, but Judd wasn't up yet. Nothing out of the ordinary seeing as she had discovered he was very much the night owl he professed to be, preferring to stay up until the early hours and sleep late until whenever his work schedule allowed. She let Betty out into the garden and made herself a quick coffee, hoping the caffeine would be the pep she needed, and took it back up the stairs, followed of course by her canine companion. As she walked by Judd's room, she was surprised to hear him talking. She held her breath and listened.

'Yeah, I know, the ending was abysmal. I can't believe they

did that. I mean, Steve went back in time and totally ruined Peggy's life. They could've done so many things with that ending.' There was a pause. 'Yes! I totally agree! I can't even bring myself to watch it again, it makes me so angry.' Another pause. 'Aye... but they're not going to listen to the Marvel Comics fans, are they?' Another pause. 'Nah. You're so right, Selina. So damn right, Captain America deserved so much more.'

Esme sighed. *Selina, the girl from the barbecue. They definitely hit it off then.* Why did sadness descend at knowing Judd had potentially met the love of his life?

She showered and dressed and checked her phone again. There was a text from Zach.

> Two breaks, wrist and shin. Not great news. Surgery overnight. Now out of action for goodness knows how long. Filming will have to stop. Producers will be pissed. Thanks again for last night. You're very special. Z x

Esme wasn't sure how to respond so sent a simple:

> I'm here if I can help. E x

* * *

She left Judd chatting to Selina, and Betty snuggled up on the rug in front of the fire. She hadn't even let Judd know she was heading to work considering the fact he was definitely preoccupied. Neither her nor Parker's matchmaking services were any longer required, clearly.

When she arrived at the castle, it was a hive of activity. There seemed to be more people than usual, and everyone seemed to share the same harrowed look of concern. As she reached Olivia's office, loud voices halted her from knocking. Apparently it was a day of catching conversations through doors.

'I'm telling you we can't just stop filming,' came Zach's voice, strained and pleading. 'I'm aware we've shot some of Lucille's scenes but it's not irreparable at this point. As one of the producers, I think my opinion should matter, Victoria. And I'm telling you Della is the right person to replace Lucille.' Things sounded heated. And Esme was shocked to hear that Zach was a producer on the film.

'I'm not so sure, Zach. Maybe this was all a little too ambitious. I didn't even want to cast Lucille, as you well know. But you're too kind and I was too gullible. Face it, you're not cutthroat enough to be on this side of the business, Zach. She may be a good actor, when she's sober, but Lucille causes mayhem wherever she goes, and she was never going to complete this film. She's in self-sabotage mode and has been for months now. But, of course, you wouldn't be told. And now you're expecting me to accept your replacement, like I'm going to trust your judgement again? You were the one who guaranteed Lucille would be fine, and considering the way you broke up, I still can't understand why you support her. Personally, I think we need a break to rethink this whole thing,' the female voice, who Esme guessed to be Victoria, replied. 'As executive producer on the film, I think my opinion is what counts. I hate to pull rank, Zach, but my reputation is on the line.'

Zach wasn't giving up without a fight. 'Please, just audition Della. It's not like she's new to this. She could act every single member of this crew under the table. With the exception of Ruby Locke, of course. No one can beat Ruby, in my opinion. But this woman is special. Trust me.'

'There are those words again, Zach. I have so much money riding on this project that I have to think with my business brain, not my heart. I'm aware Della is good. I've seen her on screen, and I agree with you there, but this project has been delayed once before and it feels jinxed. We should maybe just cut our losses.'

'Come on, the initial delay was out of courtesy to Lady Olivia and her husband. They'd just had a baby, for goodness' sake. How can you think of that as a jinx?'

There was a pause. 'I'm not saying the baby is a jinx. I would never insinuate such a horrible thing. I just mean that there has to be a cut-off point. People have other projects lined up, meaning that further delays will be detrimental to more than just us, Zach.'

Olivia appeared by Esme's side and made her jump. 'Are they still going at it?' she asked.

Her insinuation that this had been going on for a while made Esme wince. 'It appears so. They're discussing a replacement for Lucille, some actor called Della, but the woman, Victoria I think Zach called her, isn't too keen. She wants to shut the shoot down.'

Olivia's eyes widened. 'Oh, no. I hope they don't do that. I'm worried they'll want their money refunded. We've already allocated the funds to... something.' She chewed on her nails, something Esme had not seen her do before, and it concerned her.

'I'm sure they'll come to some agreement,' Esme replied but of course she knew nothing of the sort.

'I wonder how much longer they'll need to be in my office, they've been in there over an hour.' Then, almost under her breath, she mumbled, 'Maybe we should hang fire on signing the contracts.' Esme wasn't sure to which contracts she was referring and didn't like to pry.

The heated conversation behind the door continued. 'Victoria, you know she can match anything Lucille can do. You've already said you've seen her for yourself. I'm telling you we can reshoot the scenes Lucille has shot, and we can get back on schedule. It's not just our money we're talking about. Lady Olivia has sacrificed so much for this shoot to go ahead. We can't let her down now. Please rethink. I can't stress enough that Della is 100 per cent the right replacement.'

'In that case why wasn't she your first choice? Hmm?'

A heavy silence hung in the air and Esme and Olivia seemed to simultaneously hold their breath.

'Scheduling conflicts!' Zach blurted as if he'd had some kind of epiphany. 'Which are no longer an issue.'

'Ugh, fine, we'll audition her. But I'm not agreeing to signing her until *I'm* 100 per cent certain. Set up the audition. And let's hope she's even free. She's a very busy actor and very much in demand from what I've heard. I'm not holding my breath.'

'Leave it with me, Victoria. I'll set the whole thing up.'

A tall, dark-haired woman in a sharp skirt suit that reeked of Chanel exited the room and stopped in her tracks to look the two women up and down.

'I hope you weren't listening in,' she snapped.

'Victoria, allow me to introduce Lady Olivia MacLeod and Esme, her PA. Lady Olivia, Esme, this is Victoria Morrisette, our executive producer.'

Victoria's expression immediately changed, and she held out her hand. 'Oh, I see. Thank you for the use of your office, Lady Olivia. What a stunning castle you have here. Thanks again for allowing us to film in your ancestral home.' There was no apology for the mistaken identity or the way in which she had spoken to her host.

'You're more than welcome,' Olivia replied graciously and

before anyone else could add anything Victoria walked away. Zach gave an apologetic shrug and mouthed the word 'sorry' before following her like a little dog chasing his owner.

* * *

Romeo and Juliet rehearsals were set for every night that week in a last-ditch attempt to make sure everyone was up to speed now the play was being performed much sooner than originally anticipated. But before she set off for Inverness, Esme video called her parents.

'Oh, hey, pet. I was going to call you. You'll never guess what's happened,' her dad said with a wide smile that even twinkled in his eyes; something that had been lacking lately.

'What's that then? Have you won the lottery?'

'No need now!' her mum added. 'Dad's had some fantastic news, haven't you, love?'

'Aye, it's all down to your boss actually.'

Esme was confused, but wondered if it was something to do with the contracts Olivia had mentioned earlier in the day. 'Go on,' she said.

'Lady Olivia has hired everyone from the distillery and has even bought up the remaining stock and equipment. How about that?'

Esme's eyes widened. 'Seriously?'

'Seriously. Lady Olivia came with her uncle to meet with Hamish McIver, and they agreed on terms. It's all signed and sealed. I'm now an employee of Drumblair Castle distillery. We'll be moving all the equipment to Drumblair. I'm over the moon. I think, from what I can gather, the remaining McIver whisky stock is to be rebranded to Drumblair or MacBain, I'm not too sure which yet. But the distillery at the castle is going to start with a line of its own gins until the first batch of their own single malt has matured. And guess who'll be heading up production of that at the castle?' He held out his hands and glanced around at a non-existent audience. 'Aye, we'll be colleagues, pet.' Her dad's eyes were filled with joy and Esme wished she had gone around to visit in person so she could hug him.

Her eyes began to sting. 'Aw, Dad, that's absolutely brilliant. I'm so happy for you.'

'Aye, pet. No need to sell the house. But I've got you to thank.'

Esme frowned. 'How so?'

'Well, because Lady Olivia requested me personally to head up the castle distillery. I presumed you'd put a word in for me.'

Esme held up her hands. 'No, this was all you, Dad!'

'Aye but let's face it, if it hadn't been for you working there already she would've never heard of me, so I'm sticking with my thanks.' His smile faltered for a moment. 'Now I know you're not fulfilling your dream in this job. And I know Mum and I have a lot to do with that but we want you to know how proud we are of you. We spoiled your chances of becoming an actor out of our own fear and if this past week or so has taught me anything it's that doing what you love is so important. And that even jobs you think are safe as houses can suddenly be lost. We're going to support you in whatever you choose to do from now on. If you want to go back to college or reapply to the Conservatoire, we'll support you. You can always move back home.'

Esme felt tears escape from her eyes and swiped them away quickly in a futile attempt to stop her parents from seeing them. 'Thank you but... I'm actually happy in my job. And you were right. Acting is a hit and miss career. I've witnessed firsthand how rapidly things can change. So, it's all good. I've got my am dram.' She made jazz hands to try and lighten the mood.

'We're just so sorry, love,' her mum said, wiping at her own eyes. 'So very sorry. But we know you're going to be an amazing Juliet.'

* * *

Esme floated all the way to the theatre that evening. She wouldn't allow the worry that tried to spoil her fun to wangle its way into the forefront of her mind. If her dad had been offered a job then the film must be going ahead too. *All the metaphorical ducks must be flying in a row*, she surmised.

The rehearsal was intense. Bryce ended up ditching the false teeth and lisped his way through their first dress rehearsal. In the interval, Esme and Parker went outside for fresh air. The late April evening was mild which Esme was grateful for as the fabric of her costume was tissue-paper thin.

'It's going to be a complete disaster, Esme,' Parker huffed and kicked at the gravel beneath their feet. 'I think we should duck out now while we still have some dignity intact.'

Esme gasped at his suggestion. 'Parker, we can't just abandon Sylvia now. Not like this.'

'Look, I know you don't want to upset your boyfriend by ditching his aunty, but this is a total shit show,' he hissed. 'We're going to look like such idiots. I mean, let's be truthful, it can't get much more ridiculous. And you can wave goodbye to any chance of rekindling your acting career when anyone who's anyone sees this poor excuse for a play. The only positive is we all make you look even more talented through our lack of it.'

He had a valid point about the career bit. 'Zach's not my

boyfriend,' she snapped, annoyed that he was right about the other stuff.

Parker tilted his head and gave a humourless laugh. 'That's all you chose to comment on about my whole rant?'

Esme shrugged. 'He doesn't even like me like—'

Parker slammed his hands onto his hips. 'Then why did he ask me what flowers you like and if you wear jewellery?'

Esme swallowed hard past the air that had become trapped in her throat. Her head began to swim, and she had to lean on the wall to steady herself. 'He did what?'

'I've been telling you for ages now that he fancies you. He's just waiting to make his move. But honestly, I'm not sure I can even do opening night slash closing night,' he said in a sarcastic tone. 'I mean, how stupid is the fact that we're doing two performances in one day and then calling that it? It's unheard of. Most people, those with any sense anyway, would have called this whole thing off and rescheduled, not let it go this far. We're going to be laughing stocks. I can't decide which would be worse, a bald Romeo with Turkey teeth or a bald, toothless Romeo. For feck's sake, Esme, what is Sylvia thinking? Surely any director worth their salt would know when to quit.'

'Bryce is wearing his hair piece.' Esme's words just added to the ridiculousness of the whole situation. 'Look, we can't give up now. We've got the rest of the week. We just need to plug on through and give it our best shot. Everyone is remembering their lines now... mostly.' She wasn't convincing herself, never mind Parker. She wanted to change the subject immediately. 'Oh, I forgot to mention I think Judd has a girlfriend.'

Parker's eyes widened. 'Ooooh! Tell me more.' The news, thankfully, had the desired effect.

'Yeah, he met her at the barbecue. She's called Selina.'

Parker's eyes narrowed. 'Selina the film set runner?'

Esme tilted her head. 'You know her?'

Parker nodded. 'I've met her a few times. She's very sweet. But I felt sure she's gay. My gaydar must need new batteries.' He shook his head. 'Anyway, she was telling me she was diagnosed with ADHD as an adult which seems to be becoming more frequent.'

A wave of sadness washed over Esme again. 'Ah, well, that's something they have in common. Although Judd isn't diagnosed but...'

Parker raised his eyebrows. 'Oh, he has ADHD all right. And he's 100 per cent on the spectrum. I'd recognise the traits anywhere.'

'How would you know the traits?' Esme asked.

'Girl, I get stuff on my FYP every single day on TikTok. You really need to get yourself on there. You learn so much.'

'Oh, aye, and of course if it's on TikTok it must be factual,' Esme replied with a roll of her eyes.

Sylvia poked her head around the door. 'Darlings, let's crack on, shall we? Chop chop! We're all waiting for you two.'

'Whoops! Sorry, Sylvia, we're coming,' Esme said as she tugged a reluctant Parker along behind her.

17

Judd was sitting at the kitchen table when Esme arrived home from her rehearsal. Betty was on his lap, snoring, as usual. He seemed to have such a calming effect on the little dog. A pot sat in the middle of the table complete with a lovely flowering narcissus. Their cheerful yellow trumpets brought an immediate smile to her face.

Judd pointed at them. 'For you. Positive energy and happiness, in case you were wondering.'

As always, his actions touched her. 'They're so beautiful, thank you.'

'So, how did it go?' he asked with a wide smile.

She nodded, aiming to put a positive spin on things in light of the flowers before her. 'Yeah, it was... erm...' She couldn't quite manage it and flopped onto a chair. 'Oh, God, Judd, it's awful. Parker wants us to quit. He's suggested we have a secret meeting with the rest of the cast and try and get them all to agree we can't put on a show like this after so few rehearsals. Get them to all walk out.'

Judd's eyes widened. 'Is it really that bad?'

'To quote Parker, "we have a balding, toothless fifty-something-year-old playing Romeo", does that tell you enough?'

Judd pulled his lips in and was evidently trying not to laugh. 'But he's wearing his hairpiece, isn't he?'

'He is. And that sort of makes it worse. He's such a lovely man. And I'm worried that people are going to laugh at him. He doesn't deserve that. None of us do.'

Judd wagged a finger. 'You know what you should do? You should ask Zach to come in and give you all some acting tips. Some hints on remembering lines and such. He's your director's nephew, surely he'd agree to it? He won't want her to be made a laughing stock, will he?'

Esme beamed. 'That's actually a great idea. Maybe it'll help. I mean, let's face it, it can't make things worse. We only have four more rehearsals though. Perhaps we should have done this when he first turned up.'

Judd shrugged. 'Better late than never, I reckon.'

'You're right. I'll find him tomorrow and ask him. Thanks, Judd.'

Judd's face tinged with pink, and the eye contact was gone. 'Aye, no bother. Although why not just call him or text him? No time like the present.'

'Yes, maybe you're right.' She fired off a quick text to Zach asking for his help and he was quick to respond.

> Absolutely! Happy to help in any way I can, just for you xx

She smiled and her own cheeks warmed. 'Well, that was easy peasy lemon squeezy.'

'See, I told you.' Judd grinned. 'Always strike while the iron's hot, I say.'

'Anyway, how are things with you and Selina? Have you heard from her?' she asked, knowing full well he had.

The pink tinge intensified to a hot fuchsia and he began tapping his nails on his mug of coffee. 'Aye, we were chatting about films this morning actually. She's a lovely lassie. We have a lot in common really. Makes a change. She doesn't seem to think I'm weird, which is a bonus.'

That little twinge of sadness ate its way into Esme's heart. 'I'm really happy for you.' Why then didn't her feelings match her words?

Judd frowned for a moment, which she found confusing. 'Aye, thanks.'

* * *

When Esme arrived at the castle the following morning things seemed pretty normal; lots of activity, people wandering around with headsets or walkie talkies looking serious, various pieces of equipment being relocated, actors in period costume. She was relieved to say the least.

'Morning, Esme, how was rehearsal?' Olivia called from across the gravelled area in front of the castle. She was standing with Mirren, whose hands were on Freya's pram.

Once she reached them, Esme smiled. 'Good morning. It's going well, thank you,' she replied, refusing to be negative about it all again.

'Ah, that's great, I can't wait to see it.'

Esme's stomach dropped. She hadn't thought that other people from the castle might come to watch the play. Olivia continued, 'Mirren is taking Freya for a few hours, and I'd like you to come to a meeting with me. The crew are being updated about the shoot. I thought it would be good if we went along to make sure we're also fully up to speed.'

'Yes, sure, of course.' Images flashed through her head of people sitting in the audience laughing and pointing at the stage, their faces bulbous as if being filmed through a fisheye lens. 'You know you don't have to come to the play. I wouldn't want you to feel obliged,' she added.

'Nonsense. We're looking forward to it!'

'We?' Esme asked, her heart racing.

'Brodie and me, Mirren and Dougie, Noah and Paisley, the rest of the café and gift shop crew. We're all coming to support you.'

'Oh, great,' Esme said, trying to sound much more enthusiastic than she felt.

'Mummy will see you later, beautiful,' Olivia said, crouching to kiss her baby. 'Thanks, Mirren, I'll come over later for her. Brodie is at the distillery today to oversee the installation of the mash and the fermenter. It's all coming along really well.'

'Exciting!' Esme waited until Mirren had gone. 'I want to thank you for employing my dad. I can't say how grateful I am.' A lump of emotion tightened her throat, but she wasn't sure if it was over her dad's job or the play. 'He was so worried he wouldn't find another job at his age, and it was so hard seeing him feeling defeated like that.'

Olivia smiled and reached out to squeeze her arm. 'Hey, I hope you know how important you are to this place, and I wouldn't leave your family stranded if I could do something. The urgent meeting I was called to was with his boss Hamish, who couldn't speak highly enough about your dad. It was a no brainer, really. I just hope you don't mind that he'll be here on site every day.'

Esme laughed. 'Not at all. He's such a loyal worker, I can

definitely vouch for that. He's been at the distillery since he was in his late teens.'

'Great. These things happen for a reason. Right, let's stop by the art space quickly and check on the artists in residence. I haven't called in for a while.'

They walked across the grounds where the trees were in bud all around them and there was a fragrance of grass and green shoots filling the air. The sky was a little overcast, however, and threatening April showers, but the temperature was decent. They reached the old converted barn and walked in through the glass doors. Each art space was separated by partition walls, and some had a large work table in the centre. There were painters, sculptors, a potter and a felt worker in there and everyone was beavering away at their respective crafts. The space was buzzing with positive energy and Olivia lit up when they walked around each unit. She chatted to each of the artists in turn and they all had only positive comments on their whole experience. The place was painted in a vibrant array of colours with art from the tenants applied directly to the walls. It was a real eclectic mix, and Esme felt a little jealous that she wasn't as talented as these people.

Olivia's space was upstairs and filled the whole upper floor. She had been designing and creating some of the costumes for the film shoot which meant that Esme had been left running the place. It had been a challenge but one she had embraced and thoroughly enjoyed.

They left the art barn and made their way back to the gallery where the meeting of crew and actors was to take place, and stood at the back. Esme took out her notebook and pen in readiness.

The woman she had encountered leaving Olivia's office, Victoria Morrisette, took to the front to speak. 'Good morning, everyone. Now, as you know, Lucille Delgado, one of the main cast, is now incapacitated due to a broken leg and wrist. Her recovery time is going to be quite significant and so we have released her from her contract.' A collective mumble travelled the room. 'We discussed the option of shutting down, but Zach has convinced me he has found the ideal replacement. This means all of Lucille's scenes will now potentially be reshot. If the weekend's audition goes well, and it's a big if...' She gave a sideways glance at Zach, who didn't look at her, he just clenched his jaw and flared his nostrils, clearly annoyed at her. 'But until then we will be carrying on as normal. The latest development is that we have enlisted the help of a sound crew that I've had the pleasure of working with before. This means that, in theory, some of the scenes, where Lucille was filmed from the back, may only require a little sound dubbing by Lucille's replacement. But I'm very grateful that Gadigal Films have agreed to come over from Australia to assist. If anyone can make this hitherto, shall we say *difficult* shoot, a success, it's them.'

Esme felt the colour drain from her face. Why did that name sound so familiar? Was it just the mention of Australia? She glanced around the room as her stomach knotted and her legs went a little numb.

Oh, no. It's Rhys... Rhys is the connection. He took a job in the sound division of Gadigal. That was why we split up. But they wouldn't send him all the way over here, would they? Surely this kind of stuff can be done remotely.

She shook her head to rid her mind of the silly and somewhat intrusive thoughts. Of course Rhys wouldn't be here. That stuff literally only happened in movies.

'Are you okay? You've gone really pale,' Olivia whispered.

Esme nodded and smiled. 'Just a little warm in here,' she

replied. There was movement behind Victoria and Esme's stomach flipped. Her eyes widened and she gripped Olivia's arm involuntarily. It was him. Rhys had just entered and was standing in the background as Victoria carried on speaking; her words were no longer coherent to Esme. They were just a barrage of senseless noises like the teacher in a Peanuts TV show. She covered her mouth with her hand.

Her stomach lurched. 'I have to... sorry,' she mumbled as she dashed from the room and down the stairs to the visitor toilets, just making it into a cubicle before her breakfast vacated her body. Her heart pounded and her stomach continued to roil as her skin became clammy.

'Esme, is everything okay?' came Olivia's out-of-breath voice from outside the cubicle.

Esme took a deep, calming breath. 'I'm so sorry. I think it must be something I ate,' she lied.

'Oh, my goodness, what on earth did you have for breakfast?'

Esme cringed. 'Erm... tea and toast.'

'That can't be it.' There was a silent pause where Esme could only hear the sound of her pulse pounding in her ears. She heard Olivia take a couple of steps closer to the cubicle where she was crouched on the floor. 'Would you like to talk about it, Esme? I can tell it's something more. I'm here to listen.'

Esme flushed the toilet and unsteadily clambered to her feet. She sheepishly opened the cubicle door and walked over to the sink to rinse her face and mouth when the tears came. 'I can't believe it. I've been doing so well. I don't even want him back. I just don't want to see him. Least of all here, on my home turf. It's too much.'

There was a pause until Olivia's reflection in the mirror changed. Her hands reached up to her cheeks, her mouth opened, and her eyes widened. 'Rhys? Oh, my word, Rhys is here?'

Esme nodded and her body was racked with uncontrollable sobs. 'He works for Gadigal. It's just so unexpected. I had no idea they were going to be involved in the shoot, so it came as a massive shock. I mean... Did he know I was here? Is that why he came? Has he not hurt me enough? Or is it all just a horrible coincidence?'

Olivia enveloped her in a hug. 'Oh, Esme, I don't know but I'm so sorry. We'll get through this together though. We can ensure you avoid him. Don't worry, please. We'll figure this all out.'

Esme thought back to how Rhys had looked. His hair was much shorter, and she was sure she could see little flecks of grey, meaning he must have stop dyeing it, and he had a smooth, stubble-free face which he rarely ever had. He wore a smart pale blue and white button-down checked shirt – not really his style – and beige chinos – again not the Rhys she knew. But he had still been incredibly handsome, just a little more mature perhaps.

'Look, why don't you take an early lunch break and go home to freshen up?' Olivia said, pulling her from her reverie.

Esme peered at Olivia through vision blurred with tears and nodded. 'Thanks, I think that would be a good idea.'

'Take as long as you need. But whatever you do, don't let him win, Esme. Don't let him cause you to fall back into depression. He isn't worth that.'

Esme nodded again and left the toilet block. As she rounded the corner to the front of the castle, a voice called out, 'Esme Cassidy, I thought it was you.' Oh, no, the Australian accent she would know anywhere. It meant he had seen her.

She froze on the spot, her heart trying in earnest to escape from her chest. She closed her eyes but could hear his footsteps bringing him closer.

'Esme?'

She took a deep breath and plastered on the fakest of smiles before turning to face Rhys Carlson once again. 'Rhys! Hi! How are you?' She was aware that her voice sounded strained and a little too high pitched. 'Long time no see,' she added for an air of nonchalance.

He smiled and closed in on her, wrapping his arms around her and pulling her close. She inhaled the scent of him and was dragged back to more intimate moments they had shared when they had been together.

'God, it's so good to see you,' he said, releasing her and holding her at arm's length. 'You look... beautiful, but then you always did.' There was a fondness in his expression that she tried not to notice.

'What are you doing here, Rhys?' she asked through gritted teeth, her face now aching from the fake smile.

'I was going to ask you the same thing, but I asked someone, and they said you're working here as Lady Olivia's PA. What happened to your dreams of being an actress? I felt sure that must've been why you were here on the film set when I saw you.'

His question irked her. 'You knew that I hadn't gone to the Conservatoire though. You knew I'd taken a different path.'

He nodded and rubbed the back of his neck. 'Yeah, but I just thought you might have come home and had a rethink I suppose. After you and me... You know.'

'Well, no, I'm very happy here. I love Drumblair and I love my job.' She shrugged even though she knew she sounded defensive.

'I'm really glad to hear that. So... how have you been?'

Since you broke my heart, chewed me up and spat me out, you mean? 'Good. I've been good. You?'

He nodded and glanced down at the ground. 'Yeah, I'm... erm... I'm engaged actually.'

The ground fell away from beneath her feet and Esme glanced around for something to steady her but there was nothing within grasp. 'Oh? Congratulations. That's lovely,' she lied.

'Are you seeing anyone?' he asked with narrowed eyes; a strange expression to accompany such a question. And a strange question to ask of your ex.

'I am. I'm living with someone actually.' *What the hell did you just say, Esme Cassidy? Are you mad? Have you completely lost your marbles?*

His smile disappeared. 'You are? Oh right, great. Who's the lucky bloke?'

'His name's Judd and he's one of the groundskeepers here at the castle.'

Rhys nodded. 'Right, right. Well, that's good. I'm glad you're happy.'

'I am. Now, if you'll excuse me, I have to nip home. I have a touch of food poisoning and want to take something to settle my stomach.' She turned to walk away, in desperate need for the conversation, and lies, to be over.

'I'll walk you to your car.'

'No need. I live on site,' she replied quickly.

'I see. Maybe we could meet later for a catch-up?'

'Hmm, I'm not sure about that. I'm really busy just now. The castle is being used as a film set, you know,' she said with an awkward laugh.

He held up his hands. 'Kinda why I'm here.'

'Well, durr.'

'Maybe we can meet up later? After work?'

'Sorry, no can do. I have a rehearsal.'

His eyes widened and the colour seemed to vacate his tanned face. 'A wedding rehearsal?' He swallowed. 'You're getting married?'

Her confidence spiked when she realised he was taken aback by the thought, regardless of his own betrothed state. But she wouldn't take the lie that far. She still had to convince Judd to pretend to be her partner. 'No, silly. I'm in a play. *Romeo and Juliet*.'

He seemed to exhale a rapid breath, albeit silently. 'Ah, right. Great! I'm glad you're acting.'

You don't know the half of it, mate. 'Yeah, it's am dram but it's good fun.'

'That's really great, Esme. Well, I'll let you get going. But I hope we can meet for a chat while I'm here.'

She turned and began marching towards Garden Cottage. She lifted her hand in a wave. 'Can't promise anything!'

18

By the time she arrived back at the cottage, she was out of breath and feeling lightheaded. Her face was damp with tears and a knot of anxiety scrunched her insides until it was almost painful. After she closed the front door behind her, she slid to the floor, rested her head in her hands and let the crying begin unabashedly. On hearing her, Betty ran into the hallway from the direction of the living room and jumped into her lap. She licked at her tears and Esme nuzzled her fur.

It had been so long since she had seen Rhys that she thought, stupidly, if she ever happened to see him again, which was so unlikely anyway, she'd be fine. After all, she knew she didn't want him back. She could never trust him again. But having him turn up here, *now*, was such a shock. Her visceral reaction, however, made her question herself so much. Was she getting over him at all? Had she ever even started to? Did she still have feelings for him? Would she take him back?

She spoke to her dog as if she had questioned her. 'No, I don't have feelings for him, Betty, not positive ones anyway and

I would absolutely bloody *not* take him back!' She shook her head. 'Get a grip, Esme Cassidy!'

The front door opened slightly, pushing her forward a little. Betty barked and jumped from her lap as Esme angrily got to her feet and shouted, 'I can't believe you followed me here! I told you I was busy!' She yanked open the door fully and was greeted by a startled-looking Judd.

'Oh, I'm sorry, I'll go.' He turned and made to leave.

'No! Sorry, Judd, I wasn't expecting it to be you. I was expecting...' She shook her head, unsure how the heck to put things into words. 'Never mind.'

He turned to face her. 'Are you okay? Because I saw you running towards here as if you were being chased so I wanted to come and check on you. You looked really upset... or angry... or both.'

He was so thoughtful, and it made her smile. 'I'm okay... well, maybe not okay but...'

He gestured into the cottage. 'Shall I come in? Do you want to talk about whatever's bothering you?'

She thought about it for a moment and considering that she'd inadvertently involved him, she nodded. 'I think it's best.' She had to explain before he heard something from someone else, namely Rhys.

He made tea for them and for the next twenty minutes she explained all about Rhys and what he had done to hurt her in the past, and how he had turned up on the film set right at the point when she genuinely thought she'd moved on.

He huffed. 'Bloody hell, Esme. No wonder you're angry and upset. I'd be the same in your shoes. But you just need to avoid him. I can have a word with him if you li—'

'No!' Her heart leapt and she inhaled slowly in a bid to calm herself. 'Sorry, no, that won't be necessary. Although... there is something you could do to help.'

'Aye, anything.'

'I kind of told him I was living with you.'

Judd laughed. 'Well, that's not a lie.'

She slowly shook her head. 'No, I mean I told him I was *with* you. That we were a couple. And now I feel awful because of course there's Selina.'

He scrunched his brow. 'Selina? I don't... I mean what about Zach? Why would you tell him you were in a relationship with me when Zach likes you so much and you like him? Surely that would've had more of an impact. He's a famous actor.' His tone was sharp, and he tapped relentlessly on his mug.

She shook her head. 'I'm so sorry, Judd. I didn't mean to drag you into this. I acted without thinking, he said he was engaged and asked about my relationship status...' She was aware of how ridiculous it all sounded. 'I'll tell him the truth as soon as possible. Will you excuse me while I go freshen up?' Before he could answer or get angrier, she went straight up to her room.

Why was everything suddenly turning to crap when things had been going so well? She went to the bathroom to brush her teeth and wash her face then reapplied her makeup. Eventually, when she felt human again, she made her way downstairs, but Judd was nowhere to be seen. She found a note on the kitchen table from him that said:

Gone back to work. Sorry if I seemed off. It's all just a bit weird. I hate lying because I'm pretty crap at it and always give myself away. But I'll help you as long as he isn't here long. Judd.

His note was short and to the point, and Esme felt terrible. She wished the churning in her stomach would stop. She knew she'd have to come clean to Rhys the next time she saw him.

* * *

That evening she met early with Parker to tell him about Rhys being part of the crew now, and how she had lied about her relationship with Judd.

His face crumpled. 'He's here? In bloody Scotland? You can't tell me he didn't know you worked at the castle. I wouldn't trust him as far as I could throw him. Load of bull. Of course he knew you were here and he's going to try and get you back, you mark my words, Esme. Why else would he turn up? The audacity of the man!' He paused his tirade and scrunched his face. 'Why Judd though? Zach would've had a much bigger impact.'

Esme growled out her frustration. 'Judd said the same thing. Why is Zach more impressive than Judd?'

Parker gave her a look of incredulity. 'You have to ask? Erm... hello! Famous actor, bloody gorgeous. Not only that but he's a better choice to play the part of your love interest. He's an actor, for goodness' sake!'

In her humble opinion, Zach was no more gorgeous than Judd if considering their physicality, but attraction went so much deeper than that. But he did have a point on the acting part. 'I wasn't exactly planning any of this, Parker. I wasn't thinking straight. But the fact is, I lied. It doesn't really matter who I lied about, does it?'

'But if you'd used Zach things might have come true. You might have manifested it. You know what they say, *fake it till you make it*. You could've got him to play along, and he might have finally admitted he does actually fancy the pants off you.' When

Esme didn't reply, he put an arm around her shoulder. 'I'm so sorry. What I should be asking is are you okay. So... are you?'

Esme thought back to some of the happier times she had shared with Rhys. But when she did there was an added feature that stood out now. Why had she never thought about the fact that he was always covering her up or speaking for her? He had commented on the amount of cleavage she'd been showing on one occasion and had remarked that *that* was for his eyes only. It felt archaic and sexist. The more she thought about it, the more she could recall other such situations.

Realising she hadn't answered her friend, she lifted her chin. 'I'm not fine as such. But I will be. I don't want him back. I think I want to understand why he treated me like he did when he had no intention of staying around but I don't want to go back to things the way they were. It's a moot point anyway.'

'How come?'

'He's engaged to be married.'

Parker's eyes widened. 'Oh, really? Huh. And you believe him? You don't think he's trying to make you jealous?'

At this point she had no clue. 'I have no reason to think he's lying.'

Parker tilted his head. 'Oh, really? Because he's never lied to you before to get what he wants?' He had a very valid point. 'You know, from what I've heard so far, I think Taylor Swift wrote *The Tortured Poets Department* album about you and bloody Rhys. It's uncanny. He is for sure "The Smallest Man Who Ever Lived".'

* * *

Zach attended the *Romeo and Juliet* rehearsal that night to give a boost of confidence to the cast. His advice was amazing and even Parker was feeling a little more positive afterwards. He gave pointers on body language, tone of voice, facial expressions, projecting and even gave a pep talk on taking risks which, even though he didn't say in so many words, felt as though he was talking about their own play and the low number of rehearsals they'd have had before putting the show on to the public.

'Being an actor is about taking risks. Even when it feels like you'll fall flat on your face. There is always the chance that you won't, and that it'll turn out to be an incredible and rewarding experience. And just think, you'd have missed out if you hadn't put yourself out there,' he said to a rapt audience.

Afterwards Esme hung back to speak to him. 'Thanks so much for coming tonight, Zach. I think you've made us believe we can actually pull this whole play malarky off,' she said as everyone left, waving and thanking him as they passed.

He smiled. 'Thank you for asking me.'

'Have you seen Lucille?' she asked tentatively. 'I was wondering how she is.'

He nodded. 'I have. She's in pieces emotionally. In the cold light of day, she hates that she's done this to everyone. She's terrified that the shoot won't go ahead because of her. And she's panicking that no one will sign her again. She has booked a place in rehab and seems determined to work at it this time. But she has a lot of regrets just now.' He glanced down at his shoes, and Esme wondered if losing him was one of her regrets. 'But there are some things that are just so hard to come back from,' he added almost as if talking to himself.

Thinking of her own situation, she absentmindedly replied, 'You're so right. I wonder if it's ever possible to trust anyone again after they've hurt you so badly.'

He lifted his chin and fixed his gaze on her. 'You're so special, Esme. I honestly don't know how anyone could hurt you.' He took a step closer. 'You helped me so much too, you know. I've yet to figure out how to thank you.'

She smiled and whispered, 'You already have.'

'Oh, good grief, you two, get a bloody room!' Parker said as he joined them.

Zach stepped back. 'Oh, no, it's not like that, Parker, my friend. Is it, Esme?' He widened his eyes briefly, as if she was supposed to understand via telepathy what he meant by the signal.

She played along. 'No, it's not,' she replied with a smile but was unsure how to feel. He was giving very mixed signals, that one thing was certain.

'Well, I'd better be going. Lucille is at a hotel now she's been released from hospital, but she isn't returning to London for a few days until she's seen her consultant again, and been given the okay to travel. Then she'll be at the rehab centre for a while so I said I'd call and see her tonight. She's having a hard time of things with the pain and… well, everything.'

'Pass on my best wishes,' Esme said, hoping she sounded sincere. Zach nodded and left, closely followed by his security guard.

'The way he looks at you is so…' Parker sighed dreamily. 'I just wish he'd bite the bullet and tell you how he feels.'

'There's nothing to tell, Parker, really. I get the feeling he's still in love with Lucille.'

Parker scoffed. 'With that bitch? No way.'

Esme nodded. 'It doesn't matter how much someone hurts you, sometimes it's hard to let go.'

'Well, I hope you've let go of that Rhys prick. I hope you're not going to go running back to him as soon as he clicks his fingers. Because mark my words, he'll click them.'

'I told you he's engaged, didn't I?'

Parker shook his head. 'My poor, sweet, naïve Esme. I wouldn't be too sure that he's telling the truth on that matter. And if he is, have you never heard of men wanting their cake and to eat it too?'

'I don't think this is one of those occasions.'

'Hmm. We'll see. Anyway, come on, I'll drop you off home.'

* * *

When Esme arrived home, Judd wasn't downstairs which was strange. Disappointment tugged at her. She always enjoyed their post-rehearsal chats. She worried she had really put her foot in it by asking him to pretend they were a couple in front of Rhys.

She found Betty curled up on her bed in her bedroom; another strange thing. She had been so used to finding her two housemates snuggled up on the sofa together. *You've really done it now, Cassidy*, her subconscious told her.

She decided on an early night, seeing as she didn't much fancy the thought of spending the rest of the evening in her own company and inside her own head, and went to the bathroom to remove her makeup and brush her teeth. She listened for a moment outside Judd's door but was met with silence. So she went to bed emotionally exhausted and with a pit of loneliness in her stomach and cried herself to sleep.

* * *

The following morning, Judd was out of the cottage before her and she was beginning to worry that this was how things were going to be from now on. That they would be merely acquaintances who passed in the kitchen and didn't really communicate unless it was notes on the table, *we're out of milk*, or *we need to put the bin out for collection*. She inwardly cursed herself for putting him in an awkward position. From the research she had done about ADHD and autism, she knew he wouldn't like it. He would feel stressed and anxious and it was her fault.

She took Betty on her morning walk and decided to let the little dog accompany her to work. She had bought a fluffy doughnut bed for the floor of her office and Betty usually just snuggled up in it and fell asleep.

Olivia was up in her studio making alterations to one of the dresses she had made for Ruby Locke to wear on screen and had left a list of things for Esme to complete. But all she could think about was Judd and how she could make things right.

At lunchtime she took Betty out for a quick walk and then began to make her way down to the little bench outside the chapel to at least try and eat some of the lunch she had packed on autopilot. She loved to sit and eat lunch with the view of the loch and the distant mountains before her. As she was walking, she spotted Judd. He was leaning on a shovel chatting to Selina. They were both smiling and seemed happy enough and guilt twinged at her insides for asking him to jeopardise that. Before she reached them, Selina waved goodbye and skipped off towards the art barn.

'Oh, hey, Esme!'

She stopped in her tracks and sighed before turning to see Rhys walking towards her. 'Oh, hi, Rhys. Sorry, I can't really stop, I'm on my lunch break and I don't have long,' she lied. She had as long as she wanted. Olivia didn't micromanage her at all.

'That's okay, I'll walk with you. I'd really like to talk to you about something.'

'Look, Rhys, can we just leave it? We don't need to talk about anything. Things ended between us and we've both moved on. Let's just leave it at that.'

'I really feel like there are things left to say. I have things left to say. Things I should have said in my letter.'

'Oh, I think your letter was pretty self-explanatory, Rhys. No further details needed.'

'You're wrong. I didn't say what I really felt. What I really wanted to say.' He glanced over her shoulder and then sighed. 'I'm guessing this is your boyfriend.' The way he made inverted commas in the air really got under Esme's skin. Clearly he hadn't bought any of it. She turned to see Judd walking towards them.

'Esme!' When he reached her, he slipped his arm around her waist and pulled her to him. 'Hi, gorgeous,' he said as he lowered his face to hers and kissed her. At first she was too shocked to respond but then she relaxed into it and slipped her arms up and around his shoulders. His lips were soft yet determined. His stubble grazed against her skin and shivers travelled her spine like little electric shocks. When he released her, he planted an extra kiss on her forehead. 'I've missed you this morning. Did you bring extra sandwiches for me?' He slipped his arm around her shoulder and then turned his face towards Rhys. 'Oh, sorry, pal, I didnae really see you there. Only got eyes for my Esme.' He wiped his hand down his jeans and held it out. 'Judd Cowan. And you are?'

Rhys smirked and held out his hand. 'Rhys, but I'm guessing you already know that, otherwise you wouldn't have felt the need to put on that display.'

Judd scowled. 'I'm not sure I get your meaning.'

Rhys's jaw ticked beneath his skin. 'Oh, I think you do. Nice to see you, Esme. Perhaps we can catch up another time. We definitely need to talk when we have privacy.' And with that he turned and stomped away, each footstep heavy and filled with anger.

Esme was lost for words. About the whole thing.

Judd's gaze flitted around, only settling on her for split seconds. 'How did I do? Was I convincing enough? Do you think he believed us?' he asked as his focus trained on Rhys's retreating form. 'He's a piece of work, eh? Are you okay? You looked angry. Are you angry? You know I'm not great with facial expressions.'

'I'm sorry, Judd, but you took me completely by surprise,' Esme hissed, still reeling from the way her stomach had fluttered, and her heart had pounded at his passionate onslaught. Angry with herself for wishing it had gone on longer. 'A bit of warning would've helped. I've spent the last two days thinking I'd overstepped the friendship boundary by asking you to play along. Let's face it, you've been avoiding me, and then you go and kiss me like that without warning me. How am I supposed to feel?'

'I was just doing what you asked,' he replied, looking anywhere but at her once again.

'I didn't ask you to snog me like that in front of him. Or is my memory betraying me? Because I certainly don't remember asking that.'

'I told you I wasn't great at this kind of thing. I apologise for not knowing the etiquette behind pretending to be something I'm not. Maybe next time you should ask a professional.' He turned on his heel and stormed away too, leaving Esme standing there wondering what the hell was going on.

19

The rehearsal that night flowed so much better. With only two to go before the event itself, everyone seemed to have acquired energy and enthusiasm from somewhere, and Sylvia was in her element. She was animated and smiling, her bright orange kaftan sleeves floating about as she gesticulated and applauded. Bryce had a new hairpiece, or rather a *hair system* as he called it, which was far better and more realistic than the original one. Esme admired his commitment to looking the part. And everyone was remembering their cues, marks and lines. *Perhaps it'll be okay after all*, Esme thought, *surely something has to be*.

After the rehearsal that night, Esme returned to the cottage to find it all in darkness again. She stood outside and looked up at the clear sky and recalled Judd's hilarious attempts to name the constellations. Ever since that conversation she had gazed up at the stars, trying to remember which cluster he had called the tiny cactus. She had also recalled the way he had looked at her on that night and how she had longed to kiss him; to feel his lips on hers. But not because of some silly act they were putting on for Rhys, she had wanted him to kiss her because he felt something too. As she peered up into the inky blue, a glittering stream of light streaked across the sky just like it had on the night of the barbecue. She wished she could've shared the view of this shooting star with Judd too, but she felt like she had completely messed things up with him and was worried she might never get to feel that way again. She had overreacted over the kiss. He was right; he had done exactly what she had asked; or his interpretation of it, at least.

She walked into the empty cottage to find the only light was the little battery-operated dinosaur nightlight that they left on for Betty. Betty was excited to see her at least. Her little curly tail wagged frantically and she yipped her excitement as Esme flicked on the lounge lights.

She plonked herself down on the floor beside the sofa and Betty crawled into her lap. 'Hello, my lovely, I've missed you,' she told the little pug. 'I'm so glad I have you to come home to. I think I'd be lost without you.' Her eyes began to sting. 'I think I've messed everything up, Betty, because I seem to be upsetting everyone and losing friends that I really care about. In fact, I think you might be the only friend I have left and I'm not sure what to do. I wish you could talk and advise me.' Betty licked at her chin. 'Come on, I'll let you out and then we'll head up to bed.'

In spite of feeling drained, sleep evaded Esme and she found herself getting up just after five in the morning. Betty had lifted her head briefly, stood and turned three times before flopping down again, choosing to stay snuggled up in her bed. Esme went down to the kitchen and made herself a cup of tea. There was, of course, no sign or sound of Judd and she wondered if he had stayed away for the night; perhaps with Selina. She sat there replaying recent events over and over, doing herself no good at all, until eventually she went to get ready for work.

* * *

'Have you seen Judd today?' Esme asked as she walked with Olivia across the castle grounds to see how the distillery fitting was going.

'He's gone with Kerr to visit a new supplier for the nursery. They went yesterday. Didn't he tell you he was going?'

Not wishing to bother Olivia with her woes, she said, 'Oh, yes, I think he did mention it. My head is full of Shakespeare so it must've slipped my mind.'

'They've gone down to the Borders so decided it was best to stay overnight. They should be back later today though.'

They arrived at the new distillery where huge copper and chrome stills, mirror-like with their newness, were fixed down to the newly laid perfectly smooth concrete floor. Pipes led away at varying angles and numbered dials were fixed at various points. The high ceilings meant their voices echoed when they spoke.

'The bottling station is all complete now,' Olivia said with a beaming smile. 'It's so exciting. I never imagined we'd have our own whisky and gin. I think my dad would've definitely approved.'

'He'd be so proud of all you've achieved, Olivia. You've created such an incredible business here at Drumblair. No one could fail to be impressed.'

'Oh, hi, pet! What a nice surprise,' came a familiar voice from behind them and Esme turned to see her dad walking towards them. 'Lady Olivia,' he added with a bob of his head that made Esme smile.

'Hello, Colm. How is it going? It's looking fantastic.'

'Oh, aye, all the professional gear and only the best. I appreciate you taking us all on so fast. My team of guys from McIver's are all very grateful for this opportunity, Lady Olivia.'

Olivia smiled. 'It just made perfect sense, and there's no time like the present. I'm so glad you're all happy and I can't wait to taste our first production of gin. I'm rather partial to a G and T.' She laughed.

'We'll be up and running in no time and we'll make sure you're the first taste tester,' Colm said with a wink and a tap to his nose.

'That sounds grand,' Olivia replied. 'Right, come on, Esme, let's leave your dad to carry on doing a fantastic job.'

'See you both later. Thanks for stopping by,' Esme's dad said.

'Bye, Dad.'

'Erm, actually, Esme, can I have a quick word?' Colm gestured to his daughter.

'I'll wait outside and make the most of the sunshine,' Olivia said, and she left them to talk.

'I've seen him,' he said when they were alone. 'Rhys, I mean. What the heck is he doing all the way over here in Scotland?'

Esme felt bad for not letting her parents know that her Australian ex had turned up unexpectedly. But she knew they would've only worried if she'd mentioned him. 'He's working on the film. But please don't worry, I'm not planning on spending any time with him.'

He reached out and pulled his daughter into a hug. 'He'll be best to stay out of my way or I might rearrange his face.'

'No, don't go doing, or saying, anything that will ruin things for you here, Dad. He's not worth it and I'm fine, honestly. I'd better go.' She tiptoed and kissed her dad on the cheek. 'See you later.'

Drumblair was a hive of enterprise and it excited Esme to see the place buzzing with the worker bees from each arm of the business. She was happy to be a part of something that was thriving and in a place she had always loved. The café was doing a roaring trade feeding the film crew and the accommodation was all full. Thanks to where the kids' play area was situated, families were still able to make the most of it without disrupting the film set. The gift shop was having to restock regularly and, of course, the art space was incredibly popular. Whenever Olivia talked about the changes she had seen at Drumblair, she oozed happiness and there was a glow about her that was unmistakable. Having Brodie close by meant they got to see each other whenever they wished; something that many couples would tire of, but not Olivia and Brodie. Their love for each other was evident for all to see, and Esme hoped that one day she would find that for herself.

* * *

The weather had started off rainy but by the time Esme had reached the office that day the sky had been a vivid cerulean with white candyfloss wisps of cloud. It was still pleasant at lunchtime, so she took herself for a walk around the grounds, hoping to bump into Judd on his return from the Borders, but he'd become like the elusive pimpernel. She decided it would be best to let him calm down and hoped that, eventually, he would forgive her, and they could get back to being good friends.

After her walk, she wandered down to her favourite spot on the bench by the chapel and sat overlooking the loch. She watched as an osprey dove headfirst into the water and came up seconds later with a wriggling fish in its mouth.

She closed her eyes for a moment, tilting her head back to feel the warmth of the spring sun on her face.

'It's a stunning location. I can see why you stuck around.'

Rhys.

Esme opened her eyes and gave a deep sigh. 'Aren't you supposed to be working?'

He chuckled. 'Nice to see you too. Mind if I join you?'

Do I have any choice? 'Actually, I'm heading back to work in a minute.'

He sat down beside her. 'Come on, Esme, can we just talk, please?'

That familiar knotting began in her stomach again. 'What is there to talk about? It's not as if you came here specifically to see me. You came across me purely by accident and now you think we have things to say to each other. But I have nothing to say to you, Rhys. You broke my heart, and I've spent the year since that happened working on mending it. I was doing great until you turned up here.'

He leaned closer. 'So that means seeing me has affected you.' Why was his voice filled with hope?

She scowled. 'You're engaged. Or was that a ploy to try and make me jealous?'

He rubbed his hands over his face. 'No, I am engaged. Kim is... she's lovely. She's everything I thought I wanted.'

Esme was shocked at how little his words bothered her. 'So, what's the problem? Go home, marry Kim and be happy.'

He slid closer still and took her hand. 'The problem is she's not you, Esme.'

Esme opened and closed her mouth, completely taken back by this revelation. 'You broke up with me. You had a litany of reasons for doing so, so forgive me if I'm not doing a happy dance or flinging my arms around you.'

He swallowed hard and nodded. 'I understand that but I've regretted my decision ever since. I sent that letter hoping that it'd help me to move on, but I would've reached back into the post box and retrieved it if I could've. I wanted to call you so many times, Esme. I've missed you so, so much.'

Her Taylor Swift ringtone sprang to mind, and she tried not to smile. 'You haven't missed me so much that it stopped you from asking someone else to marry you though,' she replied with an indignant shrug.

He closed his eyes for a moment. 'Fair point. I know. And the awful thing is Kim is perfect for me. She's only three years younger than me, she's beautiful, she's intelligent, she's... just not you.' He sighed.

'So you've said. I'm sure she'd love to hear you talking to me like this and betraying her trust just like you betrayed mine.'

He clenched his fists in his lap. 'I know. I do know how shitty this is of me. But the heart wants what it wants.'

Esme curled her lip involuntarily. 'Until it doesn't.'

'What can I do to prove to you that I've changed and that I'm serious about us?' He reached forward and stroked her cheek and for a moment she forgot herself. She closed her eyes and relished the familiarity of his touch.

But she took his hand and removed it from her face. 'You don't need to prove anything, Rhys, because I'm not interested. You're engaged to be married to someone else and what you did to me at the airport was the worst kind of betrayal. There's no coming back from that. Just let it go, please. I'm finally happy.'

Rhys scoffed. 'With that lanky doofus who would've happily pissed on you to mark his territory?'

'How dare you talk about Judd that way? You know nothing about him. He's kind, funny, intelligent and considerate. None of which are traits I can say you have in common.'

Rhys gave a humourless laugh. 'You're joking, aren't you? He's weird and scruffy. You and me have history. Our feelings are deep, not just some fleeting bullshit crush.'

'And now you're becoming a cheater too. Pardon me for not jumping at the chance.' Esme stood. 'My break is over. Goodbye, Rhys. Please don't waste your time bothering me again. We're never getting back together.'

He stood and grabbed her arm, pulling her to him and pushed her back into the stonework of the chapel, banging her head. He held her tightly so she couldn't move. 'I'll change your mind. I'll make you see how you feel about me.' She could smell the distinct odour of alcohol on his breath before he crushed his mouth into hers. She pushed against his chest as she struggled to breathe. As she wriggled and hit out at him, she managed to force out a muffled squeal, and then there was a sharp breeze before Rhys went flying backwards.

'That's called assault, pal,' Judd growled. 'And you'll not be doing it again.' He dragged Rhys back until he fell onto his bottom on the ground.

'Who the hell do you think you are? You utter moron.' Rhys scrambled to his feet and swung for Judd with his clenched fist.

Luckily Judd dodged, grabbed his assailant's arm and twisted it up his back. 'I'd think very carefully about adding more problems to your current list,' he told Rhys through gritted teeth. 'As it is you'll no doubt be fired for this behaviour.'

'Need a hand, Judd?' Zach asked as he came jogging around the corner of the chapel. 'I heard a commotion and thought I heard a woman scream.'

'Aye, you did. This arsehole has just assaulted Esme.'

'Oh, really? Right, you shithead, let's be having you.'

Between them they tugged a swearing and flailing Rhys back towards the castle. Neither of them had hit him, just restrained him, and Esme had never been more grateful to see either of them.

* * *

Parker, Noah and Paisley had been to Olivia's office to check on Esme, all angry and upset on her behalf. But when things quietened down again, she sat with Olivia on the sofa with a glass of untouched brandy in her hand.

'Are you sure you're okay? And are you sure you don't want to call the police?' Olivia asked as she sat beside Esme on the sofa in her office.

'No, no, I'm fine, honestly. He didn't really hurt me. I was just shocked because I've never known him to be like that. The look in his eyes... It wasn't him.' She shuddered as she remembered the way he had glowered at her before forcing her back against the chapel wall. 'I'm just glad my dad wasn't around to witness it. Rhys may not have survived that.'

'Dads are very protective of their daughters. You'll need to tell your parents though as word has a tendency to get around.'

'I know. That won't be fun.'

Olivia chewed her lip for a moment as if she had something to say but was hesitant. 'Just so that you know, I've spoken to Rhys's boss at Gadigal and he's definitely going to be disciplined, and probably even fired. It turns out he was here under his own steam. He wasn't here with his employer's permission or blessing. He must have found out that you worked here, somehow, and took it upon himself to come over and try to get you back, using the film as his excuse. They were all quite surprised to see him when he turned up but he told them he was on holiday and it just happened to coincide with the shoot.'

Esme shook her head. 'Oh, wow. I still can't quite believe it all to be honest. He could've called me and saved himself the air fare. I can't believe he behaved like that. So aggressive. And he's engaged too. What was he thinking?'

'I know. Apparently his fiancée thought he was going on a work trip to Melbourne for a conference. She had no idea he was over in the UK. She's been contacting his employer for the last few days because he's been avoiding her calls. It seems he's been lying to everyone. Nice guy.'

Esme didn't have the words to express how bizarre she felt the whole situation was. 'I should get back to work. I have things to still check off my list.'

Olivia frowned. 'You'll do no such thing. Go home and have a rest before your final rehearsal. There's nothing on the list that can't wait.'

Esme shook her head. 'Honestly, I'm absolutely fine.'

'Boss's orders, I'm afraid.' There was a knock on the door. 'Come in!'

'Erm, hey, hi. Sorry to interrupt,' Judd said as he stepped into the room, fidgeting with a ring he always wore on his right hand.

Olivia stood. 'I'll leave you two to talk. Be back soon.' She left and closed the door behind her.

20

Once Olivia had gone, Judd stepped further into the room. 'I just wanted to check you're okay,' he said. 'Are you? Okay I mean?'

Esme stood and walked over to him. 'I am, thanks to you.' She reached up and hugged him and at that point tears spilled over and down her cheeks as she sobbed. It was beginning to sink in that the Rhys she had once adored had just attacked her. She hadn't known Judd that long, but it felt like she had; he felt like her safe place. And even though she leaned towards feminism, on this occasion she saw him as her hero. 'I honestly don't know what would've happened if you and Zach hadn't shown up.'

He hugged her too. 'Hey, it's okay, you don't have to think about that. You're safe now. He can't hurt you again. Anyway, they've taken him to the police station.'

'They have?'

He nodded. 'Aye. He tried to punch several other folks, and was quite mouthy so they called the coppers on him. He needs to sleep it off.'

'It's just all so out of character for him. Well, for the Rhys I knew, anyway. I don't understand why he acted that way. There must be some reason for it. Maybe I did—'

Judd released her from his embrace and stepped back, holding her at arm's length. 'Stop. You did nothing wrong, and I don't want to hear you blaming yourself for this. It's all on him.' He shoved his hands into his pockets. 'Actually, someone from the Gadigal sound team told Selina that Rhys has been drinking heavily for a while back in Aus, he's been turning up to work intoxicated and behaving erratically. He's been disciplined and threatened with the sack, and was on his last warning. They said that he asked if he could come on the UK trip for the shoot, but he was told no. They were apparently concerned about him flying, but he came anyway on his fiancée's money. What an idiot thinking he could manipulate you like that. I'm just glad you see through him and weren't sucked in.'

Esme placed a hand over her racing heart. 'I don't get why he did any of that. He was the one who ended things with me, and he was adamant we wouldn't work out. The strange thing is, he had moved on enough to propose to someone so he must have been happy at some point. And it's been so long since we spoke. I had no clue he still felt this way.'

Judd smiled. 'Well, obviously you're a hard woman to get over. Come on, I'll walk you home. I know a furry, four-legged little lady who'll cheer you up.'

As they walked across the grounds of the castle, the sun had disappeared and clouds had replaced the bright glow. The weather now seemed to match her sullen mood. The windows of the castle glowed amber where lamps had been switched on inside and the place looked magical, in spite of the downturn in temperature.

Esme linked her arm through Judd's. 'I was so worried you'd

fallen out with me when you didn't come home last night. I felt so bad about dragging you into everything and I'm truly sorry about that. It was a horrible thing to do.'

He winced. 'Aye, sorry about disappearing on you. Sometimes I just...' He shook his head. 'Sometimes I can't communicate what I'm feeling. I sort of shut down. It's not that I don't want to talk, it's more that I... I can't. I'm sorry I made you feel bad. It wasn't intentional. And I need to say...'

He fell silent so Esme wanted to encourage him. 'And you need to say what? You can be honest with me, Judd. If I've hurt you or upset you then just tell me.'

He stopped in his tracks and turned to face her. His eye contact was a little hit and miss but he was clearly trying. 'I'm so sorry I kissed you without your permission. I should've warned you somehow, told you that next time I saw you with him I'd do something to help you. But... the thing is I had no clue I was even going to do it until it happened. I'm no better than Rhys, really, am I? Forcing myself on you like that.' He visibly shivered with disgust at his actions and his chin trembled. He cleared his throat and fixed his gaze on her as if he felt that was the best way to prove his sincerity. 'Just please know that I would *never* hurt you deliberately, *ever*. I saw him bothering you and it felt almost like a call to action, Judd the fake boyfriend to the rescue. The trouble is I have no clue how to even be a boyfriend, so it probably looked totally fake anyway. It was stupid and I'm so sorry, Esme.'

Esme placed a hand on either side of his face. 'Hey, it's fine. You were trying to help me just like I'd asked. It was my fault for putting you in that position, Judd, so you have nothing to apologise for. And you are *nothing* like Rhys. Nothing at all, okay? Come on, let's go home and have a cuppa and pretend today never happened.'

* * *

Zach came to the final dress rehearsal that night and morale was once again boosted by his words and more simply by his presence. Although Esme had been wondering who they would even be performing for. With such a short amount of notice, had any tickets even sold? She knew her colleagues had said they were coming but would they actually turn up? Sylvia hadn't mentioned ticket sales and clearly no one else had dared to broach the matter with her.

At the end of the evening, Zach approached her. 'You blow my mind, Esme Cassidy. I had tears in my eyes tonight.'

She laughed. 'Because of how awful I was probably.'

'Hey, don't do that. You're such a talented woman. Take a compliment. The others are excited to see the play and I can't wait for them to come tomorrow.'

Esme's heart tripped over itself. 'I'm sorry, what?'

'The crew have all got tickets. In fact, I'm pretty sure it's sold out.'

Esme's shoulders slumped. 'Oh, great, a pity audience. Or worse still a piss-taking one.'

Zach lifted her chin with his forefinger. 'That's not it at all. I've been raving about the show to everyone. Especially about you. You're amazing, Esme.'

'Thank you, but I'm dreading it when I should be excited. It feels like my stage debut will also be my final curtain call.'

'You should have more confidence in your abilities. You really make this role your own. Take it from someone who knows talent when they see it.'

'Hmm,' was all she could muster.

'Anyway, how are you doing after today? I hear your ex was arrested. Rightly so too.'

She shrugged. 'I'm okay, just a little perturbed by his behaviour.'

Zach reached out and tucked a strand of hair behind her ear. 'You're clearly a hard woman to let go of.'

She laughed. 'So people keep telling me. I had no clue.'

'By people do you mean Judd, by any chance?'

She narrowed her eyes. 'I do, why?'

Zach shrugged and smiled. 'No reason. Come on, let's get back to the castle. Max and I will give you and Parker a ride home.'

When they stepped outside the theatre, Esme was shocked and horrified to find a huge crowd had gathered. Cameras flashed and girls screamed. This was the first time she had experienced this because his team had been so good at keeping his trips to Eden Court a secret.

'Oh, my! Is this what it's like to be famous?' Parker asked, his eyes gleaming. 'I love it!' He posed a few times and the gathered crowd cheered in between shouting Zach's name.

'What do we do?' Esme asked as fear sent a shiver up her spine. She had seen this kind of situation on TV but didn't think it would ever be something she experienced in real time.

Thankfully the police had been tipped off early and were already there. A female officer approached them. 'Evening, sir. PC Mel Sherburn. Are you okay, Mr Marchand?' the woman asked in a Yorkshire accent. Esme recognised her from her visits to the castle.

'I am, we all are, thank you for coming. We weren't expecting this but it's fine. Occupational hazard,' he said with a smile.

Screams of, 'Zach! Can I have a selfie?' and 'Zach, please sign my t-shirt!' rang out into the chilly evening air as the crowd pushed into the police officers in their high-vis jackets who had formed a barrier in front of the theatre. 'Marry me, Zach!' was followed by 'I want your babies, Zach!' It was cringeworthy really.

'How would you like to handle things, Mr Marchand?' PC Sherburn asked.

'We'll say a quick hello, sign a few autographs and then be on our way,' Zach replied.

'Are you sure you want to do that?' Max, his security guard, asked. 'There's no pressure, you know. We can just get you out of here.'

Zach shook his head. 'No, it's fine. It's what I signed up for.' He shrugged.

Zach proceeded to pose with fans for selfies, scribble on a variety of items that were thrust in his direction and chat briefly to as many fans as he could, all under the watchful eyes of Max, PC Sherburn and her colleagues. Esme admired him for taking it all in his stride. Once he was finished, he waved to the gathered crowd and was rewarded with a loud cheer and whistles. As they rounded the corner they were greeted with camera flashes and shouts from paparazzi that had gathered to get the money shot of the famous actor.

'Are you on a date with your new lady, Mr Marchand?' one of them shouted out. 'Are you dating a nobody now?'

Zach stopped in his tracks and glared at the journalist who had asked this question as cameras flashed away, capturing everything. 'You should *never* refer to someone as a nobody. It's the worst possible insult. Every person is *somebody*,' was all he said before lowering his head and marching to the car, shielded by Max.

They made it to the car with a large crowd following and the police officers formed a barrier in order that they could climb into the back of the black car with its blacked-out windows.

'Bloody hell, that was exhausting,' Esme said as she slumped into the rear of the car.

'You get used to it,' Zach said. 'That was pretty tame to be honest though.'

'Do you think we'll be in the national papers tomorrow?' Parker asked, checking his reflection in a small compact mirror he had pulled from his satchel. 'I think I looked tired. I hope they touch up the photos to get rid of my dark circles.'

Zach laughed. 'Unfortunately, the press rather like it when celebrities look like crap. I suppose it shows they're only human and can't be airbrushed 24/7.'

'I honestly don't think I could cope with that every time I left the house,' Esme said with a shiver.

'Nah, you'd soon get used to it.'

* * *

Along with a rather conspicuous police escort, they dropped Parker off at his parents' house and then set off for Drumblair Castle.

'Are you okay? You went a little pale back there and I know this has already been a difficult day for you,' Zach said as he reached across and squeezed Esme's hand briefly.

She smiled. 'Yes, I'm fine. It was just a bit full on.'

'Welcome to my world,' he replied and there was a tinge of sadness to his tone.

'Do you ever get really tired of the fame?'

He huffed air through puffed cheeks. 'Sometimes. But then I remind myself that this is the life I wanted. This is what I strived for. And so yes, I can't walk down the street to call for a pint of milk, and okay, I can't go clothes shopping whenever I feel like it but... it's what I signed up for.'

'It's hard to believe that it was once what I wanted too. But seeing that crowd tonight made me wonder if I'm actually better off just as I am.'

Zach turned a little in his seat. 'It's not for everyone, admittedly. But you're a tough cookie, Esme. And I really do think you should pursue your acting career again. Maybe the time is right.'

She laughed lightly. 'I doubt that I'm going to get snapped up from an am dram performance of *Romeo and Juliet*. I know that kind of thing happens in movies but this is real life and I'm just Esme Cassidy.'

'You sell yourself short. I have contacts I can make available to you. All you have to do is say the word.'

The car pulled into the long driveway of Drumblair Castle which was lit with solar-powered mini torchieres. In the distance the castle was aglow, lit up with amber spotlights. It never failed to take her breath away.

'It's stunning, isn't it?' Zach said. 'But I can't imagine how Olivia felt knowing she had inherited it as a dying duck. She's worked miracles, hasn't she?'

Esme nodded. 'She really has. It's an amazing achievement.'

The car stopped along the lane outside Garden Cottage and just before she opened the door to climb out, Zach reached for her hand. 'Maybe now is the time for you to achieve your own dream instead of aiding others to achieve theirs.'

'I'll give it some thought,' she replied. 'Goodnight, Zach. Thanks for the ride home.'

21

Esme stood outside Garden Cottage looking up at the night sky again. A shooting star streaked across the navy blue in the centre of her vision, and she smiled. Her granny always used to say you had to wish on them for your heart's desire. So why did she not have a clue what to wish for? What did she truly want? For the play to go well? Definitely. To be swept off her feet by the man of her dreams? That would be nice but he didn't seem to feel that way about her, which was a bit of a barrier to that wish. To become an award-winning famous actress? And put up with what she had just experienced? With only one wish available, she wasn't sure how to use it, so she silently told the universe she'd save it for another time. She wasn't sure it was allowed but no one had ever said it wasn't.

Judd was waiting at the kitchen table, a pot of tea ready and a plate of fancy biscuits sitting beside it. 'How did it go?' he asked with enthusiasm as he stroked Betty's fur where she sat on his lap, again.

'It was great. Everything ran smoothly until we left the building and were mobbed by Zach's fans.'

'Oh, shit, are you okay?' he asked with wide, alarm-filled eyes.

'Yeah, absolutely fine. The police came, it was all good. Parker loved it.' She laughed. 'Tried to make them photograph his good side.'

'Figures,' Judd said with a chuckle. 'So, what's the plan for tomorrow?'

'Ugh... get up at the crack of dawn and try to eat something, drop Betty at Parker's mum and dad's house for a sleepover with Gladys.' She huffed. 'Don't you just hate when your dog has a better social life than you do? After that I'll head to Eden Court for a final run through. The first performance is at two and then the evening one is at seven.'

'I'm coming to both,' he announced.

'What? Why? You don't have to do that.'

He shrugged. 'You're my closest friend and I want to support you.'

Esme's heart melted a little. 'That's so lovely, thank you, but please don't feel obliged.'

'I don't at all.'

'The rest of the film crew are apparently coming tomorrow night,' she said, scrunching her nose.

'Aye, Selina said that too. Why don't you seem too happy about that?'

She heaved a sigh. 'Because I'm worried it will be a disaster and that I'll fail in front of a room full of professionals.' Betty jumped from his lap and made her way around the table to Esme as if she knew she needed comfort. Esme scooped her up and nuzzled her fur.

Judd leaned forward. 'If the play fails, that's nothing to do with you. You've learned your lines until you can recite them effortlessly. You play the part incredibly well according to Zach and Parker. You're a star, Esme, in more ways than one, so, you can't fail. And even if things go wrong, no one can blame you for that.' He was right but that didn't stop her from worrying. 'How long is it since you acted on stage?'

'I was in the panto that Sylvia wrote at Christmas but that was just a fun mess about, really. This will be the first time I've acted in a Shakespeare production since I was at school. I'm excited and terrified all at the same time. I'm also a little worried that Rhys will show up and make a scene.'

Judd shook his head. 'No chance of that happening. There are too many people who have your back. We wouldn't let him near you so don't worry about that. Just go and enjoy your moment in the spotlight.'

'This was my dream for so long,' she said wistfully. 'All I ever wanted was to be on stage or screen. And now I have this chance, I'm panicking I'm going to fluff my lines or fall over my own feet.'

'Not a chance. You're going to be amazing. A real shooting star.'

22

Matinee time. The theatre lights dimmed, and the curtain went up in readiness as the audience settled. Sylvia, taking the role of narrator, began the monologue that opened the play. There was a rapt silence as Sylvia left the stage. The Capulets' servants Sampson and Gregory were next to take their marks and they proceeded to make rude jokes and banter back and forth. The audience laughed in all the right places and things seemed to be off to a flying start. Esme began to relax. She glanced at herself in the dressing-room mirror and hoped the beads of nervous sweat wouldn't be visible under the stage lights. She dabbed her face with a tissue, only to get bits stuck to her skin. She panicked and picked them all off again quickly, then went back to watching from the wings and chewing her lip.

Partway through the first fight scene, the backdrop began to wobble. Two of Sylvia's volunteer stagehands, found at the local high school, along with much of the backstage crew she had acquired, rushed on to hold it up as the audience began to chuckle. Esme's face flushed and sweat beaded all over again. She glanced down at her tissue-paper-thin white dress and wondered if her underwear was going to be visible under the stage lights. Perhaps she should have thought about that much sooner.

Bryce tripped over his own feet when he made his entrance as Romeo and for some reason called Mercutio *Mercury*, as in Freddie. To be fair, Parker was sporting a rather Freddie-esque fake moustache for his part, so it was easy to see why Bryce made the mistake. But Parker then got the giggles and added in a couple of Mr Mercury's signature fist bumps when he delivered his lines, which, of course, the audience found hilarious; only serving to encourage him further.

'They think it's a comedy,' Sylvia said in a strained voice as she arrived backstage and stood beside Esme. 'They're laughing at us, Esmerelda.'

Esme wanted to shout *I told you so!* But instead she reached out to comfort her. 'To be fair, Sylvia, the audience is mostly made up of school kids. I doubt that many of them have even studied *Romeo and Juliet* yet, so they'll have no clue whether this is all meant to be happening or not.'

Sylvia turned to her. 'Do you think so?'

The hope in her expression tugged at Esme's heart and she nodded. 'Absolutely. And look at it this way, this performance will be a way to iron out any issues for this evening, which I suppose is the main attraction really.' She knew it probably wasn't the best way to view the matinee performance, but she immediately saw Sylvia's eyes brighten.

Sylvia nodded and a look of relief spread across her face. 'Yes, oh, yes. My Charlie and his fellow actors are coming this evening, so it has to be right. I can't make him a laughing stock too. I won't allow that.' At first Esme was confused by the name *Charlie* until she remembered it was Zach's birth name.

'There you go. What's that saying, *it'll be all right on the night?*' Esme said with a smile that she hoped was more convincing than how she really felt.

'Yes, teething troubles, that's all it is. Every play has them. Teething troubles.' And just as Sylvia uttered those fateful words, a piece of the background scenery came crashing down to raucous applause and laughter and luckily missing everyone on stage.

* * *

Thankfully, nothing else too drastically negative befell the performance; there were a few real names injected into dialogue instead of character names, and the odd mispronunciation, but in the end the audience gave a standing ovation.

Afterwards, along with the other cast members, Esme stood in the foyer to chat to audience members as they left.

'That was banging!' one teenage boy told her. 'I always thought Shakespeare was dull as shit but that was brilliant.'

Sylvia, who stood beside her, lifted a finger to speak, and Esme had a feeling she knew exactly what her director was going to say, so she intervened. 'Ah, well, we're so glad it's opened your eyes. Thanks very much for coming.'

The young man left, beaming from ear to ear and Sylvia turned to scowl at Esme. 'I was only going to tell him that it was supposed to be a tragedy so that he understood.'

Esme smiled. 'Yes, but remember they don't need to know that. So long as they've enjoyed their trip to the theatre that's all that matters, right?'

Sylvia sighed and huffed like a sulking toddler. 'I suppose so.'

Once the audience had gone, Sylvia called a meeting. Everyone gathered on the seats as Sylvia took to the stage once more, only this time there was no smile on her face. 'That was a disaster!' she exclaimed with her hand on her forehead as if shielding her eyes from the glaringly obvious. 'I can't believe the audience weren't leaving in droves.'

'With all due respect, Sylvia, they seemed to love it,' Bryce said, adjusting his tights for about the hundredth time.

'Aye, they were laughing their heeds aff!' the actor who played Sampson added.

Sylvia sighed. 'But it's not a comedy. Romeo and Juliet are star-crossed lovers who meet a tragic end. It's supposed to be emotional and heartbreaking, not hilarious!'

'Aye but who knows what any of it means? It's written in gobbledegook,' Gregory, aka Alec, chimed in.

'It's just early modern English, Alec,' Sylvia said with no little exasperation and a deep sigh. 'It's how people used to talk, that's all.'

Alec's eyebrows shot up. 'Oh, right! I didnae ken people used te speak in rhyme in the olden days. You learn sumhin new e'ry day.' He glanced around to check if anyone else was surprised.

Sylvia stared at him blankly for what felt like an age, clearly unsure whether or not Alec was joking. She chose to treat his comment with the contempt she felt it deserved and addressed the cast and crew again. 'Right, we have only a couple of hours until we need to be ready for the evening performance, so please, for goodness' sake, and for my tiny shred of remaining sanity, can we ensure the scenery and backdrop are all secure. Make sure our shoelaces are knotted, and can we please stick to our characters' given directions without adlibbing. And yes, I'm looking at you, Parker. No one wants to see a poor Freddie Mercury rip-off at a Shakespeare play. And Bryce, his name is *Mercutio*, not Mercury. Try to remember that. And please,

please, *please*, take this next performance seriously or be the reason I have a nervous breakdown.'

A rumble of assent traversed the room before people shot off in all directions to grab drinks, food and to do Sylvia's bidding.

Parker sidled off to a corner and stuck his earbuds in, so Esme went over to check on him.

'Whatcha doin'?' she asked in a sing-song voice as she plonked herself down beside him.

He handed her an earbud. 'Trying to regain my sanity by listening to Mother.'

Taylor Swift's 'Fortnight' played into her ear. 'Why do they call Taylor Swift Mother anyway? She's not that much older than us.'

'Because with her music she provides the emotional support pillow we sometimes need to get through the day.'

'So why not call her pillow?' Esme feigned seriousness and Parker glared at her until she started laughing.

'So, on a scale of one to ten, how much are you shitting yourself about the next performance?' Parker asked as he took out his remaining earbud and turned in his seat to face her. 'Because I'm at around one hundred and fifty.'

Esme giggled. 'Probably only ten behind you, to be honest. There's so much riding on this that I can't really think about it too much because if I do I may just run away.'

Parker groaned. 'I can't believe all the castle staff and film crew are coming. Oh, God, we could've been having a night out instead of doing this, Esme. What were we thinking?'

'Come on, Mercury, I mean Mercutio, where's your fighting spirit?'

'Not seeing the light of dayooooh, ayyyyoh, ayyyyyoh, deededayohayohayoh,' Parker sang in his best Freddie Mercury

Band Aid concert style, and they both burst into a fit of hysterics.

* * *

Evening performance time.

Lights down.

Heart pounding.

Sylvia pacing.

Curtain up. Here we go...

The applause at the end of the performance was incredible. Loud, heavy clapping, whistles and cheers. Single flower stems flew onto the stage from the audience. The cast walked out to take their final bow and Esme was gobsmacked to see everyone on their feet again. Only this time everything had been perfect. No fluffed lines, no tripping, no falling scenery. It had been as professional as any rushed Shakespeare play by a group of amateurs could have been, and a lump of raw emotion lodged itself in Esme's throat as her eyes welled with tears of joy and relief.

Sylvia was brought out on stage and handed a beautiful bouquet and a microphone.

'I just want to say a huge thank you to my wonderful cast and behind the scenes team. Without you, things would neither have been possible nor have been as fabulous. I also want to thank my darling nephew Charlie for offering advice to my cast. His words of encouragement have created some amazing actors and I'm forever grateful. This play wasn't supposed to have been performed for many weeks but due to a personal scheduling conflict I had to bring the whole thing forward. I wasn't going to cancel because it's been a lifelong dream to put on this play and I had never before had a cast so willing to commit to it and so wonderful to work with. I can now head off into hospital safe in the knowledge that we finished what we started. Thank you all!'

More appreciative applause and whistles ensued.

So that's what the conflict was. Sylvia's having surgery, Esme thought, and her eyes welled with tears again. Once they were all off stage and everyone had hugged Sylvia, Esme walked over to see her.

'I'm so sorry, Sylvia, I had no idea you were having to go into hospital.'

'Oh, don't worry, dear. I didn't tell anyone, only my close family. The last thing I needed was for people to stay in the play out of pity. I just wanted to do this one thing before I'm laid up and incapacitated for months. I hope you're not too upset with me for keeping the truth quiet.'

Esme pulled Sylvia into a hug. 'Not at all. I think you're incredibly brave. And thank you for all you've done. This has been a memorable experience, that's for sure.'

'Thank you, my wonderful Juliet. Your talent really is wasted, you know.' She turned as more people came towards her. 'Oh dear, I expect I'm going to have to explain myself several times over tonight. Wish me luck.' She turned and walked towards a crowd of people and was enveloped in a group hug.

* * *

Esme and the rest of the cast and crew made their way out to the foyer again, only this time to a different reception. Lots of praise about how well executed such a complex piece had been, how exceedingly good the cast was, how the costumes and scenery were just enough and very classy. Esme felt like she had floated into an alternate reality. It felt good.

She scanned the crowd looking for Judd. She knew he was here. He had been at the matinee but had just waved and given her a thumbs up before leaving the theatre afterwards. This time she hoped to actually speak to him. But she couldn't see him anywhere.

'There's our Juliet!' came her dad's voice. 'You were amazing, pet. Absolutely brilliant. I'm beyond proud of you. We both are, aren't we, Sal?'

'Oh, absolutely in awe,' her mum replied, and they both hugged her. 'I was telling the people sitting by us that you were our daughter. They thought you were a professional. The woman said, "Ooh, I thought it was an amateur thing so how come they've got a professional to play Juliet?" and she was so surprised when I said you weren't.'

'Oh, that's lovely.'

'Anyway, we'll see you tomorrow, there's a queue of folks wanting to talk to you.'

Olivia and Brodie came over next. 'Wow! Just wow!' Brodie said. 'I mean... wow seems quite fitting, I think.'

Esme laughed. 'Thank you.'

Olivia hugged her. 'I'm beginning to think I'm destined to never have a PA, you know,' she said as she beamed at her.

Esme frowned. 'Are you firing me?'

Olivia laughed. 'Absolutely not! But you're my third and now everyone knows you're this good at acting the film crew will be kidnapping you.'

Esme shook her head and grinned. 'I sincerely don't think you have anything to worry about there. I think you're stuck with me. And anyway I love working for you.'

'Yes, but now we know why Parker said you're wasted as my PA. Anyway, we must dash, Mirren and Dougie are babysitting again but we're missing our little girl.' They hugged her again and left.

Once they had gone, a huge bouquet of stunning flowers came towards her as if floating under its own steam but when it reached her a head popped out from behind it. 'I knew you'd be incredible,' Zach said as he handed her the bouquet.

'Oh, wow, these are beautiful. What are they?' she asked.

Zach chuckled. 'Erm, flowers according to the florist in the very fancy shop I went to.'

'Well, of course. I just wondered... never mind. They're lovely. Thank you.'

'I'm so glad you like them. Everyone was so impressed by you. I mean stunned to the core impressed. I reckon some of our cast are going to be coming to you for acting tips.'

'Oh, stop it, you're making me blush,' Esme laughed.

Zach fixed her with an unreadable expression. 'Esme, I hope you know I think a lot of you. But... can I ask you something?'

Esme tilted her head, intrigued by what he was about to say. 'Sure, of course.'

Zach clenched his jaw and scratched his head. Then he stepped from foot to foot and glanced over his shoulder before turning back to look at her. 'Do you have feelings for Judd?'

She opened and closed her mouth a few times before clamping it closed for a few moments, realising she must've resembled a dying fish. 'I... erm... I hadn't really thought about it,' she lied. But obviously she wasn't about to talk about any of this before she knew for sure and had spoken to Judd.

A crease appeared between Zach's brows, and he rubbed his thumbnail along his bottom lip several times. 'Really? Because I've seen how you look at him. And how he looks at you. The relationship you have is... I don't know...' There was tinge of sadness to his expression now. He glanced over his shoulder again, but everyone was preoccupied chatting, so he tuned back to focus on her again. 'The thing is, I've grown really fond of you, Esme, but I don't want to step on toes or even say how I feel if I know your heart's elsewhere.'

Oh, my word! Is this actually happening? Zach Marchand is telling me he has feelings for me? The Zach Marchand. My childhood mega crush! So why don't I feel anything? Why are there no fireworks? What's wrong with me?

She searched her mind for the words, any words. But before she could say anything, he leaned closer and gently kissed her lips. Her eyes closed involuntarily but there was no spark.

None.

And when she opened her eyes, she was met with Judd's. He was carrying a bunch of red, orange and pink tulips. The pained expression on his face almost broke her. She wanted to run to him but there were so many people standing in her way. She gasped and opened her mouth to call out to him, but he simply smiled, held up the flowers and pointed at them then back at her, placed them on the table beside him and left.

23

The after-show party was at the gorgeous Glentorrin Townhouse across the bridge from the theatre. It was a hotel and restaurant that had a fantastic reputation and the most stunning décor. Sylvia had prebooked a room and put money behind the bar. She had left early due to being tired and even though everyone protested and begged her to stay, she stuck to her guns and headed home. Esme was relieved because the poor woman looked drained.

Zach took her hand and introduced her to lots of people that she knew she would never remember, because all she could think about was Judd. Why tulips? What did they mean? Because she knew they had to mean something. Judd was very measured when it came to flowers. Every time she picked up her phone to try and look it up online, someone interrupted her to compliment her on her performance, which was of course lovely but frustrating simultaneously.

Parker arrived beside her with a tall, dark-haired man wearing round spectacles. He was handsome and fresh faced.

'This, my darling Ben, is the inimitable Esme Cassidy,' Parker said with a slight slur.

'It's very good to meet you. You were incredible this evening,' Benoit told her in his lovely French accent.

'Benoit! Finally we meet!' She hugged him instinctively. 'It's so good to see you.'

Parker pulled her into a hug. 'He's right, of course. Look how amazing you were tonight in spite of all the shit that's happened,' he said. 'You're the bestest actor I know, and I know quite a few now.' He chuckled as he gave a theatrical wink. 'But seriously, I reckon Zach and you are going to fall madly in love and go to movie premieres every week from now on. God, I'm jealous. Think of me, Gladys and Benoit when we're eating our beans on toast and you're in some swanky New York hotel, won't you?'

She could no longer argue that Zach didn't feel that way about her in light of his earlier confession. 'Don't worry, you and Gladys will always be my best friends,' she told him.

'And Betty?' he asked with a worried, drunken expression.

'Well, that goes without saying,' she replied.

'Where on earth is Juddleberry this evening?' Parker asked as he glanced around and almost fell over.

'Juddleberry?' Esme asked with a laugh.

'It's got to be short for something,' Parker replied with a shrug. 'Is he here?'

'I think he left. But he got me flowers.'

'Aww, that's so sweet. What did he get you?'

Esme glanced over to where the flowers sat on top of her jacket. 'Tulips.'

Parker scoffed. 'Tulips? For reals? Where from? A farage gorecourt? I mean a gaffage... ugh, you know what I mean.'

She shook her head and was about to explain but there was

no point when Parker was this drunk. 'No, they're really beautiful actually. Definitely not from a garage.'

'I wonder why he didn't stay.'

Esme thought she might know the answer to that question but wasn't 100 per cent sure. Not until she could use Google.

'Come on, *mon cheri*, I think I should get you home now,' Benoit said, slipping his arm around Parker.

'Isn't he handsome?' Parker said dreamily.

'He's adorable,' Esme replied with a smile. 'Goodnight, Benoit. Look after him.'

'*Mais oui. Bon nuit*, Esme.'

At the end of the night, she clambered into a seven-seater Uber with Zach, his bodyguard, Max, and couple of the film crew. Esme clutched her beautiful flowers from Zach and Judd as she stared out of the window, watching the hedgerows whizz by, illuminated for split seconds at a time by the headlights. She glanced skywards and watched the stars as she thought back to the night of the barbecue at the loch... 'And let's not forget the falling man over there, and beside him is the great, pointed, lesser... erm... spotted spangle.' She smiled as she once again remembered Judd's attempts at astronomy and with that thought quickly pulled out her phone to load up Google.

She typed in:

What do tulips represent?

The results popped up in black and white on the screen.

Tulips can represent many things but the most important on this list is love. This can be love for family and friends, or alternatively, a more intimate romantic love.

She read silently as her heart skipped and tripped over itself. She glanced down at the flowers Judd had left for her. *Orange...*

Orange tulips often represent energy, positivity and a zest for life...

Okay, is that how he sees me? Now pink...

Pink tulips are known to represent affection, caring and love.

Her eyes began to sting; it was as if he was trying to communicate his feelings for her through flowers seeing as he felt he was so bad with words.
Lastly red... this should be the tell-all one...

Red tulips are indicative of lasting love and passion.

Esme swiped at tears that had spilled over from her eyes. She hoped he was home when she got there. But of course he had witnessed what appeared to be her kissing Zach earlier in the night and if he did have feelings for her he would have been hurt. She needed to explain. She just hoped he would let her...

* * *

When the car reached Garden Cottage, Zach jumped out to open her door. 'Are you okay? You've been really quiet tonight. And I thought I saw you crying in the cab.'

'I'm so sorry, Zach, I think I'm just a little overwhelmed by today, and tonight has been beyond my wildest dreams but it's been exhausting too, so I'm probably just wiped out and in need of a decent night's sleep.' It was the truth, after all. She glanced up at the cottage, but it was all in darkness and her heart sank.

'Okay, well, I guess I'll see you on Monday. Goodnight, Esme.' He leaned forward to kiss her, but she turned her face, so his lips simply grazed her cheek.

'Goodnight, Zach, and thanks again for all your help and support. You're such a wonderful friend.'

He gave a small smile and single nod that told her he understood what she wasn't saying. 'You're welcome, Esme. Sleep well,' he whispered. He reached out to touch her face before turning and climbing back into the Uber with the others. The driver made a three-point turn and headed back up the lane towards the castle and the stable block apartments.

The house was eerily silent when she walked inside. It was strange having no Judd and no Betty to greet her. She hated it. She flicked the hall light on and walked through to the living room where she did the same but when the room illuminated she gasped. Flowers covered almost every available surface. A vast array of colours and varieties that filled the room with the sweetest fragrances. A hand-painted banner above the fireplace read 'Future Oscar Winner Esme Cassidy Lives Here' and it was clear why Judd had dashed off after the matinee performance. He had prepared all of this for her. But where was he?

She removed her coat and climbed the stairs in a hurry to his door. She knocked lightly. 'Judd, are you awake? Is it okay if I come in?' There was no answer, so she turned the handle and opened the door. 'Judd, it's only m—' His bed was empty, the duvet piled up in the middle as it usually was when he got up. 'No point making the bed when I'm going to unmake it again tonight, seems like a waste of energy.' His words rattled around her head, making her smile.

'Oh, Judd, where are you?' she said aloud.

***

Esme awoke at seven the following morning feeling a little disoriented. She had dreamt that she had walked out onto the stage naked, and everyone had got up and walked out of the theatre in disgust. Following that she had dreamt that Judd and Betty had left her without warning and she had awoken in a cold sweat sobbing. After that she didn't sleep much until around five when she glanced at her phone, hoping to see a message from Judd, but of course there was nothing.

Once she had regained her bearings, she dashed from her bed and went straight across the landing to Judd's room to see if he had returned in the night. He hadn't.

Parker messaged to say his dad was going to drop Betty off with her around ten as he was heading out for some errands. She replied asking how his head was and received a green puke face emoji in reply. After showering, she descended the stairs and put the kettle on and while it was heating she searched the house for a note from Judd but there was nothing other than the beautiful flowers he had left. She poured herself some cornflakes that she didn't really want and sat at the table pushing them around the bowl with a spoon. She decided to drop him a message.

> Hey Judd. I just wanted to check that you're ok. I missed you last night. The flowers are so beautiful. Thank you. I think we need to talk.
> E xx

She received no reply. At ten, Parker's dad dropped Betty off as promised and when he had driven away Esme closed the front door and cuddled her little canine friend as if she hadn't seen her in months. 'I've missed you so much,' she told her in a baby voice. 'I'm so glad you're home. So, so glad.'

Her phone pinged with a text and she grabbed for it, hoping it was Judd.

> Hey Esme, are you free? If so could you come up to the castle and meet me in Olivia's office for a chat? Say around 11? Let me know.
> Zach x

She glanced down at Betty, who sat staring up at her expectantly. 'I think we're going for a walk, Betty.'

Esme and Betty set off towards the castle just before 11 a.m. It was a pleasant morning with a light breeze rustling the trees along the lane. Betty stopped and sniffed every few seconds, meaning the short walk took twice as long. As she rounded the corner, the imposing building came into view. Forget-me-nots and snowdrops skirted the stonework and the blue of the sky behind the castle created a picture-postcard image worthy of any art gallery.

The castle was quiet when Esme and Betty arrived, and she wondered for a moment if that's why Zach had chosen here for their 'chat'. She guessed it was going to be an uncomfortable one about their kiss the night before and how she had called him a *friend*. She would have to admit that she did have feelings for Judd but that he had gone AWOL again, so she was unsure if discovering this was too late. She didn't want to have this conversation, if the truth be told, but she was here now so figured she may as well get it over with.

She knocked on the door of Olivia's office, which felt strange and kind of official for a Sunday morning. Instead of shouting for her to come in, Zach appeared at the door.

'Hey, good to see you, come on in.'

Esme faltered. 'Zach, if this is about last night, I just want to say I'm sorry if I hurt your feelings. It wasn't intentional and I've come to really care for you but—'

'It is about last night but not in the way you think. Come on in,' he said with a smile. 'We'll talk about that later.'

When she entered the room there was another person in there. Victoria of the Chanel suit and terse attitude sat there in Olivia's chair behind the desk.

Esme crumpled her brow and shook her head. 'I'm sorry, I don't... what's this about?' Could this woman fire her? Had she done something she was unaware of that Lady Olivia couldn't speak to her about?

'Erm, sorry I brought Betty, I didn't know it was an official meeting. I don't usually bring her to work.' She paused. 'Actually that's not true, she often comes with me but she's no trouble and Lady Olivia doesn't mind. Sorry, I'm rambling but I'm feeling a little weirded out by this.'

'Oh, no, that's fine. All will become clear. Esme, you remember Victoria, the executive producer on the film?'

'Erm, yes, of course, hello, Victoria.' She held out her hand and Victoria stood to shake it.

'Please, take a seat.'

Zach went to sit beside Victoria and Esme felt like she was suddenly in a disciplinary meeting with two people not even connected to her job. She reluctantly took a seat.

Victoria laughed. 'You look like you're facing a firing squad. Relax,' she said in her inimitable way.

Esme responded with a nervous laugh and fidgeted in her seat. 'So, why am I here?'

'Firstly I was dragged to an am dram performance under false pretences last night to watch someone called Della Cassidy who, it turns out, doesn't exist,' Victoria said with a sideways glance at Zach. 'And then I was subjected to the worst performance of *Romeo and Juliet* I've ever had the displeasure to experience.'

Esme felt her cheeks heating and anger bubbling up from within her. 'I see. Well, I'm sorry you felt that way. The whole cast put a lot of effort into that play, and I'll have you know we were all very proud of it,' she snapped.

Zach widened his eyes, pushed his chair back onto two feet and made a throat-slitting motion out of Victoria's eyeline.

'Oh, I like you. You're feisty and you stand up for your fellow actors. I see potential in you.'

Esme shook her head. 'Hang on, did you say Della Cassidy?' She recalled the conversation she had overheard between Zach and Victoria when she had been outside Olivia's office just after Lucille's accident. 'I-I don't understand.'

Zach chewed his lip. 'I have some explaining to do. You see, I told Victoria I had found Lucille's replacement but there is already an Esme Cassidy registered through SAG-AFTRA so I did a Google search to find alternative derivative for Esmerelda and Della seemed the most appropriate.'

Esme's heart began its attempts to escape her chest; the throbbing travelling its way up to her throat making it difficult to form words. 'I'm sorry... again, *what?*'

Victoria leaned on the desk and interlinked her fingers. 'This is very much out of the ordinary and I'm not exactly comfortable with it but after seeing you last night, it pains me to say it, but I have to agree with Zach. You are incredibly talented, and I don't say that lightly. The director witnessed your performance too and she's happy for us to speak to you.'

Esme shook her head. 'Speak to me about what?'

Victoria sighed as if Esme's failure to understand was irritating in some way. 'Being Lucille's replacement, of course.'

Esme's eyes widened and her breath caught in her throat. She couldn't breathe for a moment and felt the colour draining from her face.

'Esme, are you okay? You've gone awfully pale,' Zach said as he stood and rounded the desk. 'I'll get you some water.' He dashed from the room and returned a few minutes later with a glass of ice-cold water. 'Here you go, sip this.'

Esme took the glass in shaking hands. 'I'm so sorry. This is a joke, right? You're pranking me for some reason.'

'Believe me, this is something I *never* joke about. Would you like the part or not?' Victora asked in a very matter-of-fact way.

A million things rushed around Esme's head, and she couldn't form a coherent thought. 'But this kind of thing doesn't actually happen in real life. It happens in books and movies. It's too farfetched to be real. I mean, if I was reading a book and this happened I'd roll my eyes and think yeah, right.' She lifted her head to find them both staring at her, a little bewildered. 'I'm sorry, I'm waffling, aren't I? But look at this from my point of view. You can see why I don't believe this is real, can't you? I mean it's the stuff of dreams, *actual* dreams.' Her heart pounded in her chest, and she could hear the blood whooshing through her veins. 'I mean I have *genuinely, actually* dreamt about this kind of thing happening to me but now it has I'm in complete shock.'

Her voice wobbled and her innermost emotions surfaced. 'This kind of thing doesn't happen to me... I... I think I need... Can I think about it? I need to get my head around it all. It's a huge step for me and I have so much to take in. And I'll need to speak to Olivia, of course, because she's already lost two PAs and I don't want to leave her in the lurch. What would she think of me?' Tears escaped her eyes, and she swiped them away. 'Sorry, I'm just in shock. I don't know what to do.'

Victoria sighed as she turned to Zach and folded her arms across her chest. 'You said she'd jump at the chance but instead, she's turned into a jabbering wreck.'

'Erm, Victoria, could you give us five minutes alone?' Zach asked with a strained smile.

Victoria huffed like a toddler who'd been told she couldn't have pudding and got up from her chair to leave. 'Five minutes, *max*,' she said as she left the room.

24

Esme began to hyperventilate. The shock of what she had just been asked was a little too much to take in. She saw stars before her eyes and clung to the chair, her knuckles white. Betty whined and pawed at her, clearly sensing something was wrong.

She reached down, lifted Betty into her lap and nuzzled her fur to ground herself. 'Is this... is this a joke, Zach? Because if it is, it's incredibly cruel. It's not the way I expected you to behave after I called you a friend.'

He crouched before her. 'Hey, do you really think I'd do that? I thought you'd know that's not who I am, Esme. Yes, I really like you, and that feeling was admittedly growing fast but that also means I care for you and would never hurt you deliberately. I understand I'm not the right man for you and I'd never want you to be with me for the wrong reasons. Am I disappointed that you don't feel the same? Of course, but we can't always get who or what we want in this life. But perhaps on this occasion *you* can.

'I would genuinely love to see you succeed, Esme, you have

an incredible talent and people need to see that. There'd be a lot of paperwork to complete and you'd need to be Della Cassidy or whatever name you choose for the purposes of the film but other than that you'd be on screen fulfilling a dream. But I've already spoken to my agent and she's more than happy to represent you. It will be quite intense and pretty much full time for the next few months but we're all here to guide and support you. You've seen the script already and know the gist of the story so it's just a matter of learning the lines and going for it.' He cringed. 'Okay so I may have made that sound a bit simpler than it is but you are surrounded by people who are rooting for you, Esme. You would no longer be chasing your dream. You'd have achieved it.'

She lifted her chin and saw sincerity in his eyes. 'You really do mean it, don't you?' Her heartrate began to calm, and the stars dissipated.

'I do. But I understand you'll need a little time to think it through. It's a lot to ask of you. Your first role will be a major one which means you will be thrust headfirst into the limelight. It will take some courage, but I know you can do it.'

'But what about Victoria? She seems to want an answer yesterday.'

Zach grinned. 'Leave her to me. She's a pussycat in a tiger outfit. It'll be fine.'

'How come she thought she had seen the replacement actress you had found on screen before?' Zach narrowed his eyes and Esme gasped at what she had let slip. 'Sorry, I overheard you in Olivia's office.'

'Ah, I see. So, the thing is with Victoria, you have to make her think things are her idea. I had to make her think she knew of you beforehand or she would never have entertained the idea of coming to see you perform. I may have fibbed and told her that you were taking a short break from screen acting to be in the play as a favour to your aunt who runs the drama club. She was adamant she knew who you were when I talked about you, so she had to come and see you to save face.' He grinned.

'Oh!'

He chuckled. 'I know. I'm a horrible person but it was necessary. Luckily the director thought you were perfect so that definitely helped. I have to be honest though, I knew you were the right person to play opposite me even before Lucille had her accident. You have so much more heart about you. Don't get me wrong, she's talented and there are certain parts that she's perfect for, but a romantic role isn't one of them.'

'How would she feel about me taking over her role? She hates me already.'

Zach sucked air in through his teeth. 'Let's just say she may straighten her ways once she finds out. She needs a little humbling.'

'So, what happens now?'

'Well... You'll need to speak to Lady Olivia about how this would affect your job and whether or not she wants to keep your position open if you do go ahead. Or whether perhaps you can continue to work in between shoots, because I'm aware your living situation could be impacted. And I'm guessing you may need to clear some things up with Judd too. So, take a few days, clear your head. Talk to your parents and whoever you trust to advise you and then let me know, and if it's a yes we can get the paperwork started. The sooner we do that, the sooner we can get you fitted for costumes and get you on set, okay?'

Esme nodded as she dug her nails into her palm, still expecting she was about to wake up at home in bed after another bizarre dream.

* * *

She walked back to Garden Cottage in a daze and unlocked the front door on autopilot. Betty went running inside and Esme followed her into the kitchen where she found Judd sitting at the table.

'Hey,' Judd said quickly, glancing up and then back down, returning to tapping at his mug. He bent to pick up Betty, who was sitting by him wagging her tail.

'Oh, hey,' Esme said tersely, snapping out of her stupor and suddenly feeling annoyed at him. 'Thanks for the flowers.'

'No bother. You deserved them. You were amazing last night. I was in complete awe.' Even though he didn't look at her, she could hear the sincerity in his voice and she softened a little.

How was he so nonchalant? How could he sit there as if everything was fine when he had done his disappearing act again?

'Did you have a nice trip?' she asked with a hint of sarcasm.

'Erm... I stayed at Selina's. I thought you and Zach might want to be alone.'

Her nostrils flared. 'And why would you think that, hmm?'

He lifted his chin and fixed his gaze on her. A look of confusion on his handsome, unshaven face. 'Because... sometimes couples want alone time?'

'Is that what you and Selina were having? Couples' alone time?' She was aware at how bitter and jealous she sounded but she didn't care.

His frown remained in place, and he shook his head. 'Erm... Selina is gay, so no.'

Esme raised her eyebrows and opened her mouth, but no words came out for a moment until she managed, 'Oh.' She shook her head. 'But I thought you and she... You were excited because you got her number at the barbecue.'

'Yeah because she's also neurodivergent so we clicked. She gets my quirks. I thought that was obvious?'

Esme pulled out a chair and sat as Parker's words about his gaydar rattled around her head. 'No. No, it definitely wasn't obvious.' *Well, not to me, anyway.*

'Oh, sorry.'

'You bought me tulips, Judd. Why did you do that when there were so many flowers waiting for me at home?'

He lowered his chin and stroked Betty. 'Because they're bright and cheerful. No other reason.'

'So not because you have feelings for me?'

He lifted his chin. 'Erm, no. I thought you might like them, that's all.'

She took her phone from her pocket and swiped at the screen to where she had saved the screenshots of the flower meanings. She began to read aloud:

'Tulips can represent many things but the most important on this list is love. This can be love for family and friends, or alternatively, a more intimate, romantic love... Orange tulips often represent energy, positivity and a zest for life. Pink tulips are known to represent affection, caring and love. But here's the kicker, Judd, red tulips are indicative of lasting love and passion.'

She lifted her gaze to look at him, but he sat there silently, his jaw clenching and unclenching as he stared at the table.

She leaned on the table to try and catch his eye. 'So, this information has nothing to do with why you selected tulips of these colours? You must forget that I know how you love gifting flowers with meanings.'

He put Betty on the floor and stood, still not looking at her.

'I'm guessing you'll want to move out now.' He scratched the back of his head and peered out the window. 'Or... or I can move out. I know how happy you are here, and this is *my* problem, not yours, so I suppose it's only fair.'

She walked around the table to stand before him and placed her hand on his face to turn it and make him look at her. 'Why would either of us be moving out?'

He laughed once. 'Because I doubt Zach would be happy about his girlfriend living with someone who's in love with her when it's not him.'

Esme swallowed hard. 'So, you are in love with me?'

He let his head fall back and stared at the ceiling. 'I think I have been since you came for your interview, and I saw you walking up to the castle doors. I'm not exactly great with this stuff but all I know is I wanted to be around you all the time. I wanted to look at you all the time. I dream about you. And when I saw you kissing Zach last night I felt like my world had crumbled. Like someone had reached in and yanked my heart out of my chest, so yeah, I'm guessing that means something pretty big.' His voice broke and he stuck his fingers into his eyes for a second. Then he was back to peering out the window. 'But I get it. He's a good-looking guy and he's so nice, talented too. Bastard.' He laughed. 'And he clearly adores you. But who wouldn't?'

'Judd, look at me.' He lowered his chin and fixed his gaze on her, his eyes were watery and a little red. She smiled. 'Zach and I are just friends. I don't feel that way about him.'

He shook his head. 'But you had the posters of him on your wall. And you seem so close.'

She took another step towards him. 'I realised a while ago that that was just a teenage crush. And when he kissed me last night, because *he* kissed *me*, not the other way around, it confirmed my feelings. He's a great guy but I don't see him that way.'

Judd's eyes widened and he smiled before heaving a sigh of relief. 'So, we can both stay here. Great. I have to say that's a relief. And I promise I won't make it awkward. I'll get over you in time. Well, I'll certainly try, anyway.'

Esme took the final step towards him until she could feel his warm breath coming fast and shallow. She told him, 'But I don't want you to get over me. Because I don't think I can get over you.'

'Wait a minute... you...?'

'I'm falling for you, Judd. In fact, I think I already landed.' She smiled.

A wide, handsome smile spread across his face and he cupped hers in both hands. 'I'm going to kiss you now if that's okay.'

She laughed. 'I've been waiting for this moment since the last time you kissed me, so yes, kiss me, for goodness' sake.'

He lowered his face, pausing momentarily to gaze into her eyes and then closed the remaining miniscule distance between them in a heartfelt passionate kiss that melted her heart and took her breath away. He wrapped his arms around her and held her close and the last little piece that was missing from the jigsaw Rhys left in her heart was complete.

* * *

'You have to go for it!' Parker squealed as Esme and her group of friends sat around the table at the Drumblair Arms. 'I can't even understand why you're having to think about it, Esme. You're meant to be on the big screen. You can't turn it down! I won't let you!'

'He's right, honey,' Paisley said, more calmly. 'Then you can fix me up with Hugo Delaney.' She laughed and Noah rolled his eyes.

Noah scoffed. 'Not this again. He's old enough to be your dad. You should be with someone your own age,' he said, turning his pint glass in his hands, clearly trying to appear nonchalant.

'Like you, you mean?' Judd said, giving him a nudge.

Noah's face flushed red so fast it was a wonder his head didn't explode. 'No, not necessarily me. But...' He shrugged and the group exchanged wide-eyed glances. He had almost admitted he was crazy about her.

Paisley turned in her seat. 'Are you trying to ask me out, Noah?'

Just when Esme thought he couldn't blush any more, Noah almost spontaneously combusted. 'What if I was...?'

Paisley's cheeks also tinged with pink. 'Then just ask.'

Noah's head snapped up. 'Erm... would you like to go out with me sometime, Pais?'

She smiled, appearing a little coy for the first time ever. 'I'd like that, yes.'

A cheer travelled the group of friends and Parker stood. 'That deserves another round!'

Later, as Esme and Judd walked home from the pub and reached the lane that led to Drumblair Castle, he pulled her into his side and kissed her head. 'So, you know I'm supporting you, your folks have said go for it, the crazy bunch have said go for it, Lady Olivia has said if you don't go for it she'll fire you.' He laughed. 'What else do you need to convince you to fulfil your dream?'

'I honestly don't know. It just seems so daunting and quite surreal.'

'Aye, I can understand that. But what better place to be filming than here?' They stopped as soon as the castle came into view. The moonlight was glinting on the stonework and a halo of stars seemed to circle the tallest point. 'You're trying to remember which one is the lesser-spotted spangle, aren't you?' Judd asked, nudging her shoulder.

She giggled. 'Ah, you caught me. You know I think we should get a telescope and maybe a reference book so you can learn the proper names.'

'Sounds like a plan. Although maybe an audio book because I have zero attention span unless I'm hyperfixating.' He chuckled. 'Seriously though, what are you thinking?'

'I'm trying to figure out which of the stars I wished upon granted all my wishes in one go.'

'I bet it was one of those shooting stars we saw on the night of the barbecue,' he said before kissing the top of her head.

He was probably right. After years as a child of dreaming of owning Drumblair Castle, she now worked here and could soon be appearing in a film set here too. This really was the stuff of dreams. 'It's May now, and they need an answer, so I do need to make a decision. I'm just not sure. Should I be sure?'

He turned her to face him. 'Esme Cassidy, I've known you for a relatively short period of time but in that time I've watched you take on a job you didn't think was what you really wanted to do, but you made it your own. I've seen you act in a play you thought could be a total disaster, but you took the risk and did it anyway. And I've seen you fall for some neurospicy bloke who I personally would never have imagined you loving when the seemingly perfect, neurotypical, dreamy actor guy was waiting in the wings for you. But you took a chance on *me*.' He placed a hand on either side of her face. 'Esme, if I've learned anything from you, it's that life is about taking chances. And even if you choose never to do anything like this again, you *have* to go for it, or you'll spend your whole life wondering *what if*.'

She pulled him down and kissed him with all the adoration she felt inside for her quirky, sometimes confusing man. 'I love you so much, Judd Cowan.'

'And I love you, *Della* Cassidy, future award-winning actor.'

* * *

Esme walked onto the set of *An Unlikely Inheritance*. Her palms were sweating, and her heart was dancing to a beat all of its own. Luckily her head wasn't as sore as some of her friends' as she had paced herself at the party they had thrown for her the night before.

A makeup artist stepped forward and dabbed powder onto her nose.

'Oh, heck, sorry, I'm so nervous, and I go shiny when I'm nervous,' she said to the older woman.

'Don't be, you'll be magnificent, I've seen your rehearsals with Zach.'

Her knees were knocking beneath the stunning, yet rather wide blue satin Georgian gown she had seen Lucille wearing once before. This still felt incredibly surreal. But she thought back to the note she had received from Lucille, and she smiled.

Dear Esme (or should I say Della?)

I can't think of anyone more perfect for this role than you. Thank you so much for trying to help me the night of my fall. And I'm so sorry for treating you so horribly. Just imagine the camera crew naked if you get scared… or is that audiences? And don't imagine Frank the boom controller naked come to think of it, you'll never sleep again. Just have fun.

Much love
Lucille (or should I say Hilda?)

She glanced over to the side and spotted Judd clutching Betty and chewing his thumbnail nervously. She was grateful they had been allowed in to watch her debut because they had a calming effect on her. When Judd saw her looking, he mouthed the words, 'We love you,' and her heart fluttered as she tried not to smile.

The first assistant director shouted, 'Places, everybody,' and for a few seconds people moved around the picture gallery. He then said, 'Quiet on the set. Roll camera, roll sound.'

The camera operator called out, 'Rolling.'

The sound recordist confirmed, 'Sound speed.'

Esme smoothed down the satin of her dress and took a deep, steadying breath as the clapper loader came to stand in front of her with the clapperboard. '*An Unlikely Inheritance*. Scene one. Take one.' The sticks were clapped together.

'And... action!'

EPILOGUE
ONE YEAR LATER

Esme stood in front of the full-length mirror in her hotel suite. Her long dark curls were perfectly coiffed in an up-do with loose tendrils cascading from it and her lips were a stunning crimson red. All professionally executed by a very talented makeup artist, of course. She smoothed down the fabric of her long fitted red velvet dress and wondered if everyone would be able to see her heart hammering, because she had never been so terrified. All her life she had dreamed of a moment like this but now it was here all she wanted to do was run away. She felt how she imagined Julia Roberts's character felt in *Pretty Woman* just before she was about to step into a world in which she didn't belong. Because surely this wasn't Esme's world? However, even if just for one night, it was Della's.

She was grateful that the film premiere event was being held in London because it had meant her parents and friends from the castle could attend. They had all been invited as a thank you for putting up with the filming anyway, but had each told her that she was the more important reason they were attending now. It felt good to have friends. She had missed out on this since losing touch with people she knew at school and had led quite an isolated life until she began working at Drumblair Castle; the place of shooting stars – in more ways than one – and its very own constellation called the tiny cactus. She smiled and shook her head at that particular memory.

The weeks leading up to the premiere had involved lots of shopping and fittings; and not only for her. She had accompanied her parents to Edinburgh where her dad had hired a suit from a swanky tailor. And then she had stood in Olivia's studio while her mum was fitted with a stunning midnight-blue designer dress by Nina Picarro; thanks to Olivia's connections, of course. 'Only the best for our Esme,' her parents had said when she had protested about the amount of money they had spent on hotels and travel. They had refused her offer to help. 'Just let us, we're so very proud of you.'

The only downside was that she had no one here to hold her hand and tell her it was all going to be okay. Her parents had done so, of course, but she longed to be enveloped in strong, loving arms, to be kissed and told she was beautiful. Because at this precise moment in time she didn't recognise herself. In her mind she was playing another character, and this time it was Della Cassidy, movie star. She was looking forward to getting back to being *Esme* Cassidy, PA to Lady Olivia MacLeod.

Offers had flooded in from agents and producers since the trailer reel had been released but she was definitely not seeking the bright lights of fame and stardom any more. She was considering auditioning for some smaller TV roles within the UK simply because of her love for the craft but that was where the dream she had once held so dear had ended. She had witnessed Zach's manic schedule and how hard it was for him to function in 'real life' without someone to keep his diary, someone to dress him, someone to tell him what to say, and had realised it just wasn't for her. She knew she was in the minority for feeling this way and that most of her school contemporaries would be spitting chips if they knew she was on the verge of giving it all up, especially when she had only just achieved her dream.

There was a knock on the door. 'It's time,' came a familiar voice and her heart skipped. *Zach!* She rushed to the door and opened it. There he stood in a black suit, looking as handsome as ever and every bit the man she had once fallen in love with as a teenager.

'Wow! You look incredible!' he said with a wide, heartfelt smile.

'It's not too much?'

He shook his head. 'You could never be too much, Esme Cassidy. You're stunning. And I'm honoured to be accompanying you.'

'Thank you. You may have to hold me up because I could pass out at any given moment. I can say with all honesty that I have never been so scared in all my days on this earth.'

'Take it from me, it doesn't get easier. But you're with me and this is going to be amazing. Come on, the car is waiting.'

'Not a London cab then?' Esme asked with a nervous laugh.

'Absolutely not. We're arriving in style. Shall we?' He held out his elbow to her.

Esme grabbed her bag. 'One second. I just need to check...' She took out her phone but there were no messages. She sighed deeply. 'Okay, I'm ready.'

The limousine pulled up outside the Odeon in Leicester

Square and Esme peered out of the window at the number of press photographers already waiting.

Her heartrate increased and she gulped. 'Zach, I can't... I feel like an impostor. I don't think I can...'

'Of course you can. You have every right to be here. The driver will open the door, and I'll get out first, offer you my hand and you'll climb out, okay?'

'But what if I fall flat on my face? What if my heel gets stuck in my dress and it rips?'

Zach chuckled. 'You do worry about the most bizarre things. Come on. It's show time!'

The door opened and suddenly there was a cacophony of shouting and an almost strobe effect of camera flashes.

'Miss Cassidy, over here!'

'This way, Della!'

'Miss Cassidy, you look stunning!'

'Are you and Zach finally an item?'

'Mr Marchand, is it true you've proposed to Miss Cassidy?'

Esme's legs felt weak under her long dress, but Zach held her hand as much as he could until the next photographer demanded a pose.

Eventually the next car pulled up and Esme and Zach were free to enter the cinema.

'See, you handled that brilliantly. Like you've done it a million times before,' Zach told her with a kiss to her cheek.

Esme breathed a huge sigh of relief. 'Oh, my word. I don't know how you do it and stay so calm. All the intrusive questions too.'

Zach laughed. 'Yep, they ask 'em every time, even though they know they're getting no answers. Crazy.'

For a while they chatted to their fellow actors, the director and members of the crew and the room kept on filling as more and more people arrived. Time seemed to pass in a blur.

'Hi, pet!' Esme's dad said as he and her mum enveloped Esme in a hug. 'How was it out there?'

'Terrifying! Aww, you both look so wonderful,' Esme replied, fighting back the emotions that were bubbling just beneath the surface.

'We're not supposed to have left our seats,' her mum said in a dramatic whisper. 'But we had to come and see you. We're so proud of you, darling.' Her mum dabbed at her watery eyes. 'We'll see you afterwards.'

Esme waved to her mum and dad and then looked back to Zach. 'So, what happens now?'

'Now, we grab some champagne before taking our seats for the excruciating part.'

Esme raised her eyebrows. 'Oh, God, what excruciating part?'

Zach laughed. 'The part where we watch ourselves on screen in front of hundreds of people. It's second-hand embarrassment's older, uglier brother.'

Esme chewed her lip. 'Oh, heck, I'd actually forgotten about that part.'

'Actually, before that, there's something else you need to do.'

Esme's mind whirred. What could possibly be left? There was a tap on her shoulder, and she turned around to see Judd standing there. She flung her arms around him. 'You came! You said you couldn't! But you did!'

He hugged her tightly and mumbled into her neck, 'As if I'd actually miss it.'

She pulled back to look at him. He wore a three-piece navy suit and a white shirt. 'You look gorgeous. So handsome,' she said as butterflies danced in her stomach. Then she noticed his navy tie had tiny snowdrops printed on it.

He noticed her scrutinising them. 'Ah, they're snowdrops.'

She tilted her head and smiled, knowing there was more to the tie choice than met the eye. 'Yes, I can see that. And their significance is...?'

'A promise.'

She placed her hand over her heart. 'Oh, that's so lovely, Judd. But what are you promising?'

He reached into his inside pocket and pulled something out before lowering to one knee. 'Esme Cassidy, I promise to love you with all my heart for as long as you'll have me, and I'm sort of hoping that might be forever.'

Tears welled in her eyes and the whole room fell silent as everyone was focused on them. She covered her mouth to try and stop the threatening sob from escaping.

'I've had a whole year of you. And we did say that if we were still single by the time the movie premiere came around we'd come together. Although I'm hoping you'll marry me so that next time we can just come to these things as husband and wife. What do you think?'

She lowered herself to the ground to face him. 'I think heck yes, I'll marry you.'

Raucous applause rippled around the room and Judd stood, bringing Esme with him. 'I love you so much,' he told her.

'And I love you too.'

Zach hugged them in turn. 'I'm so happy for you both. Two of my best friends!'

Judd slapped his shoulder. 'I'm guessing you'll be happy to be my best man then?'

Zach's chin trembled and he smiled. 'Well, if the chief bridesmaid spot is taken I'm all yours!'

A voice boomed over a hidden speaker system. 'Ladies and gentlemen! Please take your seats for the premiere of *An Unlikely Inheritance*!'

Judd took Esme's hand. 'It's time.'

* * *

MORE FROM LISA HOBMAN

Another book from Lisa Hobman, *A Summer of New Beginnings*, is available to order now here:
https://mybook.to/SummerNewBeginningsAd

ACKNOWLEDGEMENTS

Another book complete, another story told and another list of amazing people who helped make it happen.

Firstly, I want to thank my daughter Gee who, following graduating from uni with a BA Hons in Filmmaking and Screenwriting, was the advisor on all things film set for this book. Gee, I appreciate you more than you can ever know, and I'm immensely proud of you. If by some miracle this book or series is ever made into a movie I can think of no one else I would want to direct it than you.

As always, thank you to my family and friends for the continued love and support, and for putting up with my scatter-brainedness (not sure that's a word but hey-ho!) that always occurs when I'm writing. To Claire, my dear friend and business partner, thank you for being so understanding when I've had to swap days for writing!

Thank you to my fellow Boldwood authors for being a sounding board and font of wonderful advice and encouragement. It really is like a family, and I am very grateful to you all.

Thank you, Lorella and the team at LBLA for continuing to believe in me and advise me. It's wonderful to have you alongside me.

To the intrepid Team Boldwood – my editor Caroline and the whole team work so hard for us authors and you are very much appreciated!

Thank you, Rich. You have been my best friend for thirty-two years and you have always encouraged me to shoot for the stars. You carried my equipment when I was a singer, you clapped the loudest when I was on stage, and you make sure all your friends know about my books. You are the most wonderful husband and are still the yard stick by which all my male characters are measured. I love you to the stars and back again.

Finally, thank you to my wonderful readers. Your reviews and messages mean the world to me. I write because you read and I will continue as long as you do! Much love.

ABOUT THE AUTHOR

Lisa Hobman has written many brilliantly reviewed women's fiction titles – the first of which was shortlisted by the RNA for their debut novel award. In 2012 Lisa relocated her family from Yorkshire to a village in Scotland and this beautiful backdrop now inspires her uplifting and romantic stories.

Sign up to Lisa Hobman's mailing list for news, competitions and updates on future books.

Visit Lisa's website: www.lisajhobman.com

Follow Lisa on social media:

- facebook.com/LisaJHobmanAuthor
- instagram.com/lisahobmanauthor
- tiktok.com/@lisahobmanauth

ALSO BY LISA HOBMAN

The Skye Collection Series
Dreaming Under An Island Skye
Under An Italian Sky
Wishing Under a Starlit Skye
Together Under A Snowy Skye

The Highlands Series
Coming Home to the Highlands
Chasing a Highland Dream
A Highland Family Affair
Shooting Stars Over the Highlands

Standalone Novels
Starting Over At Sunset Cottage
It Started with a Kiss
A Summer of New Beginnings
What Becomes of the Broken Hearted

BECOME A MEMBER OF

THE SHELF CARE CLUB

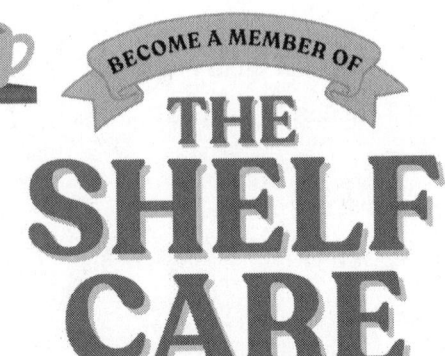

The home of Boldwood's book club reads.

Find uplifting reads, sunny escapes, cosy romances, family dramas and more!

Sign up to the newsletter
https://bit.ly/theshelfcareclub

Boldwood

Boldwood Books is an award-winning fiction publishing company seeking out the best stories from around the world.

Find out more at www.boldwoodbooks.com

Join our reader community for brilliant books, competitions and offers!

Follow us
@BoldwoodBooks
@TheBoldBookClub

Sign up to our weekly deals newsletter

https://bit.ly/BoldwoodBNewsletter

Printed in Dunstable, United Kingdom